DOWNFALL

3
GODS & MONSTERS

LAUREN DAWES

For Phil and Evie

GLOSSARY

Aesir (n) – The sky gods. It is their belief they are superior to all other races in the Nine Worlds.

affinity (n) – the weapon that a Shadow Walker uses as their preferred weapon. It is said that the weapon will choose the Mare while they are training for the Final Test

Asgard (n) – The former home of the Aesir.

fade (v) – to dematerialize to another location with a thought.

Fall, the (n) – The time when the Norse gods were no longer worshiped and therefore lost their power. The Fall was the tipping point that destroyed the Nine Worlds, breaking down the highly organized and coveted hierarchy built by the Aesir. Factions split and different species within those Nine Worlds were strewn across the human world. Some prospered while some merely survived. The gods favored the cities created by humans while others, like the dwarves, preferred the furthest outposts of human civilization.

Fenrir – A monstrous wolf that was imprisoned by Odin. He is also one of Loki's children.

Freki – One of the wolves who once served Odin loyally.

Freyja – The goddess of sexuality, beauty, war and death.

Frigg – Odin's wife; the goddess of fertility, love and marriage.

Geri – One of the wolves who once served Odin loyally.

Glasir – the giant, golden tree that grows outside Valhalla.

Gleipnir **(n)** – The silken ribbon created by the dwarves in order to bind the giant wolf, *Fenrir*.

Hel – The goddess of the underworld

Hreidmar – The king of the dwarves.

Huginn – One of the ravens that serves Odin.

Loki – The god of trickery.

Mare (n) – A dark elf. Pure-blooded Mares are widely believed to be extinct, after a campaign by Odin over a thousand years ago to eradicate their species. To escape persecution, dark elves bred with light elves, creating half-breed children whose features helped them to pass as light elves. Mares are usually no shorter than six feet tall. Their appearance is humanoid; however, they have fangs. They are not for the taking of blood for sustenance; rather they are used for sexual gratification.

Midgard (n) – The home of the humans.

Mimir's Well – The well where Odin sacrificed his eye to drink the wisdom from the water.

Mjolnir (n) – Odin's hammer.

Muninn – One of the ravens that serves Odin.

Muspelheim (n) – "The Land of Fire" is home to the fire giants and fire demons. It is ruled by the giant *Surt*.

Nidavellir (n) – The land of the dwarves.

Nidhogg – "The Corpse Eater" is a dragon that gnaws at the roots of Yggdrasil.

Odin – The father of all gods and men. Sometimes referred to as the *All-Father*.

Old language (n) – The language spoken by human and gods alike at the height of the Aesir's power.

Ragnarok (n) – The prophesized and feared end of the world for many gods including Odin and Loki.

Shadow Walker (n) –*Shadow Walker* is the ancient name for any Mare trained to be an assassin because of their ability to "wrap" shadows around them to conceal themselves. However, due to the extensive inter-breeding with the light elves, many dark elves lost the ability to shadow walk, but the name remains the same. Shadow Walkers were feared for their ability to enter a person's dreams and manipulate them.

Sleipnir – An eight-legged horse ridden by Odin. Sleipnir is also one of Loki's children.

Surt – The giant who is a major figure in the events of *Ragnarok*.

Thor – The god of thunder. He is also Odin's son. Thor gets his power and strength from the hammer *Mjolnir*. In order to have that power, Thor must be touching his hammer.

Tyr – The god of war.

Valhalla (n) – An enormous hall within Asgard that housed fallen battle heroes.

Valkyrie (n) – A beautiful warrior female created by Odin to take the bodies of men slain in battle to Valhalla. They are immortal only while their swan feather cloak is in their possession. If this cloak is stolen, the thief is entitled to seven years of service from the Valkyrie. If the feathers are plucked from the cloak, the Valkyrie can be killed by a mortal wound.

Yggdrasil – The holy ash tree that connects all the Nine Worlds together.

PROLOGUE
ASGARD – 500AD

Bored, Fenrir snarled, the message reverberating through Loki's mind with as much vehemency and irritation as if the words had been spoken out loud. Hot, viscous saliva oozed from Fenrir's jaws, dripping from his gums and onto the skins covering the stone floor beneath him.

Loki sighed, reaching up to touch his son's jet-black muzzle. "I know you are. And it's Odin's doing."

Fenrir growled at the mention of the All-Father's name, the sound vibrating through his throat. Loki was starting to see why his son hated Odin. For too long, Fenrir had been confined to Asgard. For too long he had been subjected to the controlling rule of the All-Father. For too long he had been tethered to the social conventions of the Aesirean fuckers who had kept him there because of their fear.

What would Fenrir do if he were free to roam the Nine Worlds? Whatever it was, he knew it would be disastrous and destructive and oh, so satisfying. Loki grinned as an idea formed. He gazed into Fenrir's blazing, golden eyes, seeing his face reflected back at him. "How would you like to have your freedom, son?"

Freedom, Fenrir replied, his voice a guttural growl in Loki's mind. He nodded. "Freedom."

———

As a wolf, Fenrir stood five times taller than an ice giant. His rough fur was as dense and black as tar, his fangs as sharp as a newly forged blade. But as a man . . .

As a man, he was magnificent.

His inky hair hung over his forehead, his jaw was strong, his aristocratic nose straight and narrow. His eyes were the only thing that couldn't be changed. They were still that brilliant gold – dangerous and menacing to look at. But that was the limitation of the magic Loki had used to transform him from a wolf to a man. He had needed to use a great deal of power, and had no way of knowing how long Fenrir would remain in this new form.

"How do you feel?" Loki asked, staring into Fenrir's hard eyes.

His son flexed his hands into fists. "Small," Fenrir said. "Weak."

Loki smiled. "I can guarantee you are not weak, Fenrir. Now, what would you like to do? In this form, you can leave Asgard and the Aesir would never know . . . *Odin* would never know."

"Experience . . ." Fenrir managed to say, swallowing hard, "everything."

Yes, Loki wanted to see how Fenrir would experience everything there was in the Nine Worlds. "Come with me and I will take you to a place where you can truly experience everything you want to. I will make sure this opportunity is not wasted."

Loki led the way, fading them both to a marketplace on Alfheim

– the land of the light elves. All around, tall, lithe and beautiful beings strolled past them, going about their daily lives, completely unaware of the destruction and devastation that walked among them. The stalls of the market were filled with fruits and vegetables native to Alfheim, as well as fresh fish and meats, all filling the air with a mix of tantalizing aromas.

As the pair moved through the crowd, Loki took delight in the way the elves looked at them – their curious expressions slowly morphing into fear as they started to feel the menace rolling off Fenrir's body in thick, choking waves. Harried whispers broke out around them and females picked up their young children to take them out of harm's way.

If only they knew just how much harm they were really in.

Without turning to his son, Loki asked, "Where would you like to go?"

"Thirsty," Fenrir replied, his feral, yellow gaze traveling over the quickly thinning crowd, his top lip curling off his upper teeth.

Clapping him on the back, Loki led him in the direction of a tavern. "Then we shall have to remedy that."

He pushed open the pale wood door, the heady scent of the sweetest Alfheim honey and hops greeting them as they stepped inside. All conversation ceased, every set of eyes landed on them. A low, rumbling growl escaped Fenrir's throat as he glared at them all.

Loki simply smiled and moved toward the barkeep. "Two tankards of ale," he announced, keeping that smile firmly locked in place. These elves could have no way of knowing who they were, but their reaction to them certainly made it seem as if they did. When the elderly elf behind the bar remained still, Loki added, "Please."

Jerking into motion, the male poured the ale into two large

horn cups and handed them over. Loki fished some coins from his pocket and placed them on the counter.

"Thank you."

He turned around and walked to the table Fenrir had requisitioned from a group of elves. The chatter of conversation was yet to resume, leaving the atmosphere inside the tavern on a knife's edge.

"Unwanted," Fenrir said, eyeing the throng wearily. Loki picked up his own drink and took one long pull, his eyes never leaving the golden gaze of his son. "Scared," Fenrir added.

Loki glanced around at the light elves watching them. "They're right to be scared."

"Normal?" Fenrir asked, his one-word questions coming a lot more easily from his tongue now.

Loki shrugged. "For some. We're strangers here and although the light elves are the most trusting of all the beings in the Nine Worlds, aside from Odin's *precious* humans," he sneered, "they can sense the danger in you."

Fenrir snarled, this time turning his glare to the elves. All averted their eyes, getting busy looking at the table or at their drinks.

"Try your ale," Loki muttered absently, taking another sip from his own tankard. Fenrir picked up his drink and sniffed at the contents, his nose wrinkling a little. After a beat, he put his lips to the side of the cup and tasted it.

Swallowed.

Grimaced.

"You . . . like . . . this?" he managed to spit out. His vocal cords were getting stronger.

"Drink some more and tell me in an hour if you can't see its merits."

It took less than that for Fenrir to begin feeling the effects of the alcohol. It took his nature even less time to come forward. His fierce yellow eyes were darting around all the time, seeing what people's weaknesses were, watching the women like a starving man. Fenrir had never known the feel of a woman, or heard her pant his name. He had never known the joy of making a female scream out in ecstasy as he spilled his seed inside of her.

That was when Loki saw the new idea form in Fenrir's head, the desire mirrored in his golden eyes. He wished for a woman.

"You've thought of something else you'd like to do, haven't you?" he asked his son softly. Fenrir's eyes found his face, his gaze intense. His son nodded, slowly, just as a shadow loomed over them.

Both of them looked up at the light elf blocking the light. He was as tall as Loki but had short, pale hair. His eyes were the color of the midday sky, his nose straight. He was doing his best to look intimidating, but the tendrils of his fear were polluting the air. Fenrir's nostrils flared, taking in the scent, identifying him as prey rather than as the predator he was trying to portray.

Loki arched an eyebrow at the elf in amusement. "Can I help you?"

The male's eyes slid toward Fenrir for a moment before fixing back on Loki's face. "Yeah. We don't like having strangers around here, so we'd appreciate it if you just finish your drinks and get going."

He spoke with careful precision, the cultured tone of a high-born light elf. Although why he was slumming it down here in this tavern Loki had no idea.

Making sure to keep a benignly pleasant smile in place, Loki simply stared at the male then said, "We'll leave when we're ready."

Loki picked up his ale again, stopping abruptly when the elf's hand landed on his wrist. His long fingers tightened, causing

Fenrir to start growling. Loki narrowed his eyes at the light elf.

"I said, I think it's time for you to leave."

Fenrir stood up, but remained where he was at the slight twitch of Loki's free hand. His growling, however, didn't stop. The light elf's gaze skated over in Fenrir's direction, his already pallid skin paling further. A bead of sweat rolled down his temple.

"I'd advise you to release me," Loki said softly, watching the elf's eyes return to his face. Behind them, a group of a half dozen elves stepped up.

"We've got your back, Morgan," one of them said with a cocky grin.

Morgan, bolstered by the appearance of his friends, said, "Or what?"

Loki stared at the new arrivals over Morgan's shoulder, not at all concerned by their appearance. They thought they could handle this situation when they knew nothing of what Loki was capable of, what Fenrir was capable of.

"Or what?" Morgan demanded again, more forcefully this time.

Loki fixed his green eyes back on the elf and nodded his head slightly. Fenrir was nothing more than a blur. His strength and speed were the same in this form as when he was a wolf, and the light elves didn't stand a chance.

Fenrir's thick hand wrapped around Morgan's throat, fingers squeezing until the elf began gasping for air. His friends were struck dumb for just a moment before they leaped into action. Two elves jumped on Fenrir's back, trying to pry him off while the other four were yelling at Loki, demanding he stop the attack.

Eventually Morgan's hand released Loki's wrist, which, in turn, released Fenrir from Morgan's throat. A second later, Morgan was being thrown across the room, crashing into a table and scattering the elves sitting there. Splintered wood rained down around him, leaving him motionless on the ground.

This time it was four elves who attacked Fenrir, and in one sweeping motion, he discarded them all. They crashed to the floor, stunned and sucking in deep breaths of air, not really sure what had just happened. The other two had watched their friends sail past them, but now their sights were firmly set on Fenrir.

"We'll make you pay for that," the larger of the two snarled, pulling a blade out from the inside of his tunic. Fenrir saw the weapon he was being threatened with and bared his teeth.

"I'd put that away if I were you," Loki said in a sing-song voice, watching the scene unfold. He wasn't scared for what could happen to his son. He knew Fenrir would dominate any enemy who was foolish enough to challenge him. "He doesn't take threats well."

The elf remained where he was, his hand flexing around the handle of the knife, waiting.

Loki stood up, pulling at the bottom of his tunic. "Have it your way, then."

———————

Splattered in blood, Loki and Fenrir left the tavern. A tear in Fenrir's shirt revealed the slashes in his skin were already starting to heal. Behind the door, some elves were still moaning pitifully as they waited for death to take them.

Wrapping an arm around Fenrir's strong shoulders, Loki said, "What do you wish to do now?"

With eyes practically glowing, Fenrir rumbled out one word. "Woman."

The god smiled. "As you wish." He'd seen a brothel near the tavern, and was now leading his son in its direction. As they approached the unassuming building, a barely-dressed woman stepped out of the front door with a man who looked well-used and incredibly satisfied.

She pressed her painted lips to his cheek, rubbing her body along his erotically. "Until next time, lover," she whispered, cupping his crotch possessively. The guy gave her a lazy smile and sauntered off, staggering ever so slightly.

The woman watched him leave, but her attention was soon fixed on them. Her eyes were a darker shade of blue than Loki was accustomed to, but her hair and height were right on par with that of a light elf. Her smile brightened when she looked at Loki, but dimmed considerably when she saw Fenrir.

"How much, female?" Loki asked, stalking closer to her. She took a step back, her hands coming up to cover all the bare flesh she had no problems flashing before.

"I'm finished for the night," she managed to stammer, her wide eyes still fixed on Fenrir.

Cocking his head to one side, Loki pushed on. "Perhaps one of the other girls, then? Surely one of them is interested in making a lot of money tonight."

The light elf looked behind her quickly, licking her red lips.

"Want," Fenrir said, inching closer. A whimper escaped the woman's mouth.

"Well?" Loki inquired. "The choice is yours. We can do this on your terms, or we could simply take what we want."

At Fenrir's next step, the female bolted inside, setting off Fenrir's hunting instincts. He went after her and Loki stood outside for a moment longer, listening to the screams of the women. With a smile on his face, he followed his son inside and made sure nobody could escape the building.

No one was safe from Fenrir's desires. He took every single

woman by force, smiling when they begged him to stop, laughing when he injured them with his savagery. After he had spilled himself in each of them, his aggression had to find another outlet.

And that outlet was with his fists.

He beat the women until they were unrecognizable.

And only then did he stop.

Panting, he turned to Loki. Fenrir's face was spattered in blood, his hands still curled into tight fists.

"Satisfied?" Loki asked, crossing his arms over his chest, waiting for Fenrir's clipped reply.

"For . . . now," he replied, his eyes glowing. "Want . . . more."

Loki laughed, standing up and slapping his son on the back. "Of course you do."

Turning around, Loki reached for the door handle, but he was suddenly pushed backwards, causing him to lose his footing. He crashed into Fenrir, sending them both toppling onto the floor and into a slowly growing pool of blood.

"What have you done?" a voice boomed into the room. Loki didn't have to look to know it was his blood-brother come to ruin his fun. Loki glanced up at Odin. The All-Father's obsidian eye reflected back the scene of the room and his green eye showed his fury.

Standing up, Loki fixed his tunic and faced the other god, making sure a smile was firmly in place. "Ah, blood-brother, how nice of you to come along and join in the fun."

Odin's eye scanned the gruesome scene behind them. "You call this fun?" he spat back in reply. "This is monstrous, Loki, and who is this man with you?"

Loki glanced over his shoulder at Fenrir. Could the All-Father truly not see who he was? "Do you not recognize my son?"

Odin's eyes narrowed on Fenrir, scanning his face. "Your son?"

"His current form is unfamiliar to you, but I'm sure those golden eyes will convince you I'm telling the truth."

Loki watched Odin's study of Fenrir once more, his eyes widening when realization struck.

"Fenrir?" he asked.

Loki nodded.

"What magic created this?" the All-Father asked in a harsh and disbelieving whisper.

Loki smiled and shrugged. There were still some things the All-Father did not know, and he wanted to keep it that way.

"When will his form return?"

Again, Loki shrugged, infuriating Odin.

"Why did you bring him here? The light elves are gentle, peace-loving beings."

"What better reason than that?" he retorted.

Odin looked over the bloody and broken bodies of the women splayed across the floor, their robes askew, revealing their already bruising bodies. "Why?"

It was only one question, but it was loaded with so much more meaning.

Once more, Loki shrugged. There were a million different reasons why; he didn't like to see his son suffering; he wanted to see what would happen if Fenrir was released upon the world . . .

Loki was bored.

"You are both returning with me to Asgard, where Fenrir will be returned to his true form."

Fenrir snarled down low in his throat at Odin's threatening tone. The All-Father's gaze fixed on him, challenging him to try something. Loki reached out and motioned for his son to stop.

"We will return with you, Odin, but whether or not Fenrir will transform back into a wolf is not up to me."

———

Running his hand through Freki's ruff while Geri sat at his feet, Odin closed his eyes against the bloody images burned into his retinas. He could not believe what he'd seen. The women at the brothel were not the only ones to have suffered at Fenrir's hand, but at least they were still breathing. Fenrir had laid waste to the men at the tavern. Not one of them had survived his fury. Arms and legs had been removed; hearts had been dug from chests as if Fenrir had wolf's claws rather than a man's fingers.

Odin knew Fenrir was a dangerous creature, but Loki was starting to look more dangerous. His unpredictability alone was enough to warrant a higher degree of caution. Fenrir's many years of restriction to Asgard were necessary, but now Odin realized that he'd grown lax, especially in his vigilance of Loki.

With a thought, Odin faded from his palace in Asgard and traveled to Nidavellir, to the home of the dwarves. It was a dark land with impenetrable, black, jagged mountains rising from the ground like daggers. The air was infused with petrichor, the smell of rain on dry earth. A few sparse trees dotted the landscape, but serrated chunks of black stone prevented any other type of vegetation to grow. Although the sun did try to break through the thick clouds hovering over the mountains, it did little to bring any light to the landscape.

Despite the dimness, the palatial home of the dwarf king loomed ahead of Odin. Made of gold and gems, the whole building glowed as if backlit, the gems gleaming brilliantly. A path of gold led the way to the front gates, proof of Hreidmar's avarice. Odin walked the short length, knocking on the golden door and waiting.

A few minutes passed and then the small sliding door in the

center of the larger door slid open, revealing the stone-colored eyes and bulbous nose of a dwarf. His flinty eyes narrowed for a moment before widening.

"All-Father? What are you doing here?"

"I have come to see the king."

"Yes, of course," the dwarf stammered, quickly sliding the door closed. The larger golden door swung open a moment later. Odin's gaze fell low to the ground, taking in the small creature looking up at him. Only coming up to Odin's hip, the dwarves were a small, ugly race of beings. This dwarf was dressed in a dark gray tunic and pants, both made from a rough fabric that reminded Odin of the crude shale covering the land around the palace.

But despite their small stature and hideous appearance, the dwarves were experts in smithing and crafting and were a valuable tool to Odin.

"Is the king expecting you?"

Odin smiled. "No, I don't believe he is."

"Follow me, then, and I'll take you to him. He would want to see you."

As they walked, Odin glanced around at the building Hreidmar called home. Everywhere he looked, he saw the king's greed. Precious rubies and diamonds were embedded in the walls, around the windows and doorways. Even the floor was inlaid with sapphires of the deepest blues and amethysts large enough to rival the size of his fist.

They eventually came upon an intricately carved golden door, a large gilded knocker in the shape of a dragon's head placed somewhere near Odin's knee. As the dwarf knocked on the door, the rubies of the dragon's eyes glittered with the movement.

"Enter," came the booming voice beyond the door. Odin's

escort gave him a small smile and pushed against the solid gold. Inside, Odin squinted against the brightness of the room, the sconces on the walls reflecting back the radiance of the gilded surfaces.

"Odin, my old friend; it's been too long," Hreidmar said, drawing the All-Father's attention his way. The king of the dwarves was only slightly taller than the man who had led Odin to Hreidmar, but his features were much the same.

Flint-colored eyes.

A large, misshapen nose.

A shaggy beard.

But there was one thing to distinguish him from any other dwarf in his kingdom. And that was the ostentatious crown perched on top of his head. Made from a mix of yellow and rose gold, diamonds traced the scalloped edge of the crown. A combination of rubies, emeralds and sapphires adorned the curved edges wrapping around Hreidmar's head.

"It has been too long, Hreidmar. How are you fairing?"

The old dwarf gave him a broad smile that showed his yellow teeth. Gesturing to the small seat beside him, he said to Odin, "Please," before lowering himself onto his golden throne. "Been doing just fine, Odin. What can I do for you?"

Giving the king a nod, Odin took the other seat, shifting to get into a comfortable position, which proved nearly impossible. Gold was not a forgiving metal to sit on.

"I have come to collect what you owe me."

Hreidmar's gray brows rose slightly. The dwarves were a self-sufficient race, but they still needed help from time to time. And Odin had provided them with it in their hour of need. But Odin never wanted to have the roles reversed; to be indebted to the dwarves meant to promise something without knowing what it might be. It could be small like jewels or gold, or it could be large like the gifting of a child for nefarious purposes.

Hreidmar sat back into his throne, carefully studying Odin. "What is it that you need of me, All-Father?"

That was simple: he needed a way to control Loki. Imprisoning him had crossed his mind before, but he always decided against it; he simply couldn't bring himself to do it — his love for Loki was just too strong. But family had always been Loki's weakness, and that was how Odin would gain the upper hand.

"A chain strong enough to bind Fenrir forever."

"Loki's son? Is this the same Fenrir of whom you speak?"

Odin nodded, knowing the dwarf had many more questions and bracing himself for them. But . . . to his surprise, none came. The dwarf king nodded just once and stretched out his hand.

"Agreed. My best craftsman can do that for you."

"Can you guarantee its strength? Fenrir has broken free of his bindings before. He is a dangerous beast that needs to be taken to heel."

Hreidmar looked over at the dwarf who had shown Odin in. "Rago, fetch Brok. Tell him to come immediately."

Rago nodded briskly and excused himself from the room. A few minutes passed before Rago returned with another dwarf. The pair could have been brothers — their likeness was that strong. Brok was the same height as Rago, with the same wiry, gray hair. The only thing to set him apart was the fact that the dwarf had only one eye, a jagged but faded scar criss-crossing where the appendage used to be.

The heavy leather apron hanging from his shoulders almost scraped the ground as he walked to the dwarf king, his shoulders rolling forward as he lowered his head. In his hands, he twisted a pair of leather gloves nervously.

"King Hreidmar, you summoned me?" he asked, his voice like gravel.

"Yes, Brok, I did. I have need of your skills."

The dwarf looked up. "I would do whatever you ask, my king."

"You will be paid handsomely for your work, since this is a special task for the All-Father," Hreidmar said.

Brok turned his attention to Odin. "What do you need, All-Father?"

"A binding strong enough to ensnare and keep Fenrir bound forever."

The craftsman's small smile turned into a knowing grin. "I've been working on something that would be perfect for that. I call it *gleipnir,* and it has been made with six things that are not of this world, or any of the Nine Worlds."

Intrigued, Odin sat forward in his seat. "Go on."

"I created it with the sound of a cat's footfalls, the beard of a woman, the roots of a mountain, the breath of a fish, the spittle of a bird and the sinews of a bear."

"And where is this binding now?" Hreidmar asked.

"At my workshop."

"And you are sure of its strength? Fenrir is the largest and fiercest wolf in existence. A simple chain will not suffice."

Brok met the All-Father's eyes. "I am sure. If it does not hold, you can feed me to the wolf yourself."

"Go fetch it then. Let me see it before I decide."

The craftsman looked to his king first before leaving the large room, his heavy leather boots slamming against the gold floor as he hurried away.

"You will not be disappointed, my friend. Brok is the best we have. I trust him and his products."

The master craftsman returned no more than ten minutes later with the supposedly unbreakable bonds, but as Odin cast his eye over the object in his hands, he could hardly believe the claim.

Brok's hands were gently cupping what looked to be nothing more than soft gray ribbon. He offered it to Odin, his head bowed. Skeptical didn't even begin to cover how Odin was feeling, but he took the proffered ribbon and ran it through his hands.

"What is this?" he demanded, still studying the fragile-looking object.

"*Gleipnir,*" Brok replied. "Don't be fooled by its appearance. It is much stronger than it seems."

Odin fixed his green eye on the dwarf. "Impossible."

Hreidmar's booming laugh rang out beside Odin. "The All-Father does not believe in your abilities, Brok. Rago, take him and go and fetch the giant we captured trying to pillage from the village. Show the All-Father how much strength *gleipnir* has."

Both dwarves disappeared out the door. The silence was cut by a thunderous roar, which echoed through the room. Odin sank farther into his seat, his eyes fixed on the open doorway.

Hreidmar's grin was splitting his face in two, the anticipation shining in his eyes. "A fire giant," he announced proudly. "He wanted to steal from me."

"How did you capture it?" Odin quizzed, still watching the doorway. Giants were known to be the physically strongest beings in the Nine Worlds. They were hard to catch and even harder to restrain.

The king's gaze settled on him, that same smile still firmly in place. Leaning forward, he said, "I'm not in the habit of revealing all my secrets, Odin."

Odin nodded, turning his face back to the door. Long shadows formed outside, getting shorter as the captive and its master approached.

Brok walked through the door, *gleipnir* firmly wrapped around his fist. Odin followed the other end of the gray ribbon up, up, up until it finished around the throat of the fire giant. With red scales covering its entire body, and two small horns protruding from its head, the creature was dressed in nothing else but a loin cloth. Odin wasn't sure if it was a male or a female as both sexes wore the same thing and looked the same. The fire giant's red eyes scanned the room as it hunched over to get through the doorway. As it straightened, Odin could see there were wounds on its body. Shallow cuts covered its chest, but they looked to have been self-inflicted.

As Brok gave one last tug, the giant began gripping the ribbon with its huge hands, trying to break it – but no matter how much it struggled, it could not sever the bond. Intrigued, Odin stood up and took a step toward the pair.

"It's quite safe," Brok said, yanking violently on *gleipnir*. The giant bellowed in pain. The ribbon tightened around its neck and it fell to its knees. The whole room shuddered with the impact, the flames in the sconces flickering.

Odin walked up to the now felled giant and studied it. He had business with the giants, but that business was always conducted at a distance and through intermediaries. Up close, he could see the iridescent sheen to its scales, and the almost fragile makeup of its horns. The giant's red eyes were defiant, yet broken at the same time. Odin did not know what its fate would be, but if it had been trying to steal from the dwarves as Hreidmar claimed, then its punishment would be drawn out and bloody.

Brok handed the thin ribbon to Odin. "See how little effort is needed to control it."

The All-Father took the end of *gleipnir* and gave it the smallest tug. The giant howled in pain as the noose around its neck tightened further. With its clawed hands, it attempted to shred *gleipnir*, but no matter how much it tried, it could not undo what had been done.

Odin studied the knot. "How is that possible?" he asked.

"Only the hand which ties the bonds has the ability to undo them. There is nothing stronger than *gleipnir* in all the Nine Worlds."

Odin felt sick to his stomach. This was the only way he could see to secure Fenrir successfully. This was the only way he could bring Loki into line again. He wished it hadn't come to this, but Loki had made his bed when he'd transformed Fenrir into a man. Now he would have to lie in it.

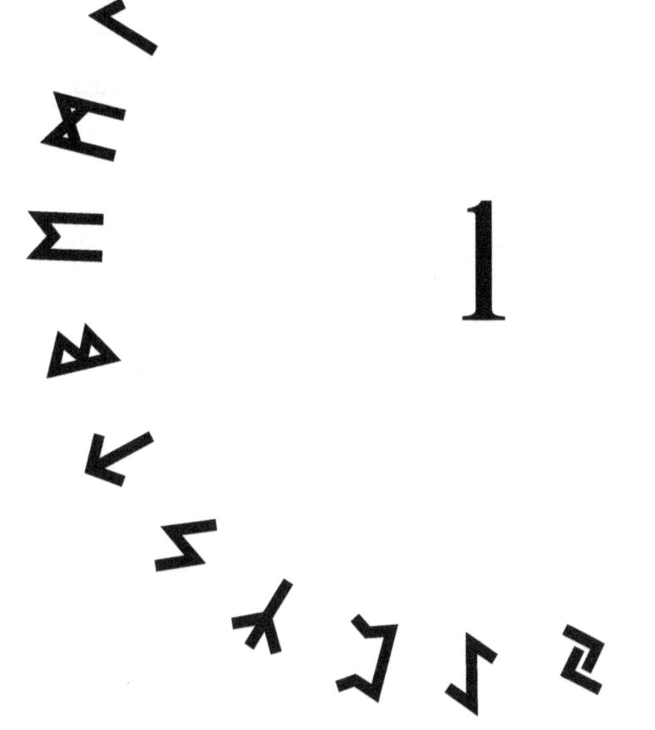

Chicago – present day

Odin peered out of the curtains like some goddamn recluse, his eyes scanning the area directly beneath his hotel room. The sidewalk was scattered with a few dozen people, but other than that, everything was quiet.

Perhaps a little too quiet.

He'd been laying low for the past month. One reason was because he was still in mourning for the loss of his wife, Frigg. Despite the estrangement, despite the infidelity, he had still loved her. The other reason he'd been more vigilant about protecting himself was because he had a target painted on his back, and his dear blood-brother Loki was the one taking aim.

Loki had always been difficult to handle – even when he was among the Aesir in Asgard. A long time ago, Odin had laughed off Loki's behavior as nothing more than harmless pranks meant to make people laugh, but it was the Trickster's involvement in the death of Odin's most favorite son Baldr that changed everything. Loki had simply gone too far. Driven by a rage Odin had not felt since that day all those thousands of years ago, he had done what he said he never could and imprisoned the man he called brother, killed Loki's wife and his son, and not felt a shred of regret for it.

The bonds that held Loki were supposed to hold him forever...

But now Odin was being hunted.

Once powerful, once feared, he had been reduced to skulking from shadow to shadow to protect himself. After the Fall – a time when the humans stopped believing in the gods – everyone had abandoned him. His wife, his Valkyries, the other gods, but the biggest blow had been losing Brynhildr. She was his first Valkyrie, the one who he had poured most of his soul into when he gave her immortality. They were unequivocally bound in life and death – if Brynhildr died, then he could be killed by a mortal wound too.

All he'd ever wanted was to protect her, but she never saw it that way. She claimed that he was controlling and manipulative, but all of his actions had been in her best interests, always. The last time he'd seen her – had tried to speak reasonably with her – she had been...unreceptive to what he had to say.

And now he was powerless and the only person he could depend on was himself.

He had to get rid of Loki. Imprisoning him again was an option, but Odin was thinking of something much more permanent and much more painful. Odin had to protect himself, and if Loki's death was the only way, then that was the way it had to be. But how was he supposed to kill him?

Loki was a god, just like any other Aesir, but Odin had gifted him with extra protection so it was as if he were Odin himself. He didn't know whether he could be killed by conventional means, and the only weapon he could think to use against him was a Valkyrie's sword. All it would take was one of them to cut Loki and he would die. There was just one problem: Odin was not on good terms with any of his warriors anymore. They would sooner watch him burn than throw water on him to douse the flames.

Despite Odin's vast knowledge, he could not see into the past and future. He needed to call upon the Norns again – three women who knew all that has been, all that is and all that will be. After striding over to his desk, Odin picked up the bespoke letter opener and pressed the tip to his finger. Blood welled instantly. He approached the fire burning in the hearth and allowed three drops of his blood to fall into the flames – one for each of the three sisters.

"Skuld, Verdandi, Urd, I summon you to me," Odin announced. The fire hissed with each droplet of blood, consuming the small part of him hungrily, yet nothing more happened. He turned around, unbuttoned his suit jacket and rolled his shoulders. He didn't like to wait. It only confirmed his fall in station. He walked toward the window and peered out once more. His paranoia was getting worse with each passing day.

"You called for us, All-Father?" Verdandi's voice was a gentle caress, a whisper that could barely be heard over the crackle of the fire. He spun around.

The three sisters looked as different from the other as they could; Urd had black hair and eyes, Verdandi had blonde hair and blue eyes and Skuld had red hair with green eyes.

"I did," Odin said. He sank into his wing-backed chair and crossed his legs at the ankle, studying all three of them. "What took you so long?" he demanded.

Urd gave him a disapproving look, something she would not have dreamed of doing one hundred years ago. "We're here now. What do you want?"

He bit the inside of his cheek. The impertinence of the woman was infuriating. "I need information."

"Clearly," Urd shot back. Odin settled back in his chair and leveled her with a hard stare. Crossing her arms over her chest, she jerked her chin up a little and stared right back.

He could antagonize the woman, but he didn't have time for that. Instead he shifted his attention to her sisters. He knew that both Verdandi and Skuld still feared him. "Verdandi," he said loudly. The woman flinched a little, her blue eyes widening as she looked at him. "I need to know about Loki."

"All-Father?" she replied.

"I need to know how to . . . kill him," he said carefully.

Verdandi's gaze flickered first to Skuld then to Urd. She looked at her oldest sister for a long time, an unspoken conversation passing between them. "Kill your brother?" Verdandi eventually replied.

"Isn't that what I said?" he ground out.

"Forgive me, Odin," Skuld said, "but there is no way."

"There must be *some* way to kill him, just as there is a way to kill . . ." He clamped his lips shut. Urd snorted derisively. Biting his tongue, he added, "Loki *must* have a weakness."

"There is a way to kill the Trickster." Urd walked toward him. She was the only one of the three who was curvy – more seductive. "Loki's greatest weakness is his family," she said smugly. "Only a true blood relation can kill him."

That was a fact Odin had already been aware of. Loki had four children. The first was Hel, the woman who became the goddess of the underworld; the second was Jormungand, a giant serpent who encircled the world; the third was Fenrir, the monster wolf that was still bound under the earth as far as Odin knew; and finally there was Sleipnir, Odin's former eight-legged steed. To his knowledge, all of Loki's children were fiercely protective of their father, even more so since his imprisonment.

"None of his children would attack their father," he said, feeling hope drain from his body.

Heavy silence fell onto the room. He was so absorbed in his own thoughts that he did not take any notice of the Norns anymore. They could have faded away from his presence for all he knew, and when he finally looked up, Urd and Skuld indeed had. Verdandi, however, remained.

"All-Father," she said quietly. "Urd will not tell you this, but I will."

Odin's eyes narrowed. "What is it?"

"Do you remember what happened on Alfheim over fifteen hundred years ago?"

He studied the woman while he rifled through his memory banks. Alfheim was the world where the light elves thrived. Their whole existence was a peaceful one, except there was one black spot in their history; Loki had been responsible for it.

"I do," he replied, recalling the event the light elves still referred to today as The Crucifixion. It wasn't a crucifixion in the sense that humans and their Christianity knew it though. There were no wooden crosses, no nails. There were, however, persecutions, torment and torture, and all because Loki had unleashed his son onto the light elves in the name of fun.

"The women Fenrir . . . despoiled . . ." Verdandi paused, obviously considering her words very carefully. "They all eventually succumbed to their injuries."

"Of this I am already aware."

Verdandi grasped the ash tree pendant at her throat, rubbing her thumb over it repeatedly. "Yes, but did you know that one survived? The female gave birth to a son . . . a son who survives to this day."

"Are you saying that Fenrir has a son – that Loki has a grandson out there?" If it were true, how had he not known about it?

"The woman protected the identity of her child from everyone . . . even you, All-Father."

Odin glared at Verdandi. The Norns had a way of seeing his thoughts, and that fact irritated him. He huffed under his breath and turned around to face the window once more. Resisting the urge to peer out the curtains again, Odin settled for re-buttoning his jacket. "Where is this man now?"

"Here in Chicago."

2

Aubrey looked at himself in the mirror, brushing his fingertips against the lapel of his charcoal Tom Ford suit. His tie was the same shade, contrasting against the crisp whiteness of his shirt. He buttoned up the front of the jacket, then unbuttoned it, then buttoned it again.

Fuck.

He was nervous.

The question wasn't so much why, but who.

Taer.

She'd seen him in nothing more than workout gear, and she'd still wanted him . . . not that she would have admitted to that. He would break her though. He was determined to get into her panties if it was the last thing he did. He could practically smell the sexual tension whenever they were around each other, and no matter how hard she fought him on it, Aubrey was sure she felt the same way.

The trick was getting her to admit to it.

Turning around, he left his bedroom, collecting the keys to his Lexus as he strode past the hall table. Although he didn't need a car, he found great pleasure in driving. He took even greater pleasure in the looks of admiration and outright lust that came his way when he drove the high-powered LFA around the streets of Boston. Ostentatious it may be, but he wasn't afraid to admit that respect was what he craved.

Although if he was honest, he was craving Taer even more. She was a Mare – a dark elf. Revenge had motivated her to ask for his help a few weeks ago, but it was self-interest and lust that had motivated him to help her.

The car door closed with a satisfying *thump* that spoke of precision engineering and Aubrey carefully pulled away from the curb. The traffic was sparse – a phenomenon which only survived in a tiny window between the peak hour rush and the time when young professionals returned to the city to spend big at the many clubs and bars in the downtown area.

Aubrey navigated his way down to the Eye, pulling up into the loading zone outside the front of the club. He didn't need to worry about being towed though; he had more than half of the Boston Police Department in his pocket. Having that kind of backing was essential for the type of work Aubrey was in.

A line had already formed outside the bar-slash-nightclub-slash-gentlemen's club – a line Aubrey bypassed completely. A few people cursed him, but he ignored them all. Focusing his attention on the Valkyrie at the door, he met her bi-colored eyes and waited. There was something about the female that he couldn't place. With her shaved head, she was a soldier –

that was clear enough. But there was something else about her. He'd never heard her speak before, and by the looks of the scar running across the front of her throat, he thought that maybe she couldn't.

After one long eye-fuck, the Valkyrie uncrossed her arms and stepped away from the door. Stepping into the Eye, he nodded to her as he passed.

The first level held the bar. It wasn't very busy. A lot of people were going straight to the stairs, probably hoping to get access to the club on level two and the strippers up on level three. Aubrey looked for Taer, wondering whether she was working tonight when he didn't immediately see her.

He finally caught sight of her near the stage. She was wearing a shirt with the club's logo across the front of her chest, and Aubrey drank in every detail of her. The scar across her throat was on show. Her dark hair was tied back into a high ponytail that bounced on her shoulders as she moved, but the determined glint in her eye was curiously absent. Instead, she looked almost serene.

He moved toward her, reaching for her shoulder as she turned around to wipe down a table. She jumped, swinging around with a grimace on her face and a curled up fist raised and ready to strike. Recognition flooded her eyes, and she lowered her hand. Aubrey squeezed her shoulder, but when she winced, he pulled away with a frown.

That was when he noticed the bandage. Rage filled him suddenly. The feeling was so intense it staggered him. Pulling her shirt away, he stared at the bloody gauze.

"Who did that to you, Winter Fox?" he demanded, the urge to tear whoever it was apart with his bare hands wrestling with his common sense. It was just like when he'd seen the scar across her throat for the first time, only this time the feeling was ten times stronger.

Her green eyes met his. "He's dead."

He was Darrion, the Mare who had both mentally and physically tortured Taer; firstly by killing her brother and secondly by haunting her dreams. He was the reason Taer had sought Aubrey out to train her to fight him. And for Aubrey, Darrion had been the thorn in his side, the one thing stopping him from expanding his business empire.

"When?" he asked.

"Last night."

Reaching up, Aubrey ran his hand down the side of Taer's neck, feeling her pulse fighting to get out. It struck him then just how close he'd come to losing her. He'd manipulated her into killing the guild master purely for personal reasons, but after spending time with her he realized that she meant much more to him than he ever thought she would.

"Do you have any other injuries?" he asked, completely focused on her and whatever she had to say. He had tunnel vision when it came to Taer and he didn't give a damn. He didn't care that they were standing in the middle of a room filled with people. He didn't care that those people were watching them with rabid interest.

She sucked in a deep breath. "Broken wrist, internal bleeding, cut across the ribs, deep shoulder wound . . ." She rattled them off like they meant nothing, but with every word she uttered, Aubrey's blood pressure shot up just a little more.

"Are you all right?"

She shrugged. "I'm breathing."

And he was thankful for that. "Can we speak somewhere more private?"

She shook her head. "I've only just started my shift."

"Come to me later?"

Taer's expression hardened, her eyes growing cold. A tangle of complex emotions crossed her face and she shook her head tightly once more.

"Taer?" someone called. Aubrey looked over to his right to see a large man standing there. Aubrey straightened as the other male's dark eyes became two daggers trained on Aubrey's heart.

Taer stepped in front of him, a physical barrier between them. "I'm coming." Without turning around, she said to Aubrey, "I'll see you later."

As she walked toward the other male, jealousy – something Aubrey hadn't felt since he was a young man – shot through his body. Who was this other guy? And why did he care? It wasn't as if Taer belonged to him.

Although she should. The thought had come out of nowhere. He didn't want her to belong to him, did he? He wanted to get her flat on her back and begging him for more, but that was it . . . Wasn't it?

"Too much to fucking think about," he muttered to himself, moving through the crowd.

He left the Eye straight away, jumping back into his car. He hit the gas and yanked on the wheel, fishtailing onto the other side of the road briefly before straightening out. The driver he'd just cut off slammed on the horn. Aubrey wound down the window and flipped the guy off before accelerating, leaving the Honda driver staring at his vanity plates. Aubrey suddenly felt reckless and out of control and it was all because Taer might have another lover. He'd never thought to ask her, but it would explain her reluctance to give into him.

That thought unnerved him.

Was he willing to fight for Taer?

The answer scared him more than the question.

———————

It was close to three am when the doorbell rang. Aubrey was awake; his concern for Taer still had a firm grip on his mind. He wasn't expecting anyone, so when he got to the intercom on the wall, he pressed the button and waited.

"Hello?" a voice asked after a few seconds.

"Taer?"

"Yeah, it's me. Can I come in?"

Aubrey released the lock on the gate and strode to the front door. As he opened it, Taer was closing the main gate on the other side of the courtyard. Propping himself against the door jamb, he waited for her to come to him.

Her work uniform was gone and she was now wearing a black tank top under a leather jacket and a pair of black jeans. Her intense gaze never wavered as she moved toward him, until her eyes dropped to peruse his body. He'd changed out of his suit, and was wearing a pair of sweats and a tee. Nobody ever saw him so casually dressed. He was always working hard to portray an image of power to his work associates and clients. But with Taer, he didn't feel like he needed to keep up the act.

"How's your shoulder?" he asked.

Taer winced when she shrugged. "Fine."

He stared at her for a long, hard minute before stepping back and letting her into his house. He led her through to the kitchen where he filled the kettle and set it to boil.

"Tea?" he asked.

Taer climbed onto one of the tall stools set under the island counter. "Got anything stronger?"

He smiled. Fuck, he liked this woman. "What's your poison?"

"Vodka."

Aubrey walked over to the freezer and pulled out an iced bottle of Goose. Collecting two glasses from the cupboard beside the fridge, he walked back over to her. Placing the glasses down, he took off the cap and poured them both half a glass. Taer took hers before he could offer it to her, swallowing down two-thirds of the clear liquid in one mouthful.

"Cheers," he said, smirking, and then took a sip of his own drink. Taer poured herself another. He raised an eyebrow at her. "Something bothering you?" He instantly regretted the question and settled down on his elbows, leaning down to catch her eye. "What happened with Darrion?"

Taer took a deep breath and winced. "It was bad. He almost killed me." As she spoke, her voice became softer. "He talked about Adrian, and I . . . I almost lost it."

Her knee-jerk reaction to personal barbs was something they'd had to work on. "What made you stop and think about it rationally?"

Her green eyes met his and they blazed with triumph. "You."

He blinked. "Excuse me?"

"Your words pulled me back. I remembered what you told me about not being controlled by my emotions. As soon as I took them out of the equation, I was able to think clearly again."

Aubrey kept his expression serious but on the inside he was puffing up with pride. He straightened up, taking a sip from his glass. "The shoulder injury, it happened before then, right?"

She nodded and swallowed the rest of her vodka. "Yeah. The bastard threw one of his daggers at me."

"Will it heal?"

"In time."

Darrion was lucky he was already dead, otherwise Aubrey would have put him in the ground himself. "Why did you come to me tonight, Taer?" he asked. "Here, to my house," he clarified. "Why not just visit me in my dreams?" Dream walking was a skill only a few Mares possessed, but Taer was one of them. She could breach anyone's mental shields, enter their minds and manipulate their dreams.

Taer was silent. She reached for her glass, her hand shaking as she brought it to her lips. "I don't want to do any dream walking for a little while."

"Because of Darrion?"

"Because of Darrion."

Aubrey's smile made her brows rise. "What?"

He walked around the island bench, standing directly behind her and leaning down to run his lips along the same path his fingers had taken earlier. Goose bumps broke out on her skin, and her breathing hitched in her throat. Over her shoulder, he could see her fingers cinching shut around her glass, and he smirked. "I like having you here in the flesh rather than just in my dreams. It means I can do whatever I like to you."

A small moan broke free of her mouth – a sound that was abruptly cut short. Taer's shoulders tightened and she became stock-still. "I haven't touched you," she whispered.

Aubrey stopped what he was doing, her vow from when they were training ringing in his head with painful clarity.

I'll make you a deal, Aubrey. The day I voluntarily touch you – when we're not training together – is the day I'll let you fuck me.

He chuckled to himself.

They were back to playing their games.

3

Rhys blinked rapidly, squinting against the sun trying to assault his retinas. He wondered what had woken him up. His phone rang again, the sound shocking his senses for a moment. Reaching out, he picked it up and looked at the screen. It was an unknown number and his pulse quickened.

"Galen?" he asked.

"No. Moretti."

Disappointment flooded Rhys, swamping the fleeting glimpse of hope he'd felt. "What do you want?" he demanded, his free hand curling into a tight fist. Moretti was Henry Craine's lawyer, and Craine was Rhys's employer.

"I tried calling Galen but it went straight to voicemail."

Rhys sat up, suddenly uneasy at hearing Moretti's words. The same thing was happening to him. His best friend hadn't returned home from Craine's office two days ago. He figured the mob boss had sent him on another assignment before they were supposed to hit Boston. But deep down, he knew differently.

"I have a job for you."

"Why isn't this order coming from Craine?" he asked.

A chair creaked in the background. "You haven't seen the news?"

"No."

Silence.

"Craine is dead."

Rhys's mouth went dry. "When?"

"Cops think he's been dead about a week."

A week? "How?" Rhys's voice was barely recognizable.

"Looks like he disturbed a B and E. Anyway, I need you both for a job."

"It's just me. Galen is MIA."

"Still . . . are you interested?"

Rhys paused for a beat, thinking it over. He rarely worked alone . . . well, without Galen at least. Rhys was never really alone. And right on cue, the beast that shared his body stretched out in his mind.

"You still there?" Moretti asked.

After clearing his throat, Rhys said, "Yeah, I'm here. Who's the hit?"

"Kid named Valentin Romanoff. He's a supplier who's encroaching on our turf."

"When do you want him gone?"

"As soon as possible."

Rhys stood up, pinning the phone between his shoulder and ear while he pulled on a pair of sweats. It was a fucking catch twenty-two; Rhys needed to kill like he needed to breathe, but every time blood was spilled, it made things ten times worse for him.

"I'll take care of it." He hung up the phone and tossed it on the bed. The news about Craine had taken him by surprise, but what worried him more was that Galen was still missing.

Picking up his laptop, he flipped it open and took it off standby. After some hacking into the police databases, Rhys found the information he needed on Romanoff and got changed. After putting on a pair of black cargo pants and a black long-sleeved tee, Rhys strapped daggers to his body and faded from the apartment.

The Cossack had apparently been successful before he came to Chicago because the bastard had a place right on Lake Michigan. Rhys saw a guard standing by the door, and he could guarantee there were at least two more inside the palatial house. Pulling out a dagger, Rhys faded to the human at the door and slit his throat in one swift movement. The guard fell to the ground soundlessly. Rhys pulled the weapons from the other man's body and stashed them on his own.

With a thought, Rhys rematerialized inside the house, his molecules reforming on the other side of the door. He could hear five more sets of feet moving around. Closing his eyes, Rhys let his beast come a little closer to the surface, taking advantage of its sense of smell. Two men were on the first level and the other three, whose scents were fainter, were upstairs. Stalking around the bottom level, Rhys found one guard standing watch at the back door. Rhys even let the bastard see him in the reflection of the glass door before striking. The second guy just happened to round the corner as Rhys lowered the first one to the highly waxed floor.

The guard reached for his weapon, but it didn't matter. Rhys was faster. Taking another blade from his arsenal, he threw it at the human. The man dropped to the ground, the dagger firmly buried in his chest. Rhys yanked the blade free as he walked past him and made his way upstairs.

The floorboards creaked and groaned a little, but nobody came to investigate. Rhys dispatched the other two guards silently, stalking toward a room at the end of the hall. Nudging open the door with his foot, Rhys stepped inside and looked around. The Cossack was nowhere to be seen. Rhys was about to turn around and check out the rest of the house when he heard the sound of metal on metal, muffled by rubber.

Walking around the corner, Rhys came across another room filled with gym equipment. Three of the four walls had mirrors on them, and in the middle of the room – on the bench press – was Romanoff. The kid's black eyes narrowed as he looked at Rhys through the reflection in the mirror.

"Who the fuck are you?" he demanded, only a slight hint of a Russian accent leeching into his words.

Rhys didn't bother answering the question. He faded to the guy, grabbed him by the throat and hauled him off the bench. The fucker put up a fight, his hands coming up to Rhys's to try to loosen his grip. Rhys only squeezed harder. He threw Romanoff against one of the walls, the mirror shattering and sending shards of glass showering over them both.

A few of the edges drew blood as they hit Rhys, but it wasn't his blood he had to worry about. It was the other guy's. As soon as the smell of it hit the air, Rhys felt the grip of his self-control starting to fail. Rhys recognized he was jeopardizing everything. He was also cognizant of the fact that he didn't give a fuck. He wanted to kill. He knew that shedding more of the Cossack's blood would only fuel his beast, but he had to do it.

Even now, it was whispering to him.

Kill.

Romanoff tried to stand up, and Rhys let him struggle to his feet. His beast liked it when his prey tried to escape; it made the hunt that much more exciting. Letting the human take a few steps away, Rhys reached for one of the blades he had used to kill the kid's guards. Valentin's eyes went wide and he turned and ran. Rhys smiled and gave chase, driving the steel into the kid's spine.

Romanoff dropped to the floor, hitting his head on the rolled steel leg of his bench press as he did. Blood sprayed, coating the air. Rhys could see Romanoff's chest rising and falling slowly. The blow hadn't killed him, but blood poured from the cut to his head, dripping onto the rubber matting on the floor.

His black eyes fixed on Rhys. "Who . . ." he gasped and swallowed, "sent you?"

Rhys smiled, knowing his canine teeth had changed shape. Bringing his arm up, he drove the dagger into Romanoff's chest. Rhys wiped the blade clean and looked around the mirrored room. A flash of yellow caught his eye, and he studied his bloody reflection for a moment.

The face staring back at him was barely recognizable. Sure, his features were all the same: the same aristocratic nose, the same mouth, square jaw and the same inky hair, but his eyes were a brilliant gold. He blinked, his vision turning to shades of red.

Out.

The whisper was louder than before. With a growl, Rhys faded back to his apartment, painfully aware that it was empty. He didn't want to hope that Galen might miraculously return because he knew his friend was already dead — he just didn't want to admit it to himself. Tugging on the neck of his shirt, Rhys pulled it over his head and let the fabric skim through his fingers. Next were his cargo pants, which joined his shirt on the floor as he made his way to his bedroom.

Twisting the taps on in the shower, he didn't bother waiting for the hot water to kick in. He stepped into the cubicle. The ice-cold water felt good against his heated skin, but it did little to subdue his beast, who he could now feel pacing backwards and forwards under his skin.

More, it whispered.

It was becoming stronger, and Rhys had no idea how to gain the upper hand, how to get complete control over it; he hadn't had to manage it alone for a long, long time. He went through the regular rinse-and-repeat routine, and less than five minutes later he was clean and smelling of fucking roses. He stepped from the stall, wrapping a towel around his waist. Although the shower had helped his body to relax slightly, it couldn't help the frenetic pace of his thoughts.

What he needed was to tune out and let his mind go completely fucking blank for a while. Mindless reality TV was in order. He couldn't understand the humans' fascination with it, but at least it numbed the mind. In the living room, he turned on the seventy-nine-inch monster set against the wall, the home theater kicking in at the same time. Rhys wandered over to the bar and poured himself some bourbon. Back in front of the TV, he sat his ass down and took his first sip of Kentucky Tavern. It went down his throat smoothly, the flavor of vanilla lingering on his palate.

American Idol was on. A judge was yammering on about how transcendental some woman's performance was.

Blah, blah, blah.

He took another sip from his glass, trying to concentrate on anything but Galen's disappearance and the bloodlust still owning his body. If his best friend was dead, he wanted to give him the funeral he deserved. Murderous intent pumped through his blood like poison, his beast enjoying the slideshow of blood and gore currently streaming through Rhys's head.

Staring down into his glass of bourbon, Rhys knew alcohol alone wasn't going to cut it. He needed another release, but with Galen missing, it would be up to him to find a woman he could use. Slamming back the rest of his drink, he stood up and got dressed before fading to the alleyway beside Ice. As he stepped into the glare of the streetlight, a giant black bird cawed and landed on the stop sign at the intersection.

Rhys walked to the front door of the building and pushed it open. The cold air hit him and he shivered. At the bar, he ordered a shot of bourbon and tipped it back.

"Another one," he told Skadi. The ice giant produced the bottle and topped up his glass once more. Rhys turned around to face the room, his eyes jumping from face to face, trying to find a suitable female. The problem was there were none. They were all light elves, and he'd vowed he wouldn't ever touch one of them. In fact, the last time he'd been there with Galen, Rhys had intentionally scared off the woman his best friend had coerced to come to their table.

Rhys placed his empty glass on the bar and headed for the door. If he was going to get what he needed – not what he *wanted* – he would have to go somewhere else. He didn't want to hurt one of his kind, so that left only one place. He had to hit up a human bar.

Walking down the sidewalk, Rhys checked out the nightclubs he passed. The music blaring out of them was a strange assault on his senses. He finally picked one where a human the size of a Mini was standing outside. The deciding factor had been the lack of line to get in. Stepping up to the bouncer, Rhys looked him in the eye and waited.

"ID," the human drawled.

Pulling the wallet from his back pocket, Rhys produced the card the bouncer wanted. The guy studied it for a moment, his eyes darting to Rhys's face then down at the info. Handing it back, the bouncer took a step away from the doorway and nodded for Rhys to go in.

The lighting in the club was dim, the only real source of illumination coming from the red track lighting under the bar, in bulkheads above it, and in the inset ceilings. He walked around until he found a free table and sat down. Seconds later, a waitress appeared.

Placing a cocktail napkin on the table, she asked, "What'll it be?" As she bent down, Rhys got an eyeful of her breasts and the black lace bra that was holding them back. A girl like her would have had the matching panties too.

"Bourbon. Neat."

The woman smiled. "My kind of guy. Be right back."

He watched her walk away, hypnotized by the sway of her hips. She would do. When she returned, and placed his drink down, Rhys took hold of her wrist, careful not to be too rough.

"What time do you get off?"

"Not until two, but I have a break in thirty."

He gently caressed the inside of her wrist. "What's your name?"

"Cat," she replied.

"Come and find me when you take your break."

Want.

Rhys ignored the voice, smiling at Cat when she nodded. He slid a fifty into the glass on her tray. That was a little stiff for a shot of bourbon, but he didn't care. He was just laying the groundwork. He sat back in his chair, bringing the glass to his lips. The club had an eclectic mix of people; there were some businessmen still in suits, knocking back a few drinks before going home, some older women in small groups, and a few younger looking men who were probably in college.

He nursed his bourbon and people-watched until Cat came back over to him wearing a wicked smile.

"Are you ready?" she asked.

He nodded and threw the rest of his drink down. Standing up, he held out his hand to her. "Which way is the bathroom?"

"I've got a better idea. My boss is out for about an hour. We can use his office."

Rhys paused for a moment, thinking through his options. Being in a semi-private place was necessary. If things went bad, he needed to know there would be help for her. Being somewhere completely private – like her boss's office – heavily decreased Cat's chances of survival if . . . no, *when* things got out of control.

"Wait—" he said, but she tugged on his hand, dragging him through the crowded dance floor.

He should have pulled away. He was stronger than her, but there was a small part of him that said this was necessary. He didn't have the luxury of time; the beast would need to be sated. They climbed a set of metal stairs that led to a mezzanine where there was another bar set up and three doors along the back wall. Cat opened the one in the middle of the room. He reluctantly followed her into the office.

"Lock the door behind you," Cat said, slinking over to the desk and pulling open a drawer. A bottle of Jack and two glasses hit the table a moment later.

"Drink?"

"Sure," he replied. She poured them each a drink and handed him his.

"To new acquaintances," she said, knocking her glass gently against his.

"To new acquaintances," he murmured darkly, looking at her over the lip of his glass. Away from the red-tinted light she looked younger than he'd first thought. Her age didn't matter though. He had to get what he needed, inflicting as little damage as possible, then get the fuck out of there.

Finishing his drink, he reached for her glass and placed it back on the table. With one hand behind her neck, he pulled her close and claimed her mouth. With his free hand, he wrapped it around her waist and drew her closer to his body.

Cat raked her hands through his hair, running her fingers down the back of his neck. Digging his fingers into her ass, he lifted her off the ground and placed her on the desk, bending over her until her back hit the hard wooden surface.

More.

She gasped when his fingers found their way up her inner thighs. Impatient, he pushed aside her underwear and sank two fingers inside her.

"Oh, fuck," she hissed. A growl sat perilously close on Rhys's lips. Pressing his mouth together, he denied the sound. Inside his head, his beast bared its fangs and snarled. Sex would eventually sooth the beast, but not before aggravating it further. It was the release that Rhys was looking for. It was the release that brought him true peace.

Impatient and afraid his control would slip if he prolonged the act, he tore the underwear from her body and dragged her closer to the edge of the desk by her thighs. She gasped again when he shoved the bottom of her shirt up to get to her breasts, suckling on one through her bra. Rolling her tight nipple in his mouth, he bit down on the tender flesh then flicked his tongue over it, easing away the sting.

She arched her back, her hands fumbling to undo the clasp at the back.

"Leave it," Rhys commanded. "We don't have time."

Cat's hands fell away. His attention went to her other nipple, standing erect and begging for the same treatment. Another moan passed her lips, and Rhys could smell she was ready for him.

He lowered his fly.

"Wait," she said, propping herself up on her elbows. "I want to have your cock down my throat first."

His eyes slid shut. As good as that sounded, they didn't have the time – *he* didn't have the time. His beast was getting more and more impatient. Each pant and sharp intake of breath was just another broken rung on the ladder of his self-control.

"No time," he bit out. He flipped her over onto her stomach. Planting her feet on the ground, Rhys pressed a hand against the center of her back, forcing her to bend over further. When she was right where he needed her, he stepped back to look at the offering.

Want, his beast whispered.

Even though he shouldn't have, Rhys slapped her on the ass. She groaned in pleasure. He shut his eyes for a moment, mentally tightening his hold on his beast. He would have to be very careful now. He positioned himself against her opening, pushing in a little, giving her a few seconds to adjust before pulling his hips back and slamming into her. She inhaled sharply. He stopped. When she encouraged him with a moan, he started to move again.

A steady rhythm began to build, and he found himself getting lost in the sensation. His beast moved forward in his mind, trying to dominate Rhys's thoughts. Holding her more securely in place, he increased his pace, getting faster and faster. That was when his vision changed to red.

His beast was taking over.

Placing his hand against her mouth, he said, "Bite me."

"What?" she replied breathlessly. All the air was being forced from her body each time he slammed into her.

"Bite. Me."

For a moment, nothing happened. Then he felt her lips wrap around his hand, and her teeth sink home. The pain refocused him, allowing him to push back against his beast's hold. He couldn't hold it forever though. He needed to finish. Reaching his free hand around Cat, he found the sensitive flesh between her legs and applied a little pressure.

"Jesus," she breathed, grinding back on him. "Do that again."

He pressed against her again, feeling her inner walls beginning to spasm around his length.

"I'm going to come," she panted right before her whole body tensed and a scream rolled out of her throat. Her body constricted around him, and he felt his release coming too. He was so close, and he would finally have some peace. After Cat's orgasm crested, though, she stopped writhing against him and forced him back a step as she straightened.

No, no, no, Rhys thought desperately, his hands still vice-like on her hips.

She turned around, forcing him from her body. She started to tug her skirt back into place. "That was amazing," she said, face flushed. "Was it good for you?"

More. Blood. Now.

The animal was pacing back and forth, growing more aggressive. It bayed loudly in his head, commanding Rhys to take what he wanted. He was resistant though. He was the product of rape; he didn't ever want to force a woman. And with Galen gone, he was never in more danger of doing exactly that. Rhys gritted his teeth and shook his head. "No," he ground out.

He was stunned when Cat raised her hand and slapped him hard across the cheek. "You goddamn son of a bitch," she snarled, marching past him and out of the office.

4

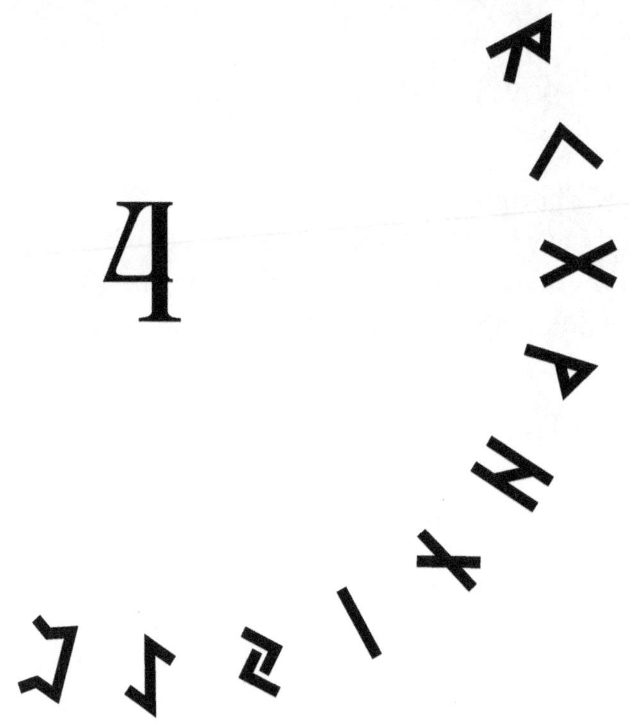

Tove yelled in triumph as she brought the wooden sword down toward Soren's stomach, stopping just before the blade struck. She was breathing heavily through her nose, her chest heaving up and down. Tossing her long braid over her shoulder, she stepped back and grinned fiercely. The dust their boots had kicked up was just settling, rays of sunlight cutting through it.

Soren slowly sat up, his brown eyes watching Tove. A frown was firmly in place by the time he stood. "How did you do that?" he demanded, rubbing the back of his head. Soren's skinny arm was sticking out of his coarse tunic. The fabric was smeared with mud and dusted with fine grit from the floor.

Tove placed her sword back into the scabbard on her hip. "I watch my father spar with his men."

"Can you show me how to do that sweep thing you did?"

"Sure," Tove said, beaming. Soren was older than her by a year, but he was her best friend. All the other boys didn't want to play with her because of who her father was, and Tove had never liked playing with the other girls in the village. They were too concerned with dolls and sewing, and they never wanted to fight with swords like she did.

"Pretend like you're going to attack me again," Tove instructed. Soren brushed the dust from his tunic and took position. Tove nodded. "Good. Now when your opponent is standing there with both feet on the ground, sweep your leg behind both of theirs and drive them backwards at the same time."

Tove completed the move, shoving Soren in the chest and sending him to the ground again. He grunted as he landed, but instead of scowling at her, he was smiling. She offered him her hand, hauling him up out of the dirt.

"Okay, you try it on me now."

Soren got the idea pretty quickly. He pushed Tove into the dust and grinned. He pulled her up. She was just finding her feet when she and Soren were surrounded by three boys from the village.

"Is that your girlfriend, Soren?" one of them taunted.

"Yeah, Soren. Are you going to marry Tove?" another said.

"Leave her alone, Jarl," Soren said, putting himself between Tove and the boys.

"What were you two doing anyway?" Jarl asked again, his eyes taking in the swords they were practicing with. "Don't tell me you were teaching her how to fight."

"Girls can't fight!" another boy said, trying to grab Tove's scabbard. She whirled around and punched him in the face. Blood streamed from his nose, his hands doing nothing to stem the flow.

"Sefi, are you all right?"

"Yeah, I'm all right, Roland," Sefi replied, spitting blood from his mouth. He turned his eyes to Tove. "I'll make you pay for this."

"I'd like to see you try," she shot back.

The boy wiped a hand under his nose, wincing a little. "Why don't you go home and practice your sewing with your mother? Oh wait! You can't, can you?"

All the boys laughed at Sefi's comment. Tove ground her teeth together, the reminder that her mother was no longer there like a rusty knife in her gut. She could feel tears stinging her eyes, but she refused to acknowledge them.

"Look, she's going to cry like a big girl," Roland announced, laughing at Tove's pain. The other two joined in.

"Don't listen to them," Soren said, hugging her. "You might not have your mother, but you have mine. She loves you just as much, Tove." Soren's parents, Gaia and Reiner, were like her own, but Sefi's words still hurt, and they were still tragically true. She let herself have the comfort for just a moment before pulling away. She looked up at her best friend, shook her head and turned away.

"Tove! Wait!" Soren called after her.

"Tove! Wait!" they all mocked. Tove ran from the marketplace, the echoes of their voices following her. Her scabbard bounced painfully on her hip, slapping her thigh and calf. She weaved through the people walking around the streets, leading horses pulling carts full of vegetables and animals.

She finally made it home, running up the shallow stairs and into the house she shared with her father. He was the chieftain of the village, so he was rarely alone. He was sitting in the great hall, a fierce fire burning in the center of the room. Her father's advisor, Ivor, stood to one side while her father listened to the complaints of the village folk.

"My wife has been unfaithful," a man said, looking disdainfully at the woman by his side. Tove walked through the shadows at the edge of the room, seeing that the woman was with child. She looked no older than fifteen – only five years older than Tove. Was that what it was going to be like for her? Was she going to be someone's wife in five years' time?

"What proof do you have?" her father asked.

"I found her in the bed of another, my lord," the man said.

Tove's father turned his attention to the woman. "Is what he's said true?" he asked, his tone softening just like it did when he spoke to Tove.

"No, my lord. I have been faithful to my husband."

"Whose child is it that you bear?"

"My husband's," the woman replied, her hands protectively cradling her swollen abdomen. Ivor leaned forward and whispered something in his ear. Her father's eyes cut to the woman's husband.

"I've just heard that you are the one guilty of being unfaithful, Sweyn."

"I . . ." Sweyn sputtered.

"I've heard that you have taken another wife in the neighboring village. So, I think the only one guilty of infidelity is you. Your case is dismissed." Tove's father took the silver arm ring from around the man's forearm and looked to Sweyn's wife. "As recompense, I will give you this." He offered it to the woman who carefully approached the dais.

"Thank you, Halvdan. You are a truly gracious ruler," she said, accepting the silver circlet.

Ivor stepped down and escorted the couple from the room. Her father slumped back in his chair, rubbing at his face. Tove skirted around the room, but stopped when her father spoke.

"Why are you crying, child?" he asked.

Tove froze. "How did you know I was here?"

He dropped his hand and stared at her. "I always know where you are," he said in reply. Tove rubbed the tears from her cheeks before stepping into the light. Her father studied her. "What has happened?"

"It was nothing."

"You cannot lie to me, Tove. Remember?"

She let out a breath and walked on to the platform, climbing into his lap. Leaning against his arm, she said, "Some boys from the village told me I shouldn't be fighting. They said I should be learning how to sew from my . . . from my mother."

Her father's brows drew down. "Who are these boys?" he demanded.

"It doesn't matter who they are," she replied.

He stroked the side of his face with his finger and sighed. "Perhaps they are right, Tove."

She stiffened in his arms. "What do you mean, Father?"

"I mean, you are going to have to stop playing around in the dust and dirt and learn the skills a woman should have. You could be married in a couple of years, bearing children of your own."

"I don't want to get married, Father. I want to fight."

Her father picked her up and set her on her feet in front of him. "You know that cannot be."

"Why not?" she demanded, putting her hands on her hips defiantly.

"Because you are too precious to me. You are my only daughter and you could get seriously injured if you fight. Those boys will soon grow into men and they will be stronger than you in every way. I don't want you to practice anymore. Leave swordplay for the boys."

"That's not fair," she pouted.

Her father laughed gently. "Life is not fair."

"Halvdan? There are still more people to be heard," Ivor announced, walking back into the hall.

"Yes, of course," he replied. To Tove he said, "Go and get cleaned up. You're covered in dirt and you have straw in your hair."

Tove walked toward the back of the hall, but stood in the shadows when her father's conversation with his advisor caught her attention.

"I have just heard that some houses on the farthest fringes of the village have been attacked," Ivor said, his voice grave.

"By who?" Halvdan demanded.

"Canute Borg and his men. They left one boy alive who was told to report to you."

"With what message?" His voice was tight.

"That they are loyal to Vadik Dalgaard and only him."

There was a crash as her father swept away the cup and plate of food from the arm of his chair. "This is the third attack this month," he roared. "Who else will join Dalgaard in his quest to unseat me?"

Halvdan's question surprised Tove. She didn't know her father's position as chieftain was a point of contention. Were there some people out there who wished to see him gone?

Shaken, Tove left the hall and went to the area where she slept. She was still so angry with the boys, but also angry with her father for not allowing her to fight. She was good with the sword. She was even better with a spear, but she would never be able to use either skill if her father denied her the opportunity to practice. Well, she wasn't going to listen to him. If what she'd overheard was true, he would need every able-bodied fighter he could find, including her.

Without changing out of her dress, Tove snuck out and made her way to the beach. She walked on the shore, watching the fishing boats coming and going. She kicked at the loose stones, sending them skittering into the water.

"Did you go and cry to your father?" someone asked snidely.

Tove looked up and found Sefi glaring at her. Blood had dried under his nose and on his chin. Patches of red were splashed on the front of his tunic. She smiled. "Did you?"

The boy's hands curled into tight fists at his sides. He seemed to be shaking with rage as he pulled on the handle of his wooden sword. He drew it and held it in front of him. Tove reached for hers too, matching his stance. Jarl and Roland, Sefi's friends, ran up, drawing their swords too. Tove looked at them, then glanced behind her. She was too close to the water. Her boots were sinking into the sand already. As if the boys had heard her thoughts, they began closing in.

"We're going to teach you a lesson, Tove," Jarl said, taking another step closer. Tove licked her lips and shuffled back another step. Her foot landed in the water, her shoes flooding with the freezing liquid. She looked at all of them, trying to decide who was going to strike first.

Her world slowed down then. She could hear her heart pounding in her ears, could smell the briny water. She blinked slowly, and when her eyes opened again, she gasped. Hovering above each of the boys' heads was a shimmer of color. Jarl and Roland's was red, but Sefi's was black and Tove knew deep down in her gut that that was very, very bad.

Sefi wanted to hurt her.

He was the first to strike. Tove deflected it, letting Sefi's momentum carry him forward. She shoved him in the back, sending him sprawling into the water. Edging away from the shore, she looked to Jarl and Roland. Roland swung his sword and hit Tove in the leg. She limped back a step, prepared for the next time he struck. Roland brought his sword above his head and lunged at Tove. Getting down into a crouch, she swept his legs out from under him and pushed him into the water with Sefi.

Jarl was the only boy left now. With a cry leaving his mouth, he rushed Tove. The fifteen feet between them was quickly being swallowed up. At the last moment, Jarl's foot hit a stone deeply buried in the sand and he was propelled forward. Tove stepped out of the way, watching the last of her attackers land in the water.

All three boys stayed where they were, too shocked to move. Tove stepped back, bringing her sword up, ready for round two. But they didn't move. A bubble of laughter burst from her lips as she looked at them, soaked to the bone with their teeth chattering.

She put her sword away and turned around, wandering back the way she'd come.

When she returned to her house, her father was lifting himself from his chair, finally done with his work for the day. He took one look at her, a deep scowl lining his face.

"What has happened to you?" he demanded. The few servants in the hall startled at his raised voice before quickly returning to their work.

Tove looked down at herself. The front of her dress was covered in water and mud. She looked back to her father and shrugged.

"You're bleeding."

That was when Tove felt the warm trickle of blood down her thigh. Roland must have struck her a lot harder than she realized. She tried to keep her gaze on her father, not acknowledging the injury.

"Tell me what happened, Tove." His voice was a command she could not ignore.

"Those boys attacked me first. They ganged up on me!"

Fury flashed behind his eyes. "You fought them?" he hissed. She nodded minutely. "How many?"

"There were three of them."

"Who? I want their names."

Tove crossed her arms over her chest and shook her head. If she told her father and he punished them, they would continue to bully her. He looked at her expectantly, but she wasn't backing down.

He frowned. "You won't tell me, will you?"

She shook her head.

He continued to give her a hard look, then shocked her when he began to laugh. Throwing an arm over her shoulders, he led her toward the dais. He gestured for her to sit down in the huge wooden chair, but she hesitated. She was never allowed to sit in it.

"Go on," he encouraged. "Sit down while I go and get some water to clean up that cut."

Tove lifted herself onto the seat and swung her legs, waiting. Her father returned with a small bowl of water and a rag. He wiped away the blood slowly.

"You're just like your mother. Do you know that?" he told her, his focus still fixed on her leg wound.

Tove held her breath, waiting for her father to say more. He hardly mentioned her mother, and never willingly talked about her. All she knew was that her name was Bodil and she was a shield maiden who had died on the battlefield.

"When she was your age, she was always getting into trouble and fighting the boys." He sighed, rinsing the rag in the water. "I guess the acorn does not fall far from the tree." Her father met her eyes. "You have spirit, Tove Norling, just like your mother did. I'm more proud of you than I could ever say, but I cannot bear the thought of losing you in battle too." Tilting her chin up, he stared into her eyes. "That's why I cannot allow you to play with swords anymore."

No! "But—"

"No, Tove. This is not up for discussion. I forbid it."

She could see the hardness in her father's expression, knew that his mind could not be changed. Whatever protests she had died on her tongue. Instead, she sat back in the chair and looked away.

"All right. All done. Go on now," her father said, sounding weary. "Change your dress and wash up. The evening meal will be ready soon."

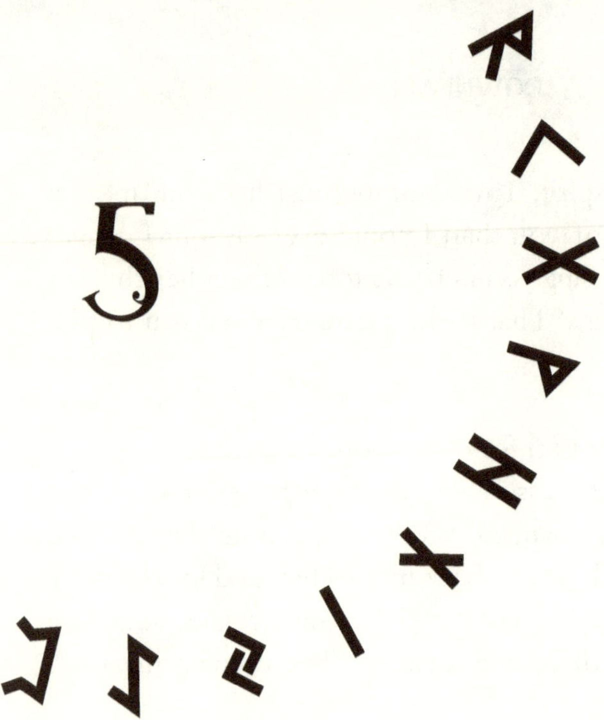

5

The steady pounding of her feet on the pavement was a sound Mav had missed hearing. She didn't know how long she'd been at it, but by the way the sun was dipping down into the horizon, it must have been at least four hours. She hadn't run like this in a long time – not since the first threats to Bryn and the other Valkyries.

Over their thousands of years of existence, nobody had managed to scare Bryn the way Loki had over a month ago. It was only now that she was starting to loosen up, and apparently the first matter of business for this new, relaxed Bryn was to force Mav to take a whole day and night off. But Mav had dug in her heels and refused. Instead, they'd come to an agreement: she would take only half a day off and Bryn would just have to accept it. The fact was, Mav's job was to protect Bryn and the only way she could do that was by being wherever her leader was.

After Korvain moved in, it helped to ease the burden on Mav. Bryn was happy for the first time in a long time with him; he had saved her life when nobody else had been able to. Although their relationship was built on deceit to start with, Bryn had forgiven him and it was stronger than ever now.

Mav ran down Boylston Street until she hit Boston Common, slowing her pace to a fast walk. Despite the fact that she was a goddess, she had to remain in the best shape possible in order to protect Bryn and the remaining Valkyries. It was a fallacy that the gods had superior strength. They all still bled just like everyone else, and you were only as strong as you allowed your muscles to become.

As her breathing returned to normal, she looked around. There were still a lot of people in the park bundled up in heavy coats while Mav ran in black shorts and a skin-tight running shirt. She checked her watch for the time and started jogging back toward the club. She wanted to get in another weights work out before she started at seven.

Dodging cars as she crossed over Tremont, Mav weaved between the pedestrians, finding herself coming up on the alleyway that led to the back entrance of the club. She punched in the code on the door and stepped inside. Moving on autopilot, she walked down the long hall, heading toward the elevator. She was still lost in her own head, her mind on the dream she'd had the night before. She had not thought on it for centuries, but for some reason she had dreamed of the day she awoke to discover everyone she'd ever loved was dead.

"Gunner?"

Maverick stopped dead, the sound of the name Odin had given her when she became one of his Valkyries bringing her up short.

She hadn't been called that since the Fall.

From inside her office, Bryn said, "Sorry, but I was calling you and you couldn't seem to hear me. Can I speak to you for a moment?"

Retreating back a few steps, Mav leaned against the jamb, her arms over her chest. Mist – Bryn's second-in-command – was sitting in the chair opposite the desk, a tablet on her lap with a spreadsheet open on the screen. Mav nodded to the other Valkyrie before turning her attention to Bryn.

"How was your half day off?" Bryn asked.

"Unnecessary." After all, it wasn't as if she'd had much of a choice in the matter. All it did was give her time to think about the biggest mistake she'd ever made in her life.

Bryn's mouth flexed into a small smile. "Well, you still have another two hours of it so don't even think about coming back down here early."

Mav nodded and turned back to the elevator. As she rode it up, her watch started beeping, telling her that her heart rate had dropped by more than thirty beats a minute. She silenced the device and stared at her reflection in the polished elevator doors. Although the image was distorted, she tracked the dark gray aura hovering over her head and shoulders; it was a slightly darker shade than it had been a month earlier. The doors sprang open unexpectedly – Mav too lost in her thoughts to even notice the elevator had slid to a smooth stop on the top level.

She stepped into the hallway, pulling her apartment key from the concealed pocket in her running shorts. Once inside, Mav went straight to the free weights she had set up against the far wall. The abdominal bench and flat bench were in the center of the room and her latest purchase – the leg press machine she had punished her body on every day since she bought it – was on the opposite wall.

After two hundred barbell rows, she did another two hundred lunges before finally finishing with her usual five hundred push-ups. With sweat pouring down her temples and rolling off her chin, she finished her last push-up and collapsed back onto her ass. Hauling herself off the ground, she swiped the towel from the top of the dumbbell rack and wrapped it around her shoulders. She had just enough time to get cleaned up before her shift started. She showered quickly, and dried off just as fast. Running her hands over her freshly shaved scalp, Mav looked at herself in the mirror, eyeing her aura warily. She closed her eyes and inhaled deeply, then let the breath go.

In her room, she dressed with military quickness and precision, pulling on the skin-hugging leather pants and black tank top she wore at the club. Out of habit, she swiped her index finger over the tattoo on the side of her neck and summoned her black sword. It materialized in her hand, the weight and smell of it as familiar as the contours of her own face. Twisting her wrist from side to side, she studied it, checking it over for imperfections that it would never have. The steel had been forged by the most skilled blacksmith, but that was not what made it so deadly. Afterward, Odin had beaten the metal — not with a hammer — but with a magic only he could wield. With it, he crafted a weapon that was deadly to anyone who received a scratch from it, but he had paid dearly for doing so.

Touching the tattoo once more, the sword disappeared. Mav sat down on the edge of her bed and pulled on her boots, lacing them up tightly. The final thing she put on was the weapon holster Bryn had insisted all her security wear. Mav couldn't see the point of having it. Why give a wolf another pair of fangs when they already had a full set of teeth?

Still, she slid in the Beretta and snapped the clip in place.

She left her apartment and took the elevator down to the club level. Walking into the Eye, she saw the head of security – a human named Mason – standing at the base of the stairs leading up to the upper levels. Mason was the only human who knew about Bryn and the other Valkyries. An ex-Marine, he had taken a knock to the head in Iraq which resulted in him being able to hear the thoughts of the gods – not that he knew that at the time.

In the last few weeks, Mason's aura had started to change color from a murky brown to a vibrant red. Eir, the goddess of healing, was responsible for that, and Mav was glad that somebody had found love and happiness. She nodded in Mason's direction, moving toward the front door. Even though he was technically her boss, Mav didn't answer to him. Her loyalty – as it had always been – was to Bryn.

Mav stepped up beside the guard Bryn had assigned as her replacement for the night. He glanced at her briefly, handing her the clipboard with the names of the parties still to come through the doors.

"Any problems so far?" she asked.

The guy cringed at the sound of her voice.

Yep, that's a real confidence boost right there.

"Nothing."

Mav nodded, her eyes scanning over the sheet of paper. Just over half of their expected groups had already entered the club. "You can leave now," she said to the human, still staring at the list of names. She didn't need to look to know a halo of dark yellow was surrounding him; she made him nervous. He let out a small relieved breath and turned away, getting lost in the crowd.

Mav's focus turned to the line of people waiting to get in. It ran the length of the front of the building and down the side out of sight. Two-thirds of them wouldn't get in tonight – the Eye was always filled to capacity by the end of the night – yet they always tried to sweet talk her into letting them in.

"Nice ink."

Mav's gaze found the guy who decided to get chatty with her.

Human.

Mid-twenties.

Too cocky for his own good.

He had a swagger about him, and Mav had seen it all before.

"I said, nice ink," he repeated, flashing his pearly whites this time around. Too bad for him that no amount of dental work would convince her to reciprocate. She stared at him, hoping he had the common sense to stop trying to engage with her. The human's smile faded and he broke eye contact.

About fucking time.

Mav waited until the line started to get antsy before she began to let people in. Mason had already told her they were only half full, thanks to the tech she had in place in her ear. Motioning to the group of women at the front of the line, she studied them as they stepped inside. All of them were already buzzed, but they were only interested in having a good night. Mav fell into the comfortable rhythm that work could offer her. It was a far cry from the warrior lifestyle she'd lived and breathed before, but this was her life now. The age of the Valkyries was over.

6

Odin longed to return home to Boston, but the news he'd received from the Norns kept him in Chicago. For the past few weeks, he had been following Loki's movements, always remaining hidden from sight, either in the back of his armored Mercedes or safely within the confines of his luxurious hotel room.

The trickster god had been wreaking havoc here in a way that Odin knew too well. Loki had been playing with the humans, assuming the identity of a businessman called Henry Craine in order to interact with two Mares who seemed to have piqued his interest. Odin had yet to figure out what part they'd play in Loki's overall plan though.

Discovering the identity of Fenrir's son was like looking for a needle in the proverbial haystack – tedious – yet it was a necessity if he was to find a way to finally kill Loki. He stared out the window as Hunter, his driver, drove them down into the university village. It was early evening, and there were a lot of people walking around in small groups. Odin noted that most of them were young men.

That was when he saw it.

"Stop the car, Hunter," he said, sitting forward in his seat to get a better look at what had caught his attention. Wrapped around one of the lamp posts was a poster advertising an event that was taking place that night. Odin looked at his watch. Less than an hour until it started. "Hunter, I want to go to the UIC Pavilion."

"You got it, boss," Hunter replied, pulling smoothly back out into the traffic. As the car traveled closer and closer to their destination, Odin began to fidget, tugging at the cuffs of his shirt and loosening his tie. The car glided to a stop, and he took a moment to look through the dark tinted window. If Frigg were still alive, she'd claim that he was being paranoid, but it was his paranoia that had saved his ass more times than he could count.

Hunter came around to open the passenger door. Odin stepped from the car and shrugged deeper into his sable-trimmed cashmere coat, trying to shake off the chill of the Chicago air and the anxiety suddenly pressing on him. He hated being exposed.

He studied the large round UIC building in front of him. The front half was made of glass, the remaining half a red brick that reminded him of Boston. There were people everywhere, all of them jostling to get inside. A flyer skidded across the ground, wrapping around Odin's pant leg. He scooped it up and looked at the poster promoting the mixed martial arts event.

All sound ceased to exist and Odin's world tilted on its axis. On the flyer in his hands, his son's hard face stared back at him. Every inch of his arms were covered in tattoos, the ink depicting everything from Odin's Valkyries riding across the heavens to lightning boiling from the clouds with a violent and bloody battleground beneath. Taking up the entirety of his chest was Mjolnir, Thor's war hammer.

Odin had not seen or spoken to his son since the Fall. He'd heard rumors, though, that Thor had been spotted in different places around the world: Athens, London, Moscow, Sydney and Ontario – just to name a few. Odin had spent many days in each of those cities, but he'd never been able to establish a connection, to find him, so he had dismissed the rumors as exactly that – rumors.

And now he had found him – finally. Determined to warn his son about Loki's presence in Chicago and his desire for revenge, Odin began walking in the direction of the doors, but a familiar caw stopped him and drew his attention. Sitting on the top of a nearby traffic signal was one of his ravens. He'd only called his birds, Huginn and Muninn, back into service within the last few weeks; Odin needed more than one set of eyes and ears out there for him. Muninn's oily black feathers puffed up then resettled as he waited for his commands.

Odin looked around quickly to see if anyone was paying him any attention, then to the raven he said, "Keep looking for Loki and the two Mares. If you find any of them, return to me immediately."

Muninn squawked before taking flight. Odin smoothed the collar of his coat and started toward the building once more. Walking through the doors, he saw there were stalls set up selling t-shirts with promoter logos all over them. He bypassed the merchandise stands, following the steady stream of people entering through a secondary set of doors into the arena. A security guard stopped him before he could walk through.

"Hey, man, you got a ticket or what?"

Odin turned to him. "No. Where can I get one?"

"Box office is out the front," the guy replied, pointing back the way Odin had come. He was already reaching for the next person's ticket as Odin retreated back outside. He didn't have time for this. Stepping away from the crowd, he faded into the arena.

Inside, the noise was nearly unbearable. Thousands of people were milling around the tiered seating rising up on three sides of the room. In the center was an eight-sided ring on top of a four foot high platform. Surrounded by a chain-link fence covered in black vinyl, the letters *XFO* were printed in the middle of the ring. Hanging from the rafters were three huge screens, currently showing advertisements for other fights coming up.

"Ladies and gentleman, ten minutes to go. That's ten minutes before our first fight begins," the announcer said over the PA system, his voice booming into the mass of noise. Moving through the crowd, Odin selected a seat a few rows behind the judges and sat down.

A man wearing a suit stepped into the ring and a hush fell over the crowd. Into the microphone he said, "Good evening, folks, and welcome to the University of Illinois at Chicago. We have six bouts lined up for you tonight, each consisting of five five-minute rounds. The final fight is for the XFO Middleweight Championship . . ."

The crowd erupted into cheers. Thor could hear them clapping at a frenetic pace even down in the locker rooms where he and his combined corner and cut man . . . woman . . . was taping up his fists.

"Big crowd," Lilith murmured, pulling another long strip of tape off the roll and tearing it with her teeth. Thor glanced at the goddess and grunted. "Nervous?" She wrapped the tape around his hand, securing the gauze bandage already in place.

"What do you think?" he shot back.

She shrugged, unaffected by his bad mood. "This guy is twenty-two and oh."

"So?"

Lilith glared at him. "You might actually have to work to win this one."

"It'll be nice for a change then," Thor replied, squeezing his hand into a fist to test the tension in the tape. "Do this one again. It needs to be tighter."

Lilith rolled her eyes and started pulling off the tape.

"You can be a real bitch sometimes. Do you know that?"

She cocked a brow at him. "Good thing you're an asshole so you don't give a shit how much of a bitch I am."

Thor tried to stifle his smile. The goddess had a point.

Outside, the sound of the announcer hyping up the crowd intruded on Thor's pre-fight tranquility. "And now, introducing our first fighters; in the red corner, fighting out of San Diego, California, at five foot ten, weighing in at one hundred and eighty three pounds. . ."

"How's the knee feeling?"

Thor had torn his ACL a couple of weeks before. Being a god, he'd healed in two weeks from an injury that would have sidelined most humans for up to six months. "Fine."

Lilith finished the strapping, shaking her head at him. "Asshole," she muttered under her breath.

Even though she was just as surly as he was, Thor couldn't have prepped for any fight as well as he did without her there. One of the other fighter's corner men came into the room, knocking on the jamb a couple of times to get their attention.

"You got any tape I can borrow?" he asked Thor, completely ignoring Lilith. Thor looked over at the goddess then back to the human.

"Ask her. I don't know," he replied, sitting back to watch the sparks fly. Lilith was overlooked by every man in the sport unless they were looking to get their cocks sucked. The guy's eyes shifted to Lilith, his gaze drifting down to check out her tits. The goddess's anger boiled over. A full roll of tape was suddenly sent flying, hitting the guy in the face. It dropped to the floor with a *thud.*

"What the fuck?" the human bellowed, stepping into the room and getting up in Lilith's grill.

Lilith stood toe-to-toe with the guy, her petite hands curling into fists. "You fucking misogynist bastard!"

"You raging bitch!" he yelled back, his face getting redder and redder. "Women have no place in this sport unless they're on their knees."

Lilith threw herself at him, tackling him to the ground. A flurry of punches rained down on his face and body. Thor stood to pull her off him. The female could inflict a hell of a lot of damage when left unchecked. Hauling her up, he held her back while the other guy recovered. He had a bloody nose and a busted lip. He pulled himself off the floor and retreated from the room, Lilith throwing more insults involving him giving fellatio to a goat.

Thor chuckled, releasing the goddess. "You're a hellcat, aren't you?"

Lilith grinned. "You're only just realizing this now?" she said, going to the ice bucket and putting a few cubes into a towel. She held them over her knuckles for a moment. "I think I broke my hand punching that bastard's hard head."

They fell into their usual pre-fight routine with Thor putting on some headphones and cranking up 50 Cent's "Patiently Waiting", while Lilith pulled out a worn and dog-eared paperback and curled up in a chair in the corner. Half an hour later, an official came and checked Thor's wraps. With about twenty minutes to go, Thor got Lilith to massage his legs, making sure his muscles stayed limber.

"Thor, you're up next," Lilith said, interrupting his thoughts. He looked at the muted TV hanging on the wall. The final match before the main event was coming to an end. The goddess threw him a sponsor shirt and picked up his towel. Together they made their way to the start of the tunnel, waiting for their cue.

Ten minutes later, Thor was walking toward the ring. People were crammed into the venue, spilling over the barricades. A lot of women were leaning over the railings, trying to touch him. Lilith did her best to make sure he wasn't harassed too much, but whatever. This was a part of fame he just had to deal with.

His career as a mixed martial arts fighter had been gradual. He'd had to work his way up through the training gym just like any human would have. He'd spent years learning Muay Thai, kickboxing and Brazilian Jiu-Jitsu along with other similar disciplines until finally someone had taken notice of him. And although he was still the god of thunder, Thor's superhuman strength only manifested when he was holding his war hammer, Mjolnir.

The ringside physician looked him over, asking him to squeeze his hands, breathe in deeply a few times. He finished by shining a torch in his eyes. Obviously satisfied Thor wasn't carrying any glaring injuries, the physician gave him the go-ahead to continue.

Thor took off his shirt. Some women standing close by screamed when they saw his naked chest. His tattoos always got him a lot of attention. Lilith applied petroleum jelly to his eyebrows to stop blood getting into his eyes and again to the bridge of his nose, then took his shirt from him. Thor climbed into the ring, pacing his side of the mat.

The announcer stepped into the center after him, his microphone in hand. "Ladies and gentlemen, this is the main event of the evening! Introducing first, fighting out of the blue corner with a professional record of twenty-two wins, no draws, one no contest; he stands five feet seven inches tall, weighing in at one hundred and seventy pounds; fighting out of Sao Paulo, Brazil. He is Anderson Souza!"

Thor watched his opponent waving to the crowd. He was confident and Thor couldn't wait to beat it out of him.

"And now, introducing his opponent," the announcer said. "Fighting out of the red corner with a professional record of thirty wins, no draws, zero no contests; weighing in at one hundred and eighty-five pounds; fighting out of Chicago, Illinois, presenting the former XFO lightweight and former XFO welterweight champion, Thor!" The cheer that greeted him was deafening. From the corner of his eye he saw a woman flashing her tits at him, but he kept his focus on Souza.

The match began with Souza coming at him, trying to get them down on the mats. The human was good at grappling, having obviously perfected the art of Jiu-Jitsu, but Thor had the superior strength. By the end of the second round, he'd put Souza into three submission holds, but the Brazilian had broken free each time. Thor had let him, of course. He wanted to give everyone value for money. They traded blows in the fourth round, and by the fifth, Thor had had enough. He got Souza into a chokehold against the cage and it was all over.

The roar that filled the arena made Thor's ears throb. He stood back while the physician hopped into the ring and checked the downed man. Lilith slapped Thor hard on the back and thrust his sponsor's shirt at his chest.

"Great win," she said, grinning. She was on a fucking high from the victory, and so was he. Souza regained consciousness a few minutes later. He got to his feet and walked to Thor with his hand extended.

"Good fight," the guy said as they embraced quickly.

"Yes," Thor agreed. It was a good fight. Souza's team crowded at his back, pulling him away while the announcer stepped toward Thor. Pulling the shirt over his head, he waited for the post-match questions.

"Thor, this makes your record thirty-one and oh. How does that feel?" The guy shoved the mic under his nose.

"Great."

"You didn't look stiff out there at all."

"That's because I wasn't." Nobody other than Lilith knew about his torn ACL. Everyone else thought he'd just sprained his knee and was out for a few weeks while he rested up.

"Did you have a plan coming in tonight?"

"To win." Sometimes Thor hated these post-match interviews. All he was here to do was fight.

The announcer hesitated, probably sensing he wasn't going to get much more out of him. "Well, it was a great fight. Congratulations." He turned to the crowd and raised Thor's arm into the air. "Ladies and gentleman, your XFO Middleweight Champion – Thor!"

He was handed his belt. He held the thing over his head for a few minutes, waiting for the flash of cameras to die down before he lowered his arms. Lilith followed him out of the ring where the physician waited to check him over. The doctor asked Thor if he was sore anywhere in particular and gave him a quick look over. When the doctor was done, Thor got the all clear to leave ringside and head back to the change room. He walked with his title belt held down at his side while Lilith followed.

As soon as the door was closed behind them, Lilith got a towel and filled it with ice. She put it on the cut above his eye. "Keep that there," she instructed. "I'll get the enswell."

The goddess held the small piece of metal to Thor's eyebrow and pressed slightly. "How are you feeling?" she asked.

"Fine."

She laughed. "Got anything else in that vocabulary of yours?"

"What do you want me to say?"

She shrugged. "I dunno."

"Look, just get me patched up and then I can get showered and we can go."

"Congratulations," someone said from the doorway. Thor's shoulders tightened involuntarily and he looked up to find Odin standing there. Dressed in an expensive sable-trimmed coat, there was nothing about his father that blended in.

"What are you doing here?" he asked caustically. Lilith had taken a step back and was now looking between the pair warily. Thor had told her about the fight that had forged a divide between him and his father.

"I've come to see you."

Thor's jaw bulged. "What makes you think I want to see you? I'm pretty sure I told you to go to hell and stay there the last time I saw you."

"You are in danger."

Thor rolled his eyes. "Say whatever it is you need to say and then get the fuck out of my life again."

His father was silent for a long time and then took a few steps into the room. "How long have you been fighting?"

"Five years."

"And you have been successful?"

Lilith laughed derisively. "He's thirty-one and oh."

Odin looked her over. There was nothing sexual about the perusal – more like an entomologist studying a new insect in his collection. "I don't understand what that means."

Thor sighed. "It means I haven't lost a fight yet."

Nothing but unspoken words filled the room. It was uncomfortable and stifling, but he wouldn't break first.

"I need to speak with you, son."

Thor ground his teeth. "I'm not interested in anything you have to say to me."

Odin let out a breath. "Please?" he asked.

He studied his father. He was hemorrhaging desperation although he was hiding it well. "I'll give you ten minutes," Thor replied. Turning to Lilith, he said, "Go and stall my sponsors."

The goddess's face screwed up, and Thor was sure he was up for a fight. Instead, the scowl disappeared and she left the room. Thor closed the door behind her and crossed his arms over his chest. "You now have nine minutes."

Odin nodded. "We have a problem."

"We?" Thor asked, moving around the room, unwrapping the tape from his hands.

"You and me," Odin replied. Thor hadn't even heard what his father wanted to say, but already didn't like it. "Loki has been freed."

That statement stopped him. He turned to look at his father. "Excuse me?"

"Loki. He's free and he's rather upset about what happened to him."

"He's rather *upset?*" Thor sputtered in disbelief. He sat down heavily on the bench. "How?"

"Your mother is dead," he said, instead of answering his question.

"*What?* When?" Gods, his father could bring the worst fucking news.

"Last month."

"Last *month?* And you didn't think to tell me?"

"I did not know where you were until two hours ago."

Thor was silent for a few minutes, his head resting in his hands. Warily, he asked, "Where is Loki now?"

"Here, in Chicago."

"Are you sure?"

"I was, until I lost him. I've been tracking him for the past month, but as of yesterday evening, I don't know where he is."

"Has he contacted you?" Thor asked.

"In his own way he has."

Lifting his head, Thor frowned. "Why do you always have to be so damn cryptic?" he asked, standing again and picking up his sports bag to get some clean clothes. "What does he want?"

Odin put his back against one wall, crossing his arms over his chest despite the risk of putting wrinkles in his suit. "I suspect our deaths."

"Why?"

"Why do you think?" Odin retorted. "We imprisoned him in a cave. We chained one son up until the end of time and we killed his wife and remaining son in front of him."

"With good reason," Thor replied.

"He needed to be punished," Odin said. "Or have you forgotten what he did to your brother?"

"I haven't forgotten." Thor's voice was dangerous. "What do you need from me?"

"I want you to come with me. I need you safe. I have already lost your mother and brother to him. I will not lose you too."

So Loki had killed his mother too. Whatever. It didn't change anything. "I'm not going anywhere with you, Odin."

His father's lips thinned at the use of his name. "Are you still angry with me?"

Angry was the fucking understatement of the century. What Thor felt toward his father walked a dangerous line between life-threatening rage and premeditated murder. Just being in his presence again reminded Thor of the day he walked in to find Odin in bed with his wife.

Thor rounded on him. "What do you think?" he snarled. He looked at the clock over his father's head. "Your ten minutes is up."

"Thor—"

"Get out. I need a shower and I need to get out of here."

"What about Loki?"

"What about him?"

"What if he comes for you?"

Thor laughed. "I was stronger than him before the Fall. I can guarantee nothing's changed. Now get the fuck out of my life. You've already turned it to shit once. I don't need a fucking encore."

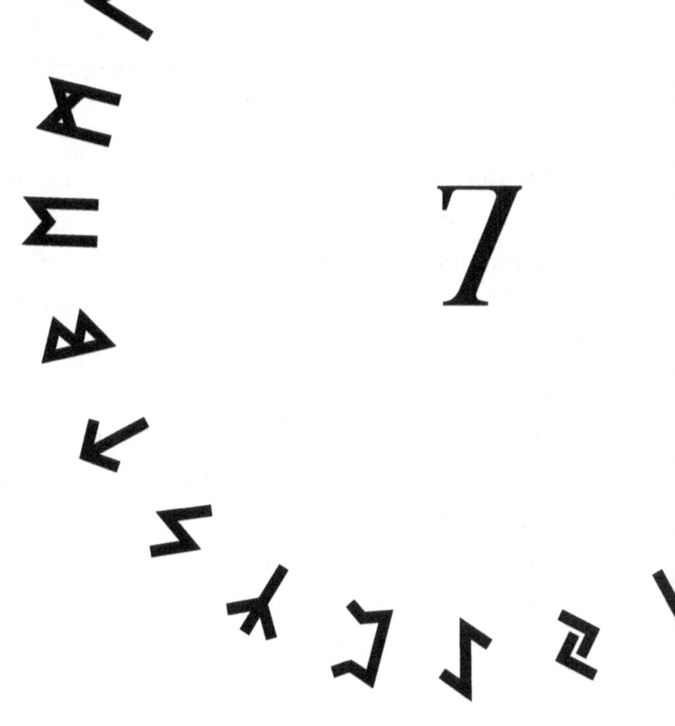

7

L oki was sitting in a stand at UIC Pavilion, no more than three rows back from Odin. If Bryn's feather cloak had been in his possession, he could have killed Odin so easily. When his blood-brother had created his Valkyries, he also created their only weakness – their cloak. If all the feathers were plucked from it, the Valkyrie would become mortal and could be killed. But for Odin, Bryn was his weakness. If her cloak was stripped and she was killed, then Odin's immortality ended along with her. And when that happened, he could be slain.

Loki's gaze gravitated back to the ring, to the spectacle everyone had come to see. He curled his lip as he watched Thor strut around the ring like a preening peacock. He had not changed at all. His arrogance was just as distasteful as it had been when they'd lived in Asgard together. The humans still loved him too, it seemed. The crowd was whipped into a frenzy when the match began, and Loki sank deeper into his seat, watching the two men grapple and fight for dominance on the mat.

Such a primitive thing – fighting. Before the Fall, Loki had lost a lot of money betting on the fights run by fire demons in Muspelheim. It was seen as the lowest forms of entertainment by the Aesir, but he'd liked nothing more than to see some black blood spilled, quickly followed by the severed limb that had been ripped from a demon's body.

The humans thought they were so evolved, so *superior* to everyone and everything else, but look at them now – they were foaming at the mouth, screaming and cheering on a fighter. These men had been elevated to superstar status and for what? To be admired? To be worshiped? Celebrity was the altar at which humans bowed down to now.

"Filth," Loki said under his breath.

He sat and watched all five rounds of the bout, growing angrier and angrier. The humans had revered Thor during Loki's time in Asgard. They prayed to him, sacrificed to him and carved idols of him. Nobody ever did the same for Loki. He was always the one they looked to – blamed – when things went badly. If their crops had failed, it had to be his doing. If a woman's husband was found in another's bed, it must have been Loki who'd poisoned his mind.

As he watched Thor, Loki had resurrected every repulsive memory he had of him. But the one that stuck out the most for him was the look on Thor's face as Loki was bound to that rock and left to endure the stench of his wife's and son's bodies as they rotted away.

The sound in the arena was suddenly deafening. Thor had his thick forearm wrapped around the other fighter's throat, choking consciousness from his opponent. The cries for him to finish the fight reached a fever pitch just as Thor did exactly that. The other fighter went limp in his arms. The referee declared the fight to be over, and Thor was once again hailed as the hero of the hour.

Odin stood up then, turned around and walked up the stairs, passing by Loki without a second glance. His blood-brother was so lost in his own thoughts that he didn't even sense his presence. With a smile, Loki followed.

———

Thor slung his sports bag over one shoulder, taking Lilith's bag in his other hand. Even though she protested, he knew she liked to be taken care of.

"I can carry that myself," she said, crossing her arms petulantly.

Thor smirked. "Of course you can, but then you'd bitch me out for not carrying it."

Lilith huffed but said no more.

"Thought so," he muttered. "So, where to?"

"I don't know why you bother asking me this. We always go to the same place after every fight," the goddess replied.

Thor dug a hand into his jeans pocket to make sure his car key was still where he'd left it. His latest model red Mustang was nearly the last car in the parking garage. It unlocked when he touched the driver's side handle before he walked around the trunk and put their bags inside. Lilith, looking good in her tight jeans and white tank top, was already buckled in by the time Thor got in. He had thought about seducing her a few times before, but never followed through on it. Lilith was important to him, and he didn't want to fuck up the good thing they had going on.

Starting up the car, the engine roared loudly for a brief second before the sound died, along with all the electrics.

"What the fuck?" he said as he hit the start button once more.

"What's wrong?" Lilith asked.

"I don't know."

"So call a tow and we'll fade to the diner. I don't know why you insist on driving this thing anyway."

"That's not the point. Veronica never breaks down," he muttered, frowning. He didn't want to give his father's words any credence, but his first thoughts went to the warning about Loki.

"Veronica?" she asked incredulously. "I can't believe you named your fucking car. What else have you named, your cock?" He grinned at her, hoping she couldn't sense his uneasiness. Throwing her hands into the air, Lilith said, "Oh, for fuck's sake."

Thor pulled the hood catch, got out and scanned the garage. When he couldn't see anyone lurking around, he walked around to the front. After propping the hood up, he put both hands onto the front of the car and leaned down, trying to figure out what had gone wrong. He checked the usual connections then called for Lilith to try and start the car.

"Yo, Lil, did you hear me? Turn her over."

No reply.

Thor peered past the side of the hood to see what the delay was, and what he saw was not what he expected.

Lilith was slumped over in the passenger seat, blood covering her throat and the front of her chest.

"Fuck." Thor pulled off his shirt so he could touch the tattoo of Mjolnir and summon his hammer. Before he could make contact though, searing pain eclipsed his senses. His legs buckled and he fell to the ground. Face-down on the cold concrete, he couldn't move at all. The pain in the center of his spine was a pretty good indication of why.

"It's been too long," someone drawled from the shadows.

Thor strained his eyes trying to see who it was, but he knew exactly who had found him.

"Loki," he gasped. "You bastard."

Loki laughed, the sound chilling Thor down to the marrow in his bones. The god walked over to him; he was covered in blood.

"Why did you kill her?" Thor demanded. He tried to move, but knew it wasn't going to happen. Whatever Loki had done to him, it wasn't wearing off quickly.

Loki flipped him over onto his back. Supine, Thor watched Loki step forward, inspecting his chest.

"Nice ink," Loki said. "I especially like the hammer. You need to touch the tattoo to summon it, don't you?" Thor pressed his lips together tightly. Loki smirked. "I thought so. It's like the Valkyries with their swords. Except they don't need to be holding their swords to have superhuman strength." Loki traced the outer edge of Mjolnir with a long fingernail. His eyes met Thor's. "Unlike you. That is unfortunate," he finished with a simpering smile.

Pulling a gun from a holster under his arm, Loki pressed the cold muzzle against Thor's chest. Thor's mouth went dry. His father's words were suddenly ringing in his ears, the warning he had ignored punctuated by the frigid barrel of a gun. He should have just listened to him, but he was still so angry with what Odin had done, with how he had destroyed his relationship and his life in one fell swoop.

"It's nothing personal, you know," Loki said. He threw his head back and laughed. "Oh, wait, yes it is." His expression sobered. "You are just as guilty as your father for imprisoning me."

The last thing Thor heard was the crack of gunfire.

8

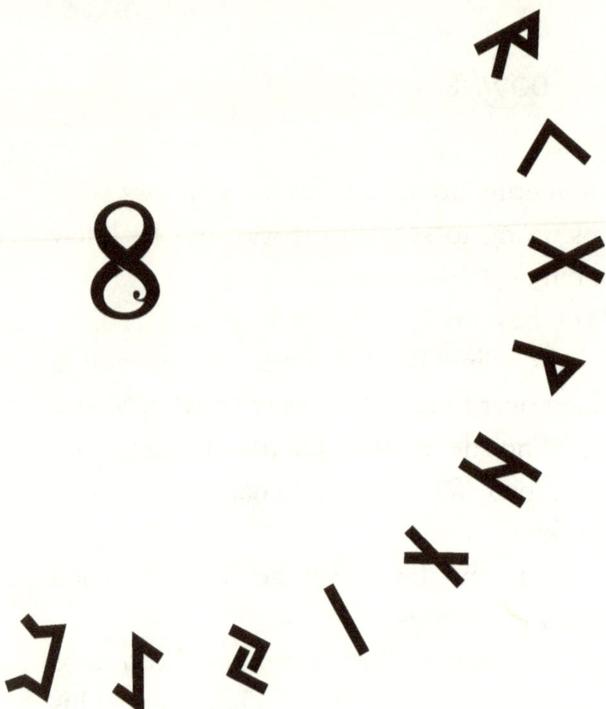

Chicago

Odin strode back into his hotel suite, and went straight to the wet bar running along one side of the living room. After pouring himself a shot of cognac, he swallowed down the amber liquid and quickly poured himself another. And then another. Thor's disregard for his warning was frustrating, but not at all unexpected. Odin had not been the best father to his son, but whatever he did in the past was in the past, and it could not be undone. He hadn't wanted to leave Thor tonight, but out of respect for his wishes and perhaps future reconciliation, he had. Odin would not give up so easily though.

The room was silent except for the sound of his pacing back and forth across the Italian marble tiles. The constant slap of his shoes was getting to him. Odin turned on the TV and sat down on the couch. He channel surfed for a while, ignoring the infomercials, the ads for late-night sex hotlines. But there was one thing he simply couldn't ignore: the feeling of dread that was squeezing his heart.

He couldn't believe Thor had been hiding in plain sight all this time. Odin let his head fall back against the cream leather sofa, his eyes closing, the liquor warming his blood. Tapping into the minds of his ravens, he began to see first through the eyes of Muninn and then Huginn. Both were flying over the city, but he could glean little else from the vision. While having them out looking was an advantage, it did have its limitations too, since he could only see what they were seeing in that moment. To see everything they had over the course of the night, he would need to be in physical contact with the birds.

"And with breaking news, we go to Jamie Reynolds down at the UIC Pavilion. Jamie," a reporter on the TV was saying.

"Thank you, Silvia. Yes, I'm down here at the UIC Pavilion where promising mixed martial arts fighter, Thor, was found dead, along with the body of an unidentified woman."

Odin's eyes became fixed on the screen as everything inside him went numb. The shot of the reporter changed to show the car where the bodies had been found, police tape cordoning off the scene. On the hood of the car was a message scrawled in blood. In the old language, it simply said: *See you in Boston, brother.*

". . . both had been viciously assaulted in what seems to be an unprovoked attack. The police have released no other details at this time . . ."

He stood up, but his legs gave out beneath him, dumping him to the cold marble floor. The glass in his hand fell with him, shattering on the floor. Loki had found his son – had *killed* his son. Odin's warnings had fallen on deaf ears, and Thor had paid the ultimate price.

A single tear tracked down Odin's cheek. Thor's death renewed the need to find Loki and make sure his punishment was permanent. Getting himself vertical again, Odin poured himself another drink and slammed it down his throat. He had to find Fenrir's son. He had to put an end to this..

At least he was in the right city, according to Verdandi. He just had no idea where to start looking. In the month that Odin had watched Loki, the god had only interacted with three people: Henry Craine, the CEO of P&C Pharmaceuticals which was, of course, a front for the Chicago mob boss, and the two Mares he had used as wet men. Craine was now dead – Odin had read as much in the newspaper – and he suspected Loki had been the one responsible.

There was a tap on the window and he walked over and pulled back the curtain. Huginn was perched on the sill. Odin opened up the window, and the raven hopped into the room.

"Who have you found?" Odin asked.

The raven screeched and flew onto Odin's shoulder. Closing his eyes, Odin looked into his raven's memories, seeing everything it had seen. Huginn had flown all over Chicago, swooping between buildings and flying low enough to see the faces of the gods and goddesses who inhabited the city with the humans. He ignored all of them until he saw the face of the Mare he was looking for. Odin didn't know his name, but it was definitely him. He was entering a building downtown and Odin knew exactly where it was – Frigg had also kept an apartment there.

He needed to get there. He would have to drive to the apartment building, and although it was time consuming, he wasn't willing to put himself in harm's way by fading especially since Loki had struck that night already. Striding over to the phone, he called his driver to get the car ready. Then, steeling himself, Odin put another glass of cognac to his lips and tipped it. The liquor was a smooth burn down the back of his throat.

At the door, Odin picked up his coat and then walked to the elevator at the end of the hall and took it. Piped in classical music accompanied him down to the lobby, the car not stopping once. Out among the humans now, he checked his surroundings and the people around him as he left the hotel. The cold air was a welcome change to the recycled air of his hotel room and he only had to wait a moment for Hunter to pull to a stop in front of him. The doorman opened the rear door of the Mercedes and Odin got in.

"Where would you like to go, sir?" Hunter asked.

"East Monroe Street."

Hunter didn't say anything more, just pulled into traffic and put his foot on the gas. The city sped by them, every mile bringing Odin closer to the Mare. He had to find out why Loki was so interested in the male. Perhaps he knew the location of Loki's grandson? Barely ten minutes had passed before Hunter slowed the car.

"We're here, sir."

Odin peered out of the tinted windows at the building Huginn had seen the Mare enter earlier. It was vast and plated in glass. The doorman standing outside opened up the door when a young couple approached. Odin stepped from the car, straightened his coat and walked up to the entrance.

"Can I help you, sir?" the man asked.

"I'm here to visit my nephew," Odin lied smoothly.

The human nodded. "Of course, sir. Welcome to The Legacy."

When the door swung open, Odin turned back to Hunter. "Wait for me." Stepping into the foyer, he strode to the elevator like he knew exactly where he was going. Once inside, he pushed a random number and waited for the doors to slide shut.

"Hold the elevator, please," someone called. Odin pressed the button to keep the doors from closing and waited as a young woman stepped in. She was dressed in gym clothes, had a towel wrapped around her neck and headphones over her ears.

He cleared his throat. "Which floor?"

She took one of the speakers from her ears. "Fifty-nine. Thank you."

Odin pressed the appropriate button and clasped his hands in front of him.

The elevator arrived at floor fifty-nine and the doors opened silently. The woman didn't move though, too lost in the device she was looking at in her hands.

"Aren't you getting out?"

She looked around and saw where she was. She gave him a small smile before walking out. Odin followed her, having no clear place to start looking. After waiting until the woman had entered her apartment, he tried all the other doors, apologizing to the occupants when he realized it was the wrong floor. He worked his way up to the seventieth floor before he was rewarded with his prize at the last door he knocked on.

The Mare stood there in a pair of jeans and a tee. For a moment, all they did was stare at each other, and that was when he saw the man's eyes change color.

One second they were blue, and the next they flashed a brilliant gold.

Odin was suddenly transported to a time – *no* – to an event that had changed his opinion about Loki forever.

He had found Fenrir's son.

Odin wondered whether Loki already knew. Was that the reason he had assumed Craine's identity in the first place – to get close to his grandson?

"Can I help you?" the Mare asked.

"What's your name?"

His eyes narrowed. "Rhys. Do I know you?"

"Not personally."

He scrutinized Odin for a moment. "Fuck you, asshole," Rhys muttered and turned, pushing the door shut as he did.

The door slammed in Odin's face. With a thought, he faded into the apartment, catching the other male by surprise. With a supernatural speed, the elf pulled a dagger from the small of his back and launched it in Odin's direction. The air whistled as the steel cut the air. Odin simply stepped to the side, hearing the weapon lodge in the drywall behind him.

"You have two seconds to tell me who you are," Rhys snarled, his voice morphing into a rolling growl. His eyes flashed to gold again, the color staying a little longer than before. "Otherwise I get to use your head for target practice."

"You worked for Henry Craine, didn't you?"

Rhys took Odin by the lapels of his coat and threw him against the wall. Getting in his face, Rhys's question was a dangerous drawl. "How the hell do you know that?"

Summoning his strength, Odin pushed Rhys away from him, sending him flying. Rhys ended up sprawled on the carpet, a look of shock on his face. He was up on his feet in less than a second.

"Who the fuck are you?" Rhys asked, wary this time.

"I'm Odin," he replied.

Rhys stared at him cautiously. It was good to see that his name was still something to be feared. "The All-Father?" he asked. Odin nodded. "Do you know where Galen is?" he asked in a rush.

Odin was taken aback by the question. But then he remembered in the whole month that he'd been watching Loki, he had not seen the pair of Mares separated, not even when it came to women. Was the other male – Galen – missing?

The idea struck him then. Odin could get exactly what he wanted with very little effort. He wouldn't even have to work at convincing Rhys of anything at all.

"He's dead," Odin replied.

There was a loud crash as a small table was sent sailing across the room. It splintered into jagged pieces, lying at the base of the wall like a broken doll. Rhys's eyes were solid yellow for a long minute, and Odin could *feel* something else was with them.

"You're lying," Rhys replied, his voice a guttural snarl.

"I'm not. I saw it happen with my own eyes, and I know who's responsible for Galen's death."

Rhys clenched his hands into tight fists at his side. "Who? Tell me."

Odin barely kept the smile from his face as he took a step closer to Rhys. "Loki."

The elf's rage was a tangible threat. "Where is he?"

Odin thought of the bloody warning Loki had left for him. "Boston."

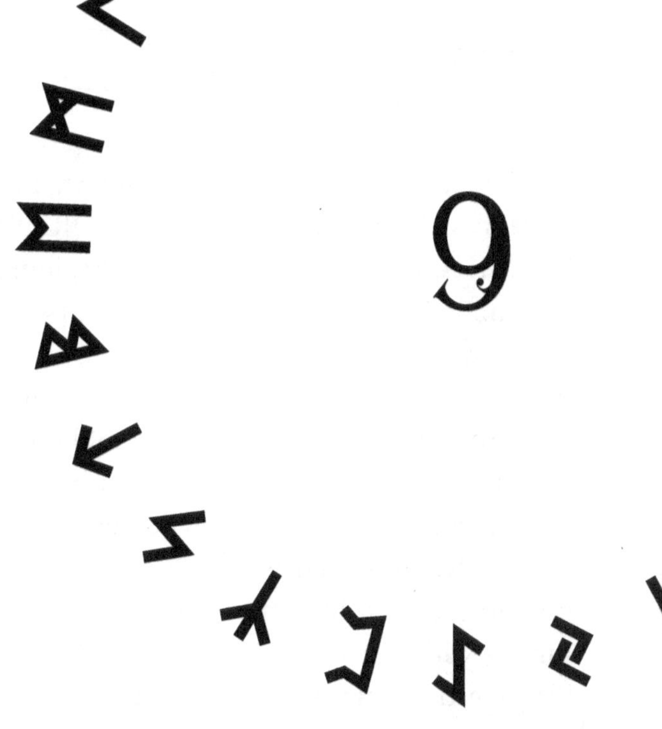

9

Taer was in Raven, the nightclub on the second floor of the Eye. Bryn had asked her to work a few hours up there before coming back downstairs later on in the evening. She had to admit that bartending was a far cry from her training to become a shadow walker – an assassin – in Darrion's guild.

It had only been five weeks ago that she'd been in the garage at the back of her house with her brother, Adrian, learning how to use a dagger correctly. It had been a little less than four since Adrian had been killed by Darrion, and now twenty-seven hours had passed since she got her revenge and murdered Darrion for his crimes.

As far as she knew, Darrion had never allowed a female to be trained before. She hadn't even known who was in her quinary – the group of five Mares preparing to go into battle with one another at the conclusion of their training – except that the remaining four members were male. Realistically the odds had been stacked against her from the beginning, but she had been determined to succeed. She wanted to be the first, until . . .

She squeezed her eyes shut against, trying to block the scene that seemed to be tattooed into her memories. Blood. Gasping. Her brother's lifeless body on the cold concrete floor.

Shaking her head, she tried to focus on the present. The problem was the hurt was just as overwhelming now as it was in the past.

There was a collective gasp of awe. She looked down the bar in time to see Dex, the other bartender who had been shamelessly flirting with her since she started her shift, performing one of his Jagerbomb tricks. As he grinned at the group of women surrounding him – all leaning over the bar to make their breasts spill out of their tops or dresses – the light glinted off the piercings through his nose, eyebrow, lip and ears.

She shook her head at the stupidity of the female species and got busy making the next drink order. As she worked, she thought about the night before. Going to see Aubrey hadn't been a good idea, but she'd had to tell him, face-to-face, what had happened with her and Darrion. Aubrey was the one who had trained her to fight after Korvain had pulled the pin and refused to do it anymore. It was because of Aubrey that she had survived.

And it was because of him that she felt her resolve not to get involved with him lessen every time she saw him. She'd been so very close to giving in when he came to stand behind her in his kitchen, but she was afraid. Once Aubrey had gotten what he wanted from her, would he simply disappear?

"Stop thinking about him," she chastised quietly under her breath. A familiar scent filled her nostrils and she looked up. Her eyes found Aubrey even through the crowd and the near darkness.

It had been less than eighteen hours since she'd last seen him, but her heart stuttered and her stomach clenched. Shaking her head, she refocused on the customer in front of her.

"That'll be twenty-five," she said.

The guy slapped a fifty on the bar and smiled. "Keep it."

She returned the gesture only because she'd learned that if she smiled more, she got bigger tips. "Thanks." She dragged the bill toward her, her breath catching when Aubrey approached the bar.

"Winter Fox," he said with a wry smile.

Taer's eyes drifted down his body. Damn, he looked good. He was in a black suit and shirt with a dark gray tie at his throat. Her whole body gave a little shudder and she sucked in a sharp breath. If this was how she reacted without any physical contact, she could only imagine how good it would be when she allowed him to touch her intimately.

"Aubrey," she said. "What are you doing here?"

He glanced from her to the customer she was serving, then back at her. For a moment there, it seemed as if jealousy had flared in his eyes. "I came looking for you," he replied smoothly.

"You found me," she said.

From the corner of her eye, Taer could see Dex watching them. After telling his customer to wait a minute, Dex approached Taer and wrapped his arm around her waist. "Is everything all right, Tay?" he asked.

A small growl came from Aubrey.

Pulling Dex's arm away, Taer said, "Fine."

Dex shrugged off the snub casually. "Who is this guy?" He jerked his chin in Aubrey's direction.

"I'm the only man allowed to touch her like that," Aubrey hissed, his pale eyes darkening with rage.

Oh, fuck. She had to diffuse the situation, and quickly. "He's my boyfriend, Dex," Taer blurted out. Seeing the smug smile on Aubrey's lips, she pulled on her apron strings, wadded up the fabric and stowed it under the bar. "I need a minute."

Shooting Aubrey a look, she walked to the end of the bar and stepped out from behind it. She watched the light elf saunter in her direction, a definite swagger in his step.

"Boyfriend, huh? Soon-to-be lover would have been a more accurate description."

Taer brushed off his comment with a huff. "Dex wasn't going to leave any other way." Crossing her arms over her chest, she said, "What are you really doing here, Aubrey?"

He studied her, seemingly drinking in every one of her features. "Where can I get you alone?"

She bit her bottom lip then sucked it into her mouth. "I'm working."

"Take a break." Aubrey placed both hands on her waist and dragged her body into his hips. Their faces were mere inches away and for a few seconds, Taer actually let him hold her that way. Those few seconds were enough for him to show her just how much he wanted her. Taer looked down at their bodies closely pressed together. Gods, she wanted him too. All this time, she'd been telling herself it wasn't true, but she'd been lying.

And just like that, her resolve crumbled.

"I'm taking my break," she said, loud enough for Dex to hear. Taer took Aubrey's hand and led him toward the back of the club. There was a storeroom there for their excess liquor, and it was the only quiet place for them to talk. She unlocked the door and ushered him inside. The space was seven square feet, and with the shelves running floor to ceiling, it made it feel two square feet. Closing the door behind them, Taer turned to face Aubrey.

The look of hard lust on his face made Taer's belly clench tightly. She rubbed her thighs together to try and suppress what her body was crying out for. She couldn't remember the last time she'd allowed someone close enough to scratch that particular itch.

"Aubrey, I—" Her words were cut off as his tongue forced its way into her mouth. Her fingers became tangled in his hair, pulling his face closer to hers, demanding more.

With a growl, he pulled away from her, but his hand on the back of her neck held her in place. "You touched me voluntarily," he said, a wicked smile on his face. "You know what that means, don't you?"

Taer's pulse was hammering, her chest rising and falling too quickly. She felt light-headed. She'd known what she was doing when she'd taken his hand: she'd finally given him permission to touch her.

Making sure she kept eye contact, Taer nodded. That same small growl – a possessive sound – came from Aubrey and he pressed her against the door. He wrapped his hands around her thighs, his fingers digging into her flesh. She whimpered, clinging to his neck.

He picked her up, guiding her legs around his waist. The new position pressed his cock against her aching core. He ground himself into her, but seemed impatient with all the barriers currently between them. He lowered her to the ground again, reaching for her jeans. He pulled at them roughly, popping the button free and sending it to the floor. Taer couldn't afford to have her clothing ruined. With a hand on his, she stopped him.

"It's too late, Taer," he growled. "You started this, and I'm going to finish it."

"I'm not changing my mind, Aubrey; just go easy on my clothes.

I still need to finish my shift with functional pants."

His grin was wicked. "Just this once," he replied. Sliding his hands onto either side of her hips, he peeled the jeans from her body and drew them down her legs. He fell to his knees and stared at her. "No underwear?" he asked. Taer shook her head, impatient, desperate for him to hurry. "I like it." His voice was all gravel.

He stood up, trailing his fingers from her thighs to her hips. He pulled her to him again, making sure she could feel his hard length. She groaned, her head falling back against the door. His mouth was on her throat, his teeth nipping, his tongue licking, his mouth sucking. His warm hands burrowed in under her shirt, finding her breasts.

"Fuck," Aubrey hissed. "No bra either?"

Taer shrugged, reaching for the fly of his pants. She wanted to undress him completely, but time was not a luxury they had. Sliding her hand inside, she pushed aside his boxer briefs and her fingers wrapped around his impressively long, hard cock. Running her hand from base to tip, she pumped him a few times, watching his eyes roll back in his head.

His fingers encircled her wrist, stopping her. She gave him a questioning look.

"As much as I'd like to take my time with you," he said, "I plan on making your submission to me hard and fast."

Taer opened her mouth in protest, but gasped instead. Aubrey had just expertly slid two fingers inside her.

"So wet," he murmured as he kissed the corner of her mouth. "I knew you would be."

Taer dug her fingers into his shoulders when his thumb circled her clit. She moaned loudly and gave in to the sensations.

"Are you ready for me, Winter Fox?" he asked, wrapping her

legs around his waist once more and positioning himself at her opening. Taer nodded, too lost in the throes of pleasure to form a coherent sentence. Aubrey didn't go slow. He slammed himself to the hilt just as he promised he would, not giving Taer time to get used to the invasion.

But she didn't care.

He filled her just like she knew he would. She never knew he'd feel this good, though.

"Fuck, you feel good," Aubrey said, echoing her thoughts. Taer thought she nodded in agreement, but she couldn't have been sure. He started driving into her, slamming her back against the door. Letting Aubrey take her roughly was like a balm to the sexual tension that had been brewing between them for so long. Perhaps this would be the only time they'd have together, but if there was a next time, she wanted to take things slowly and explore his body a little more.

Taer's orgasm took her by surprise, making her scream. Aubrey wasn't that far behind her, his hips thrusting a few more times before he jerked and then went still. They were both panting heavily, Aubrey's breath harsh against Taer's shoulder. Her fingers were tangled in the hair at the nape of his neck, her forehead resting against the shoulder of his jacket.

His lips brushed hers tenderly as he lowered her to the ground — it was a stark contrast to how he had just taken her. Aubrey did up his fly then picked up her pants, handing them to her. She stepped into them, cursing the man for breaking the button.

His thumb traced her bottom lip, bringing her attention back to him. "Can I see you after my shift?" she asked.

"I have some meetings I need to attend to tonight." Taer's stomach flipped, and not in the good way. Were her suspicions about Aubrey about to be confirmed?

He leaned forward and kissed the tip of her nose. "You look cute when you pout. How about I call you when I'm done and if you're still awake, I'll come and pick you up?"

———————

Aubrey didn't want to leave the storeroom. Taer had finally let him have a taste of her, and he was ravenous for more. She looked at him now with that same hunger.

"I have to go," he said, skimming the backs of his fingers across her cheek.

She leaned into his touch. "Then go."

"I can't," he admitted softly. He felt glued to the spot.

Taer smiled shyly. "So stay."

He laughed gently, his thumb playing with her tempting bottom lip. "I can't."

She stepped into the line of his body, pressing against him. With a groan, he kissed her again. She was a drug and he was well on his way to becoming an addict. Fighting his instincts to take her again, he pulled away and opened up the door.

He took her hand, stepping out into the busy club. "I can't wait to see you again," he murmured into her ear, making her blush.

"What the fuck are you doing with Taer?" someone snarled.

Aubrey turned his head, finding the same huge fucking male who had interrupted them last night when he came to see Taer. Only this time, it looked like he wanted to gut Aubrey. From the corner of his eye, he could see the shadows shiver. He supposed he should have been intimidated, and in a way he was, but he'd dealt with the scum of the human drug and skin trades and he knew what real insanity looked like. "What's it to you?" he asked.

One minute he was staring at the guy, the next he was getting a real intimate introduction to the wall. The guy's forearm pressed into the back of Aubrey's neck as he said, "I asked you what you were doing with Taer. Tell me what I need to know, or I'll make sure I take my time removing your spine through your mouth."

Aubrey grunted in discomfort. "I'm not sure that's anatomically possible. I've tried before." The pressure increased, cutting off his air supply. "Nothing she didn't want to happen," he said. He was usually on the other end of this situation. It was almost humbling . . . almost.

"Korvain, stop," Taer said, stepping into Aubrey's line of sight.

But Korvain clearly wasn't listening. "You know what? I don't give a fuck about what you have to say. You are not to touch her again."

"I don't see how this is any of your business," Aubrey said through a choked breath.

Korvain jerked Aubrey back then slammed him against the wall again. "Never. Again. Do you hear me?"

"Korvain!" Taer yelled. "Let him go."

A few beats of silence passed. The pressure on Aubrey's neck disappeared and he stood up, straightening his suit jacket and fixing his tie. His eyes went to Taer.

"I think it's best if you went, Aubrey," she said. "I'll walk you out."

"No," Korvain spat. "Go back to work. I'll take care of this."

"There's nothing to take care of, Korvain." Taer's hands curled into fists. "He's just a friend."

There was a snarl and Aubrey's attention went to Korvain. His dark eyes were on Taer. "We'll discuss this later. You need to go back to work. Dex needs help."

Korvain shoved Aubrey backwards, sending him sprawling.

"Korvain!" Taer pleaded. "Please."

"I'll speak to you later, Taer," Korvain replied through gritted teeth, shoving Aubrey again even as he was clambering to his feet.

"Don't touch me," Aubrey hissed at him, pulling on the ends of his suit jacket. Taer mouthed the words *I'm sorry* to him before heading back to the bar.

Aubrey turned and made his way toward the black velvet curtains hanging over the doorway. All the way down the stairs and into the lower level of the club, Korvain stalked behind him, causing his shoulders to tense. He'd dealt with a lot of powerful beings in his line of work, but nobody who felt like Korvain did. All the gods, demi-gods and humans stopped with their bump-and-grind routine to watch the show when he and Korvain emerged from the stairwell.

"Stay away from Taer from now on," Korvain said in a quiet drawl. "We clear?"

Aubrey looked over his shoulder at him, wondering once again what his relationship was to Taer. Whatever their association, Aubrey didn't take too kindly to being told what he could and could not do. Without acknowledging the threat, he stepped past the bouncer at the door, palmed the keys in his pocket, opened up his car door and got in.

Through the glass, he looked at the club. Korvain was now standing in the doorway, glaring at him. Aubrey flipped him off and started the car. As he sped away, he decided that he had to make sure he concluded his business as soon as he could so he could get back to Taer.

Fuck Korvain.

And fuck the warning.

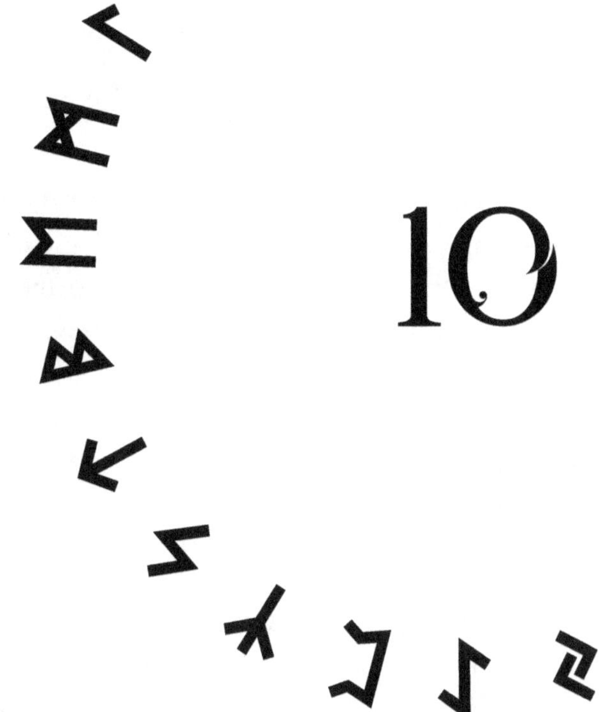

10

I t was early evening and Loki breathed in deeply, the scents of Boston filling his nose. Taking another sip of coffee, he let his gaze settle on Odin's apartment. He was sitting on a park bench directly opposite the building. He knew Odin would have returned to Boston immediately; he wouldn't have wanted to be away from his Valkyries once he'd found out about Thor's death. The message written in his son's blood would have also been a very persuasive reason to return.

Thor's death couldn't have gone any better. Loki's mouth curved into a smile as he remembered every detail. The god of thunder had been so sure he could beat Loki, just like he'd done all those years ago. But he had made sure Thor was incapacitated before he'd shown his face to him. Some would have called it cowardice to kick a man who was already down . . .

But Loki had to respectfully disagree. There was something so satisfying about gaining the upper hand through dishonorable methods. He took another sip of coffee, feeling the caffeine finally take effect on his body. The breeze had gone from freezing to arctic, and as it shifted, Loki's back stiffened.

"We thought it was you," someone said in the old language behind him. Loki stilled, caught off guard both by the words and the fact that he had not sensed the Aesirean approach.

He turned to look at the god, studying the sharp, almost lupine angles of his face.

"Do I know you?" Loki asked in the same language.

"We don't look the same as when you last saw us, Trickster," another voice said. Loki's gaze skated back toward the apartment building. He blinked at the other god that shared the same face as the first.

Standing up, he made sure he kept them in his line of sight. "Who are you?" he demanded.

"It is us, Geri and Freki," the first god said.

Loki reached a hand inside his jacket, his fingertips brushing against the gun he kept there.

"Fear not, Loki. We no longer take Odin's orders. We saw the message you left for the All-Father, and we were hoping" – Geri's eyes darted to his brother – "to join you. There is talk among the Aesir that you know how to kill Odin. Is there any truth in the rumors?"

Loki narrowed his eyes at the twins. "Why do you both have the form of a man now? The last time I saw you, you were wolves."

"The All-Father changed us after the Fall," Freki replied. "Do you know how to kill the All-Father?" he asked, impatient for an answer.

"Yes," Loki replied.

"Then we want to serve you in any way we can," Geri said.

Loki turned to him. "Why? You are Odin's creatures. You have always been that way."

From beside him, Freki growled. The sound cut off abruptly with a look from his brother. Geri said, "Odin discarded us like we meant nothing it all. We were nothing but loyal and loving servants to the All-Father, and how did he repay that devotion? He abandoned us, leaving us unable to change into our true forms. He crippled us. For decades we shied away from civilization. We had to learn how to talk, how to act like men, how to survive in the human world."

Loki didn't say it, but he knew the real reason the brothers had sought him out; they were wolves – pack animals. Without an alpha, they were flailing, aimlessly existing until somebody took charge. With that knowledge, Loki knew he had the perfect soldiers at his disposal. "If you wish to join me, you must first prove your worth."

———————

Loki faded to the Eye, the twins appearing beside him a moment later. They stepped from the alleyway and looked at the line of humans waiting to get inside. Loki noticed that the Valkyrie who was usually guarding the door was absent, and the opportunity felt too great to pass up. With a thought, he started to subtly change his features, making himself look more human.

"What are we doing here?" Freki asked, looking up at the building. "Why didn't we fade inside?"

"We can't," Loki replied. "It's too heavily warded."

"What is this place?" This question was from Geri.

He ignored it. "I need to secure a particular item that is

somewhere in this building."

"What are you looking for?"

"A feather cloak. Help me locate it."

"And if we do, you'll allow us to bring down Odin with you?"

Loki conceded with a sharp nod. "When we get inside, split up and try to get into the private quarters upstairs."

"And what are you going to do?" Freki asked.

He gave the god a hard look. "I ask the questions here, not you." Loki ignored the line of people and stepped up to the bouncer.

"Back of the line," he told them.

"I have a meeting with the owner – with Bryn," Loki said smoothly.

The bouncer narrowed his eyes and touched a small device on his shirt collar. Loki realized he was radioing the info in.

"Okay, I don't actually have a meeting with her," he said, back peddling.

The bouncer gave him a smug smile. "Back of the line, then."

With a snarl kept under his breath, Loki retreated with the twins. He joined the line, hating every second of it. He had been reduced to waiting, to standing in line with humans. He felt disgusted just breathing the same air as them. He was the god of trickery, yet he had learned patience during his imprisonment. He would bide his time.

Three quarters of an hour later, they had reached the front. The bouncer smiled at him as he let him in, a gesture which Loki returned.

I must remember to kill this one . . . slowly.

Inside, it took Loki a few moments for his eyes to adjust to the lighting. He could barely breathe. There were people everywhere, their hot, sweaty bodies pressing against him as he pushed through the crowd. Geri, or it could have been Freki, growled in irritation behind him.

"Spread out and try to find the cloak," Loki commanded, slipping away from the twins and heading toward the stairs. Another bouncer stopped him.

"Where are you going?"

"Upstairs," Loki replied, brushing past the clipboard-wielding human. He wasn't about to be held up again.

"Wait—"

Loki ducked his head and took the stairs two at a time until he reached the first landing. Ahead of him was a doorway flanked by black velvet curtains, and yet another security guard. Loki approached him slowly, eyeing him dubiously even as he was allowed to pass unharassed. House music blared from the speakers in the large, monochromatic room. There was a bar running along one wall and the rest of the space was filled with a DJ booth and more gyrating bodies.

He looked around quickly before retreating, heading farther up the stairs. The style of music changed with every step he took, and when he reached the top, he found out why. The top level, Level Three, was a club where scantily clad women paraded around in nothing more than their under things and a fake smile. There were many men and some women seated at tables facing a stage. Loki let his eyes settle on the dancer pretending to enjoy herself on the raised platform, but he could see the dead look in her eyes.

"Can I get you something, sir?" someone asked beside him.

He turned to find a pretty young woman standing there. She was wearing black lace lingerie that revealed her pert breasts and pink nipples. He cocked his head to the side. She wasn't human, but she wasn't a goddess either. The concept of demi-gods was a new one to him, but he believed that this was what she was.

"No," he replied. "I'm just, ah . . ."

She touched him gently on the arm. "You don't have to explain yourself to me, sir. I've met a lot of married men who come here without their wives knowing. What happens on Level Three, stays on Level Three," she said with a wink. "If you're looking for a dance, let me know and I'd be pleased to please you."

He watched the woman slink away to a nearby group of men. Forcing his legs to move, Loki took a seat at one of the empty tables and settled back. He needed information, and he'd learned a long time ago that sometimes just watching and listening reaped rewards. A man at one of the other tables yelled out to the woman on stage, shaking a fistful of money in her direction. The dancer sauntered over to him, lowering her body slowly and seductively beside the man. His fat fingers secured the money in her thong, his hand slithering down her thigh as she stood up. She gave the man a smile that didn't quite reach her eyes and retreated to the safety of her pole.

Sliding her back down the length of steel, Loki noticed the thick scar on one side of her neck. He sat forward, studying her features: blonde hair and bi-colored blue eyes. She was a . . .

"Valkyrie," he whispered. He frowned. All the Valkyries had their sword tattooed on the side of their necks, but this goddess didn't. When the song was over and the woman had collected all the money thrown at her feet, Loki waited for her to reappear from beside the stage. Now dressed in a leather corset and knee-high boots, the dancer walked through the crowd. She passed by Loki's table and he stood up.

"Hello," he said.

She turned to him, and that same vacant expression was in her eyes. "Hello," she replied.

"Ah . . ." – he turned and gestured to the other seat at his table – "won't you join me?"

She smiled and slid down into the seat. Loki took his place again.

"You looking for a lap dance?" she asked, reaching out and touching his forearm.

"No. I just need to talk to you."

She frowned. "Not many men come here to talk," she replied, drawing back her hand. "What do you want to talk about?"

He leaned forward, resting his forearms on the table. "You're a Valkyrie, aren't you?" When she didn't respond, he pressed on. "What's your name?"

"Kara," she replied after a long beat of silence. She lowered her gaze to the table top where she idly rubbed at a spot in the wood.

"Kara," he repeated. "What happened to your tattoo?"

She touched the scar on her neck. "I don't want to talk about it."

Loki's mind worked quickly, figuring out how to twist the situation around to his favor. "Did Odin do it to you?"

Her blue eyes became stormy. "He had no right."

So, his blood-brother had mutilated the goddess. But why? Loki knew Odin had control issues. His entire existence hinged on him having all the power, but what could this Valkyrie have done to push him to remove her sword? It was like declawing a lion – cruel, but effective. Without her sword, Kara was powerless to protect herself. If it had been a month ago and Loki was still pursuing the same path as before, this woman would have been easy pickings for him.

But he wasn't on the same path.

He was smarter now.

"You hate him."

She nodded. "I do."

A smile stretched Loki's mouth. "Wouldn't you love to get

revenge on him?"

Kara fixed her eyes on him, scrutinizing him. "Do I know you from somewhere?"

Mentally, he made sure his disguise had not slipped. "No. I've never been here before." Reaching out, he clasped her by the hand, trying to distract her. "I just think what he did was terrible. I would want to see you get some recompense for his ill treatment of you."

Kara withdrew her hand with a frown. "You don't even know me."

"I don't have to. I, too, have felt the swift and brutal hand of the All-Father."

"Oh, yeah? What did he do to you?"

Loki relived the whole scene.

He smelled their blood.

He heard their cries.

"He slaughtered my entire family."

Kara abruptly stood up, shaking the table as she did. "You're a dark elf."

Loki remained quiet, staring up at her. She began searching for someone across the other side of the room. She was right to fear him, but not for the reasons she believed.

"Everything all right, Kara?" a man asked.

Loki peered over his shoulder to see a large man standing there. He glared at Loki briefly before fixing his attention back onto the Valkyrie.

"I'm fine, Arturo. Can you escort me backstage, please?"

Arturo gave her a sharp nod and offered her his arm. Kara looked at Loki once more before the pair disappeared.

Loki stood up and left through the curtain again. Moving down the stairs, he stepped into the nightclub on the level below, finding a spare piece of wall to stand against. For a long time, he had wondered how he was going to obtain Bryn's cloak. His first attempt had almost been a success. His plan had been nearly perfect. He had blindsided them all – Odin included – but unfortunately the element of surprise could only be used once.

The second time around, he'd had to think outside the square. That was where Galen had come into play. He'd planned to make the Mare a trusted figure, someone Bryn could feel comfortable with and welcome into the club no questions asked. Unfortunately, Galen had fucked up that plan too, and Loki had learned a very valuable lesson – if you wanted something done right, do it yourself. Suffice it to say, he was cautious about having Geri and Freki working for him now. But it was different this time. They were motivated to see Odin dead. They were also well aware of what Loki was trying to achieve, unlike Galen, and this time Loki was in complete control.

This was his last chance. He had to get Bryn's cloak this time around. He knew it was futile to try and attack her here in the club, so that meant he had to get her out of it. The only problem was that Korvain followed her everywhere. If there was a way to remove him, Loki would be free to take a run at Bryn.

But what could entice the dark elf away? What would hold his interest more than Bryn, even if only for a second?

He turned to leave, but paused when he heard a familiar voice coming from behind him. Over his shoulder, he saw Korvain in an altercation with another male. There was a small scuffle and the dark elf started stalking behind the other man.

"Korvain!" a woman pleaded. "Please."

"I'll speak to you later, Taer."

Loki watched the dynamic between the trio with great interest. They passed right by him and he ghosted behind the pair, following them down the stairs. Down on the first level, he let them get lost in the crowd just as Geri and Freki met him.

"What did you find?"

Freki shrugged. "We couldn't gain access."

"But we did overhear a conversation."

Loki ground his teeth. "A conversation? How is a conversation going to get me what I need?"

"It was about you . . . well, about Thor really."

Loki's interest was piqued. "Yes?"

Geri said, "They know you're still alive. Bryn was speaking to one of her security guards about it."

Of course. Thor's death had been reported, Loki's message to Odin had been seen and now all of his enemies knew he was coming for them. "Good. They'll be afraid."

"But won't they be extra vigilant now?"

"I don't—" Loki paused as his gaze settled on someone standing at the door, speaking to the female who usually guarded the club. Both Geri and Freki turned to look at who he was staring at.

"Who is that?" Geri asked.

Loki bared his teeth. Rhys, the Mare who wouldn't ever leave Galen's side, was here. He must have found out his best friend was dead and that Loki had been responsible. He had no doubt the light elf was now out for his blood. "Another problem I don't have time for."

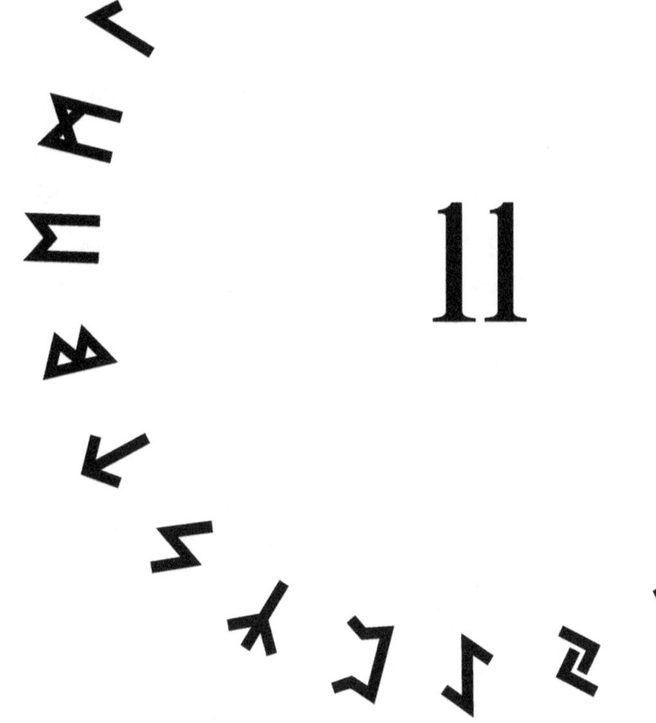

11

Midgard – 806 AD

It had been six winters since Tove had been forbidden to practice sword fighting. She was now sixteen, and, according to her father, almost ready to wed. She had grown from a gangly child into a young woman. More and more people commented on how much she looked like her mother, and Tove loved hearing their kind words and their memories of her. She'd also learned to read the colors she saw around people. According to the priest, Tove had the ability to read people's intentions and feelings by interpreting those colors.

"Sorry I'm late," Soren said, hiking up the last bit of the slope. Tove had been waiting for him just outside the village in the same small grove they had been meeting at for six years. Soren had grown too. His broad shoulders and strong back had not escaped Tove's notice, and just recently her stomach started to do this strange flip-flop whenever she saw him. She blushed as he leaned in and planted a chaste kiss on her cheek – something he'd always done – but now it seemed as if it meant more than just a greeting.

"It's fine," Tove replied, picking up the sword she had propped against a nearby tree. "Are you ready to practice?"

Soren placed his hand on hers, bringing her to stop. He stared at her for a moment before looking away. "I thought we could have a day off from fighting."

Tove frowned. Soren's aura, which was normally blue, was changing to a dark gray. "Okay," she said. "What do you want to do instead?"

"Can we sit down and talk?" His tone was unsure. Tove swept her skirts up and sat, waiting for him to sit beside her. Soren lowered himself down and took her hand. She stared at their entwined fingers, trying to calm her racing heart.

"Tove, you know how I feel about you, right?" Soren asked, staring into her eyes. Hiding beneath a fall of his dark hair, his brown eyes were serious.

She gave him a small smile. "Like I'm your sister," she replied. "Just as I love you like a brother."

He shook his head. "No . . . I mean yes, I mean . . ." He sighed. Twisting his body toward her, he reached out and pushed some of the hair back from her face. "I do love you, but not like a sister."

Tove's heart was in her throat now. "What are you trying to say, Soren?" Her whole body was trembling.

He blew out a breath, his eyes switching back and forth as he searched her face. Then, very slowly, he leaned forward, his mouth pressing to hers. His lips were warm against hers, and when his tongue swept into her mouth, a thrill went through her entire body. Her hands found their way into his hair, and his went around her waist. He lowered her to the soft grass beneath them, deepening their kiss. His hands explored her body, gliding up her ribcage to the underside of her breasts. The ill-fitting dress provided no barriers, and for that she was happy.

Soren's large hand cupped one of her breasts over the fabric of her dress, massaging and kneading it. It was unlike any sensation she'd ever felt before, but she found she liked it very much. Her legs fell open, allowing Soren's hips to fall and fit against hers perfectly. She felt his hard body pressing against her, and she wanted more.

Tove let her hands trail over his shoulders and arms, feeling his muscles bunch and relax. She'd longed to touch him in this way, but had always been afraid that he wouldn't welcome such contact. Her head fell back, allowing Soren's mouth to trail over her neck and throat. His tongue darted out and tasted her skin and her breathing was too loud, even to her own ears.

Soren pulled away, licking his lips and touching her face with his fingertips. "I have wanted to kiss you for so very long, Tove," he said, his voice hoarse. Surging his hips forward, he added, "I have also wanted to have your body pinned beneath mine for so very long."

Tove felt the blush return at hearing his words. "Me, too," she replied. Her hands skimmed over his chest, feeling the coarse hairs through his shirt.

Soren's expression grew serious. "I love you, Tove, and I want you to be my wife." He kissed each eyelid and then her nose. "Please say yes." He dropped a kiss on each cheek and then onto her mouth. "Say you'll be mine."

Tove couldn't believe how happy he'd just made her. "Yes," she replied. "Yes, I'll be your wife."

Soren's smile was both fierce and triumphant. He kissed her

again and lifted himself off her.

"Where are you going?"

Holding out his hand to her, he said, "We have to go and tell my parents, and your father."

They returned to the village and ten minutes later they were standing in front of Soren's parents.

"Oh, that's wonderful news," Gaia said. She pulled Tove from Soren's arms and wrapped her own around her. "I'm so happy for you both," she whispered into Tove's ear.

Tove squeezed Gaia a little harder, so joyful she felt she would break apart.

"What has your father said, Tove?" Reiner asked.

"We haven't asked him yet," Soren replied.

"He will be just as happy as we are," Gaia said. "Go on now."

They left Soren's home, walking through the village hand in hand, showing everyone they were now together. "What do you think your father will say?"

Tove was giddy. "My father loves you!" she exclaimed. "He will agree to this, I'm sure of it."

Climbing the steps into the hall, Tove led Soren inside. Her father was on the dais, listening to the problems of yet another farmer.

"My lord, my neighbor is stealing my pigs," the farmer said. "I had seven not one week ago, and now only five remain."

Halvdan looked grim . . . and a little distracted. He waved away the servant who was trying to refill his cup before saying, "It is summer. The wolves are starting to come into the villages, drawn by animal bones."

"Yes, my lord, but—" The farmer tried to explain further, but Tove's father cut him off.

"I must see proof that your neighbor is taking your animals.

Until then, there is nothing I can do. I'm sorry."

The farmer nodded in defeat and left the room, walking past Tove and Soren. When Tove looked up, her father was looking at her . . . and at their joined hands. Halvdan stood up and came toward them.

"Tove, what is the meaning of this?"

Soren squeezed her hand and stepped forward. "My lord, I am here to ask to marry your daughter."

Halvdan narrowed his eyes at Tove. "Has he made you an offer already?" he demanded in a hard voice.

Tove nodded. "He has. And I have accepted."

Her father's eyes clouded with rage, his lips twisting into a terrible snarl. "I forbid the union." Reaching out, he took Tove's arm and pulled her away from Soren. Tears instantly formed in her eyes.

"But why?" she asked, brushing the tears away. She didn't want to cry in front of her father. She didn't want to look weak.

"You are promised to another." His reply was curt and cold.

"Who?" Soren demanded.

"Floki Dalgaard."

Tove's stomach fell. Floki was the son of a chieftain in the neighboring village. For years, the relationship between her father and his had been strained. It was obvious that her father thought their union would be a way to stabilize the uncertain future they currently had. Floki was at least five years older than her. He was a sniveling weasel, a man without honor and without reputation. She couldn't believe her father would truly want her to marry him.

"Please, father, not him," she begged. Gripping Soren's hand again, she stood beside him, presenting a united front. "Soren and I love each other. We'll be happy together. Why can't I marry the man I love rather than the one I loathe?"

Halvdan's shoulders stiffened and he refused to look at her. "It's already been decided and agreed upon. Your consent is not required."

Soren squeezed her hand gently, supporting her silently. Glancing at him, she sucked in a breath. "When am I to marry him?" she asked, not because she was accepting the ruling, but because she needed to know how much time she had to change his mind and prove what a bad match they would be. She would rather die than have to lie with Floki and bear his children.

"At the change of season," her father replied, still not meeting her eye.

Summer was almost over. The change of season could only be a few weeks away. "And if I refuse?" Tove asked.

Turning away, Halvdan walked toward his chair. "I'm sorry, Tove, but it's done and there's nothing you can do to change it now."

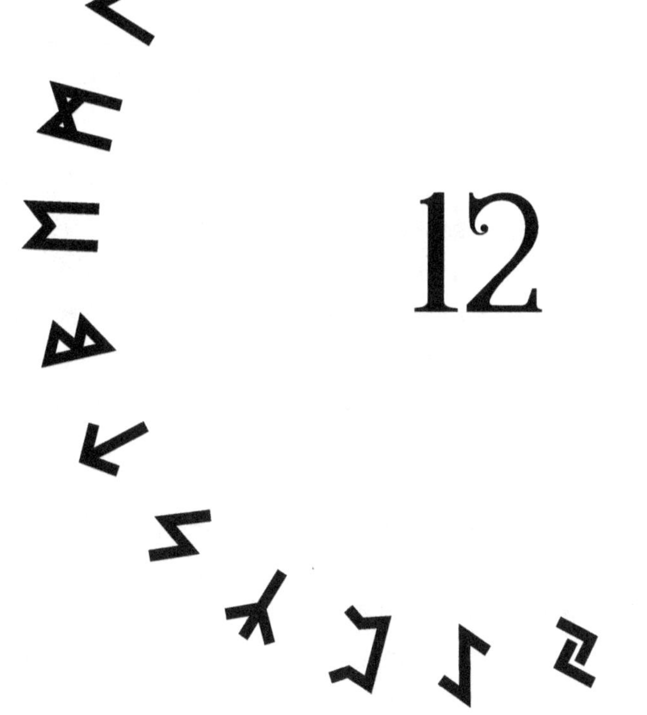

12

Rhys had faded to Boston straight after talking to Odin. His beast was feeding on his anger, making him feel as if he was losing control – something he guarded and coveted the most. He was walking a razor's edge of sanity, and the balance could be tipped at any point.

Out, his beast snarled inside his head. Rhys shut his eyes as he tried to silence the voice. If he didn't get a handle on his rage, he would have to let it out. And without Galen there to act as a buffer, it would end in disaster. The last time Rhys had given up control, it had resulted in deaths on an epic scale. He simply wasn't ready to let the animal have him. It could be days before the bloodlust wore off, and he needed all the time he could get.

Stupidly though, he had let his lust for revenge consume him. He had left to find Galen's killer without even thinking about asking Odin for more information. He had no idea where to start looking, so he was walking the streets of Boston. As he looked around, he could see . . . no, he could *sense* a lot of the other beings of the Nine Worlds walking around, mingling with the humans. They all seemed to know where they were going, and it being a Friday night, he could only assume they were going out to socialize.

Following a group of light elves, Rhys ended up standing in front of a building which the humans seemed to ignore completely. He eyed it carefully, looking for something that would identify it further, other than just being a place for the gods and goddesses.

Reaching out his hand, he breached the magic that kept the building hidden from the humans and stepped inside. One moment he was standing on a Boston street, and the next it felt as if he was standing in an armory housing weapons from the past. He stared at the elven shields hanging beside dwarf-made helmets and suits of armor. It had been too many years since he'd seen anything like it.

Rhys forced his eyes to take in the room. Directly ahead of him was a U-shaped bar where a number of elves and giants were standing. He approached the solid slab of ash wood and looked over the edge. There was a dwarf pulling beers. When he felt Rhys's eyes on him, he looked up.

"What?" he demanded, his top lip curling back from black teeth.

Rhys instantly liked the guy. "I'm looking for someone," he said, leaning on his forearms.

"How is that my problem?"

"The All-Father, have you seen him?"

The dwarf slammed the beer he was pulling onto the bar top and glared at Rhys. "Why would Odin come in here?" he snapped in reply.

Rhys shrugged. "That's why I'm asking. Have you seen him?"

The dwarf eyeballed Rhys for another few seconds before calling out to someone.

"What is it, Alistair?" a second dwarf asked when he arrived at the bar.

Alistair stopped glaring at Rhys long enough to turn to the other guy. "The light elf wants to know if Odin has been around here."

"Why would he show up here?" the dwarf replied incredulously.

Alistair turned back to Rhys with a *what the fuck did I just tell you* look on his face. "Penn says he hasn't been here."

Rhys let his gaze slide to Penn. "Any idea where I can find him?"

The dwarves shared a look. "Try the Eye."

"Excuse me?"

"It's on Tremont. Valkyries run the joint."

Rhys nodded his thanks and stalked from the bar. With a thought, he was walking down Tremont Street. He passed by a dozen clubs, but none were called the Eye. For a brief second he wondered if the Valkyries had used a different kind of magic to that of the dwarves – magic that hid the location even from him. It was only a few minutes later that he came across a line of people waiting to enter a club. The line had snaked around the corner, and it was filled with Aesireans and elves, along with humans. Walking along its length, Rhys came to the front of the building.

There was nothing on the exterior to indicate what its name was, and he thought that perhaps he had the wrong place until he noticed two things.

The first was the protection rune carved into the stonework above the door. The second was the Valkyrie standing in the mouth of the doorway, her muscular arms crossed over her chest. Dressed all in black leather, the goddess radiated a *fuck-off* vibe that even Rhys could feel from where he was standing. This was the only lead he had. He needed to get inside. He looked back at the increasingly lengthening line.

"Fuck this," he muttered. Striding forward confidently, he approached the Valkyrie. Her bi-colored eyes assessed him quickly, her inspection not going unnoticed by his beast either. It snapped impatiently, and he squeezed his eyes shut briefly.

"End of the line," she said, her voice low and gravelly.

He tried to look over her shoulder. She moved to block his view. "I'm looking for someone," he told her.

"End of the line," she repeated.

He met her eyes and exhaled. "I'm looking for Odin."

That seemed to get her attention because her gaze darted around his face. Once again, his beast balked at the scrutiny. Rhys could have sworn that he felt her in his head this time. The Valkyrie's lips thinned and her jaw tensed.

"Why?"

"Have you seen him?" When she gave him a blank stare, he added, "Look, I'm not here to cause trouble. I'm just looking for the All-Father."

"Why?" she asked again.

He shook his head. It was useless. She wasn't going to give him an inch. He figured it was her loyalty to Odin that made her so protective even though they had parted ways a long time ago. "I need him to tell me where Loki is so I can murder the bastard."

Mav watched the light elf walk away from the club. She wouldn't have thought anything of him asking questions about Odin at all, except that he had mentioned Loki in nearly the same breath. Didn't he know Loki was already dead? Bryn had killed the Trickster god over a month ago.

"Mav? I need to speak to you ASAP." Bryn's voice crackled in her earpiece.

Hitting the comms button on her collar, she said, "You got it."

Turning around, she looked for Mason, but he was nowhere to be seen. She frowned, and waved over the first bouncer she saw. The guy approached her slowly.

"What's up?"

"Cover me," she replied, stepping away from the door. She pushed through the thick sea of bodies to the other side of the bar where Bryn was waiting for her.

"We have a problem," Bryn said tightly, turning around and leading the way down the hallway to her office. Korvain and Mason were already there when Mav stepped into the room. She shut the door behind her.

Bryn slumped down into her desk chair. "Loki's still alive."

Mav stood a little straighter.

"What?" Korvain demanded, pushing himself off the wall he was leaning against. "That's not possible. I saw him die myself."

"Believe me, I'm as surprised by this as you are," Bryn said, turning to face him. She gestured to the twenty-inch flat screen TV on her desk. The news was playing, but the sound had been muted. Mav looked at the screen, seeing a story about a carjacking. She cocked a brow at Bryn.

"Give it a minute," the other Valkyrie replied.

Mav turned her attention back to the news, and the image changed to a reporter standing outside what looked to be a parking deck. The shot changed again to a body draped in a white sheet in front of a red Mustang, the ribbon along the bottom of the screen stating that MMA fighter Thor had been brutally murdered. Mav's eyes traveled up to the message written in blood on the windshield of the car.

"Fuck."

"That pretty much sums it up," Bryn said.

"Could it just be someone imitating Loki?" Mason asked. He was in the loop when it came to the long, long history between Odin and Loki. "Like a copycat or something?" When nobody said anything, he added, "That's a possibility, right?"

Bryn shrugged. "Maybe. But why? Why would anyone pretend to be Loki – to kill Thor? To what end? Simply to scare us?"

Mav started to get an itch between her shoulderblades as the information sank in. "Wait," she said. "Bryn, someone was just asking for Odin."

Bryn sat forward in her seat. "What?"

"When?" Korvain asked.

Mav glanced at the Mare for a moment before addressing Bryn. "He was a light elf if I had to guess."

"What did he say exactly?"

"Just that he was looking for Odin."

The shadows in the room shivered and shifted, making Mav look at Korvain. The male was getting agitated, which was never a good thing.

Mason asked, "Did he say why?"

Mav began to answer, but was cut off when Korvain snarled, "It was Loki himself. It had to be. He was hoping we'd tell him where to find Odin."

"I doubt he'd need our help to locate the All-Father," Bryn said reasonably.

"Besides, it couldn't have been Loki. This guy was . . . different,"

Mav added. She had read his aura, and discovered something she'd never, ever seen before.

"Different how?" Bryn asked.

"He had two auras."

"Which proves it was Loki," Korvain snapped. "If he was in disguise, of course he would have two auras."

"What do auras have to do with anything?" Mason asked, looking confused.

"Maverick can see auras and interpret their meaning," Bryn explained impatiently.

Mason looked at Mav. "Really?" She nodded. He grinned and tapped the side of his head. "Glad to hear I'm not the only special one here."

"So Loki is already trying to get into the club," Korvain said. "He's looking for a way to get Bryn's cloak after his first failed attempt."

"I don't think that's it," Mav pressed.

"What other explanation is there?" Bryn's question came out quietly. "It must be him." Korvain stood behind Bryn and rested his hands on her shoulders, lending her a strength she'd never needed before.

Mav thought back to the conversation she'd had with the light elf. She had sensed something different about him — something dangerous, something unpredictable. She had looked past his immediate intentions and delved a little deeper, something she'd only learned to do on her own since becoming a Valkyrie. For the first time ever, she had come up against a wall. It wasn't a physical barrier— rather it was a roadblock made of something organic and fluid and . . . volatile. Not being able to really see what was going through the elf's head was enough of an indication that she had to proceed with absolute caution.

"It wasn't Loki," Mav stated emphatically, but she shouldn't have bothered. Korvain and Bryn were already wrapped up in a conversation about how to protect the club and themselves better, and Mason was just getting more and more confused.

The more she thought about it though, the more she was convinced that they were dealing with someone else. Yes, the elf had two auras, and the strangest thing about them was that one was black and the other was a brilliant gold – the same shade of gold that radiated from Eir, the goddess of healing. It was almost as if the elf had two souls. One was purely good, but the other was purely evil.

Whenever Odin had taken on a different face, Mav had only ever seen one stretch of color burning around his head and shoulders.

"Right, nobody leaves this club without me," Korvain said, breaking Mav's thoughts. She looked at the Mare.

"No."

"Mav, it's for your own protection. Look what happened last time," Bryn said.

She shook her head. "I can look after myself. Besides, if this guy comes back, I'm going to get to the bottom of why he needs to see Odin."

"Maveri—" Korvain started, but Bryn stopped him by touching his hand.

"She's right, Korvain. Mav is my best soldier. I wouldn't trust anyone else to do this job."

"*I* can do it," the Mare gritted out.

"That means you have to leave me alone," Bryn pointed out.

Korvain gnashed his teeth. "That's not going to happen," he growled.

"Then it's settled," Mav said, standing up and ending the

conversation. "I have to get back to work. Excuse me."

13

Aubrey's foot slid further down on the accelerator, propelling the Lexus forward. Along with controlling the speed, he had to dodge other drivers while trying to keep his mind on the task at hand. By forcing his brain to concentrate on driving, he was starving the rest of his thoughts of oxygen, or Taer, as the case was. That little Mare had gotten under his skin in more ways than one. She had finally given in to her cravings and given herself up to him.

And it had been more than worth the wait.

Taer had been everything he thought she would be and more. But Aubrey hadn't counted on tonight being the night she would reach for him. A sharp pain lanced through his heart at the thought of leaving her to go out of town, even if it was only for less than six hours. Now that he'd had a taste, he was reluctant to leave at all.

He pushed his car to go a little faster, hearing the restrained engine growl in irritation as he was forced to slam on the brakes to bring it to a stop once more. The Boston traffic jams didn't seem to care that he was trying to outrun his own thoughts.

The traffic started moving again, but Aubrey had had enough of the stop-start routine. He yanked on the wheel, turning the car to take the Sumner Tunnel across to the east side of Boston. It was only out of habit that he went that direction – East Boston was the location where Aubrey kept most of his product. For humans, drug trafficking was difficult; they had to worry about importing the product via ports or airports, but for any of the gods or beings of the Nine Worlds, they could simply fade with nothing but a thought. The secret to his success was that he had nearly a hundred elves, gods and dwarves as willing drug mules. There was never any fear of being imprisoned, and he paid them all very well for their contribution to his ever-growing fortune. And thanks to Darrion's very recent demise, Aubrey could also employ fifty more of the former guild master's Mares if they were in need of an income.

His other business, the one he conducted as a silent partner, was in human prostitution. Not many knew about this part of his life. The whole business operated under his general partner – a light elf named Sarya. The pair had been thrown together by fate one night; Sarya was getting a beating from her pimp for not making quota, and Aubrey happened to be passing by at the time. He stopped her pimp with a warning and a bullet between the eyes, both within quick succession.

Sarya had been half starving. It had been clear that she had been forced into the business, and Aubrey wanted to give her an out. He had no issues with prostitution itself, as long as the women had not been coerced or manipulated into the business. And so his side project was born. He ran a high-end escort service with Sarya as the face. She took care of the day-to-day issues, and he made sure all his girls were paid well and in good health.

Aubrey functioned on auto-pilot, finding his way to the house where his drugs were kept. From the outside, it looked like a derelict building about to be wrecked, but there was so much more to the place. Every door and window had the latest security measure. If one of the alarms was ever tripped, a message was sent to his phone instantaneously. He could be there in a thought and happily deal with the trespasser. If anyone ever did get past his security, the unlucky soul would come face-to-face with the fire demons he kept as guards.

Stopping outside the house, Aubrey gave it a quick visual inspection. Everything looked as it should. He sat there for a moment . . .

And his thoughts coalesced onto Taer once more.

Fuck, he had to see her again.

But the meetings with his Colombian suppliers couldn't wait. Now that Darrion was gone, he anticipated the number of people in his employment was going to increase and he needed to have the supply to meet the demand.

Aubrey pulled at the collar of his business shirt, feeling the sweat trickling down his back. The humidity in Caracas was a killer at this time of year. He'd faded into the country less than fifteen minutes ago and already he wanted to be back in Boston. He'd already decided that once he was done, he would return to Taer and make love to her slowly. He would savor her.

He looked around the room he'd been shown in to by one of his supplier's henchmen, admiring the collection of Japanese Kabuki masks hanging on the wall. From what he could tell, they were all original, not cheap reproductions. Overhead, a fan whirled lazily, barely causing a draft. He loosened his tie and tried to relax back into the leather sofa cushions.

From the window opposite him, he could clearly see the giant sheds where his coke was produced. Inside, there would be barrels of kerosene and caustic soda, sacks of cement and bottles of drain cleaner along with the coca leaves to make the drug. It wasn't a pretty process to witness, but cocaine was one of the most sought after substances in the world, and Aubrey was one of the top suppliers on the east coast of the US.

"Mr. Black," someone said from the door. Aubrey glanced up, acknowledging the woman with a nod. She was a real Venezuelan beauty, and she was also Luis Perez's wife. Noely had bronze skin and dark brown hair with eyes the color of topaz. "I apologize on my husband's behalf for keeping you waiting. He'll be with you shortly. Would you like a drink?" Her English was perfect, her accent adding to her whole seductive package.

He shook his head. "I'm fine."

Noely nodded and closed the door behind her. Aubrey was getting irritated. He had given Luis the money to start production, and the little prick had gotten rich off it, but instead of being grateful, the guy had grown arrogant. This wasn't the first time that he'd been made to sit here holding his dick either. He suspected Luis had been snorting his – *Aubrey's* – product or fucking one of his mistresses the time he'd waited before. He looked at his watch, his jaw pulsing in time with the second hand as it went around and around the gold face.

He stood up to pace, glancing at the door every thirty seconds. This was getting fucking ridiculous. Luis knew he was coming. He was just doing it to fuck around with him. Aubrey ground his teeth together and turned to look out the window. Behind him, the door opened and then shut. The scent of coca leaves – something that was always around Luis's house – grew stronger.

"Where have you been?" Aubrey demanded, not turning around. He was working hard at keeping his expression neutral, and his anger in check.

"I was outside doing quality control," Luis replied. Aubrey heard him walk farther into the room. "How was your flight?"

Aubrey turned to stare at the human. His fly was only halfway done up and his shirt was on inside out. He had no idea what Aubrey was, what he could do. He smiled benignly. "Fine. But I didn't fly all this way for small talk."

"Of course." The human sat down in a large armchair opposite the couch. He gestured to the seat Aubrey had taken before. "Please, let's talk."

Aubrey didn't sit down. "I'm sending more people down to collect the product. You need to up production to meet the demand."

Luis frowned. "By how much?"

"Seventy-five percent."

"It's not possible."

"Why not?"

"I don't have the supplies to increase production by that much."

Aubrey thought he'd say that. "I've already organized another sixty thousand pounds of coca leaf from Colombia. You'll get a delivery every second week starting next week."

Luis's eye twitched as a bead of sweat traveled down his face from his brow. "What about the chemicals?"

"You'll receive deliveries every other week to make sure you can keep up. Think you can handle that?" Luis nodded. "Good. I'll start sending my men down within the month. You'll need to have five kilos of product for them . . . each."

Luis balked. "But how will they get it out of the country?"

Aubrey's eyebrows rose. "As I've told you on numerous occasions, that's none of your concern."

Luis sat forward in his chair, resting his elbows on his knees. He licked his lips again. "I've been working for you for five years, Mr. Black."

"Yes, and I've made you very rich in those five years."

Luis nodded. "But I've got to know: how do you do it?"

Aubrey studied the other man. "Do what, exactly?"

"How do you never get caught?"

Aubrey smiled at him. "That is a secret I will take to the grave." He moved toward the door, stopping just as he opened it. "And Luis?"

"Yes, Mr. Black?"

He looked over his shoulder at the man. "Don't leave me waiting like that ever again. You don't want to know what I do to the people who do."

Luis blanched. "Yes, Mr. Black."

Aubrey saw himself out, stepping off the front step and leaving the palatial house. Even though it was close to ten o'clock in the evening, and the sun had long set, the heat from the day still lingered. He had another meeting lined up with the guy who imported the chemicals he required in the cocaine production process, but that wasn't for another hour. Briefly, he considered returning to Boston, but an hour wasn't long enough to worship Taer. Instead, he thought of the room he usually got at the local hotel and faded there. At the start of each year, he paid enough to make sure it was vacant at all times.

Money spoke many languages.

He hit the button on the A/C unit in the only window in the

room and stretched out on the bed, waiting for the air to start flowing. A dull hum filled the room. His eyes began to get heavy, closing for a little longer each time until he couldn't keep them open anymore.

Aubrey woke up suddenly, blinking rapidly, his gaze swinging around the unfamiliar room. "Damn." He had forgotten where he was for a moment there. He shifted his legs off the bed, running his hands through his hair. Blowing out a breath, he looked at his watch. His next meeting was in five minutes. Moving to the small bathroom, he washed his face quickly, patted it dry, then collected his phone from the bedside table. There was a text that had come through from Taer. She wanted to know when he'd be back. He tapped out his reply and shoved the iPhone into his pants pocket. Closing his eyes, he faded to his chemical supplier's office in downtown Caracas.

He was sitting in the office chair with his back to the door when Betulio Abana stepped into the room. Aubrey turned around and faced the other man.

"Fuck," Betulio said in Spanish, holding a hand over his heart. "Mr. Black, you scared me."

Aubrey smiled and rested his hands on the desk in front of him. "Mr. Abana, we need to talk."

The human stopped breathing for a second. But then his lungs got back to working with a wheeze. "I'm sorry, but I was of the understanding that after our meeting last month, you had all the supply you needed."

"Things change, Betulio, and if you don't change with them, you get swept away." Fine beads of sweat broke out on the other man's upper lip. He'd obviously read between the lines. "Single-handedly, I'm responsible for more than eighty percent of your profits, correct?"

Betulio conceded with a nod.

Aubrey continued, "And am I not also responsible for giving you the start-up money for this company when nobody else would?"

Another nod.

"So, when I, the person who bankrolled you and provides you with eighty percent of your entire business, asks you to increase supply, wouldn't it stand to reason that you would do as I ask?"

Betulio ran his tongue over his top lip nervously. "The police have been watching me."

"Buy them off."

"I can't. I don't have enough money to do that."

With a heavy sigh, Aubrey pulled his wallet from his back pocket and pulled out the equivalent of five years' worth of salary for ten Venezuelan police officers. He slapped it onto the table, watching the other man's eyes widen. "This should cover it." When Betulio reached out to take the cash, he added, "I'll just add it to your tab."

Their eyes met and the other man nodded. "Yes, Mr. Black."

Aubrey smiled. "Excellent. Now that that's settled, I need to double my current order and have it shipped to the usual location."

"Yes, Mr. Black."

To Aubrey, there were no sweeter words. He stood, buttoning up his suit jacket once more. With a nod, he said, "Until next month."

He strode from the room and punched out another text to Taer, then faded back to his house in Boston. There was an extra spring in his step as he undressed and got showered, washing away the sweat from his skin. When he got a reply back, he slid into his new black Armani suit and finished off the whole look with a tie the color of sapphire before heading downstairs to the garage.

His Lexus gleamed when he flicked on the lights. He glided his hand over the rear quarter panel as he moved to the driver's side. Strangely, the interior light didn't come on when he got in, and he reached up to slide the small switch back into place.

The overhead light in the garage went out at the same time.

As he turned back around to see what had happened, something cold and unforgiving was pressed to the side of Aubrey's skull.

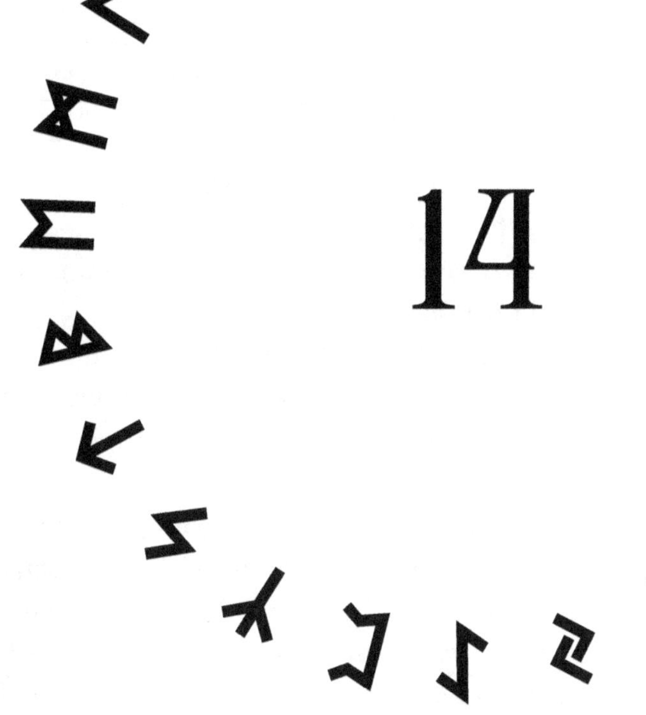

14

Aubrey's eyes cut to the side. The smell of metal and triumph permeated through his car, but he could claim neither. It belonged to the guy on the other side of the gun that was currently pressed to Aubrey's temple. Remaining calm, he rifled through his memory banks, trying to remember if he'd pissed off anyone in particular recently, and whether or not waiting in a car armed with a gun was their style.

"Put both of your hands on the steering wheel."

Aubrey didn't move.

"Don't even think about being a hero. Do it." To drive his point home, the guy pushed the gun in tighter.

Being a good hostage, Aubrey put his hands in position, and was on the verge of fading away when a metal bracelet was snapped onto one of his wrists. Squinting at it closely, he studied the runes inscribed in the steel.

Fuck.

It was an incantation to prevent fading. Whoever this guy was, Aubrey now knew he was a god.

Hating the feel of the cold metal against his wrist, he said, "I don't believe we've met." The gun was pressed harder into his temple and Aubrey ground his teeth. "That's going to leave a mark."

"Be thankful that's all it's going to leave . . . for now."

"Look, as much as I'd like to sit here with you in my garage all night and chat like girls, I do actually have somewhere to be."

There was a small growl of – irritation? Even Aubrey knew it wasn't a good idea to piss off the god holding a gun to his skull. "You aren't going anywhere right now."

"All right. Can we at least get out of my car? I'd hate to get blood all over the upholstery if I can avoid it."

"You talk a lot," the god said, easing off Aubrey's temple just a little. The movement caused blood to rush to the point of pressure, making his head throb in time with his galloping pulse. "That might serve you well . . . but then again . . ." He ground the metal back into Aubrey's skull. "Maybe it'll just make me kill you a whole lot quicker once your usefulness has worn out."

So that was the plan? "Who do you work for?" There were any number of dealers out there who could be gunning for him; Aubrey had burned a lot of bridges on his way to the top of the business.

"Myself."

"And who are you?" Aubrey tried again to get a name.

The god laughed. "You wouldn't believe me if I told you."

"Try me."

"Loki."

He was right; Aubrey didn't believe him. "Loki is chained to a boulder far beneath the earth, being driven mad by the poison of a snake."

"I told you wouldn't believe me."

"That's because it's impossible," Aubrey replied. This god – whoever he was – was just delusional. "So, *Loki*, tell me what's going to happen here."

"You're going to get out of the car and enter your home where you will be imprisoned and used as a bargaining chip."

Aubrey smirked. "By you, I take it."

The god cocked his head to one side. "You find that amusing. Why?"

Aubrey turned his head to look at the guy. "Because you aren't Loki."

The other man shrugged. "Believe me, or not. The outcome will not change."

"All right," he conceded. "You're going to imprison me, then what? Why are you doing all this? What do you hope to achieve? I'm at the top of the food chain. There's no one out there who is going to bail me out, so this whole exercise is pointless."

That statement made the god frown. "I don't understand that phrase – being at top of the food chain – but you are wrong. There is someone who will do everything in her power to *bail you out,* as you put it."

Her power? No. No fucking way. Taer was *not* being dragged into this shit. He'd rather die. "You leave her out of this. Do you hear me?" Aubrey growled, knowing his eyes would have changed from pale gray to a dark slate. "Touch a hair on her head and I will personally remove the fingers that cause the offense. I'll then proceed to remove every other finger, toe and appendage from your body, roast them and eat them, picking my teeth with your bones."

The god's mouth flexed in a small smile. "Imaginative."

"How do you suppose this is all going to go down then? You'll keep me here and she'll, what, just come looking for me?"

"Yes. In fact, she'll be here shortly. You are meeting with her, correct? That is where you were going just now."

Aubrey could feel the color drain from his face. No. *No.* Although he hated to do it, the next words to come out of his mouth were necessary. "Please, I beg you, don't hurt her."

"Get out of the car," Loki said.

Aubrey's jaw bulged as he followed the instruction, popping open the driver's side door and stepping out.

"What are our orders?" a voice asked in the darkness.

"Wait for her in the courtyard. When you capture her, bring her to me."

"Yes, Loki."

Aubrey's heart dropped. It really was Loki.

The god added, "And don't inflict too much damage when you capture her. I still need her whole."

The gun was shoved into Aubrey's spine, forcing him to go through the door connecting the garage to the house. Once inside the kitchen, Loki directed him to the basement. A small flicker of hope ignited in his chest. All of his weapons were down there. With his mood buoyed by the knowledge, he led the way, flipping the light switch at the top of the stairs.

When they reached the bottom, Aubrey was horrified to find his training equipment and weapons were gone.

"Surprise," Loki said. Aubrey's phone vibrated then for a long second before his ringtone for Taer started to play; he'd programmed Marilyn Manson's version of "Sweet Dreams" just for her. Loki smiled. "Oh, that might be Taer now."

"Leave her out of this!" Aubrey demanded fiercely.

Loki's returning smile made him shiver. "I'm afraid I can't do that." Shoving the barrel of the gun into his face, Loki forced Aubrey to a chair in the center of the room. "Sit down, or I'll make you sit down."

Aubrey bit the inside of his cheek until he tasted blood. He spat on Loki's shoes as he lowered himself into the chair, glaring up at him. With the gun still on him, Loki retrieved a metal chain from the corner. He tied Aubrey up quickly, wrapping the links around his chest and securing the ends behind the chair.

"I still don't understand," Aubrey ground out. "What does Taer have to do with this? She's not involved with the business."

"I don't know what business you're referring to, light elf, but my business is with Odin." Loki was behind him when he spoke. Aubrey strained his neck in an attempt to see what the god was doing. His mind raced, trying to connect the dots to a puzzle where he had no idea what the final picture was. How could Loki get to Odin through Taer? It made absolutely no sense.

The only thing he could come up with was that Loki was insane.

Whiskey Saigon was a popular nightclub in Boston. Taer had never been there before; she'd been too busy training to kill indiscriminately to go out and drink and enjoy herself. When she arrived, there was a small line of people waiting to go in on one side of the door. She stood on the opposite side, folding her arms over her stomach and leaning back against the glass wall. This was where Aubrey had said he would pick her up. She checked her phone to see if she'd missed any other messages from him. There were none.

For fifteen minutes, Taer watched the people come and go from the nightclub, checking her phone every few minutes like a love-sick woman. When the time stretched out to thirty, she called him to see where he was. It went straight to voicemail. She left a message and hung up. After forty-five minutes, a little unwanted voice started to whisper in her ear.

He got what he wanted from you already.

She shook her head, angry at herself for even thinking it. It just wasn't possible. He said he was home. He said he was coming to see her, and he was. There had to be a logical explanation for him being late. She waited until the bouncer at Whiskey Saigon started giving her strange looks. By now, Aubrey was an hour and a quarter late.

Taer walked away, finding the closest alleyway to fade to his house. After materializing in the courtyard, she looked up at the redbrick building, seeing that the lights were on upstairs. Standing on tiptoe, she peered into the garage through one of the side windows. His car was still there.

She slowly lowered herself down when the hairs on the back of her neck stood on end. She couldn't shake the feeling that she was being watched. She glanced around, wishing she had her katana with her. Unfortunately, toting around a giant Japanese sword wasn't as easy as she'd like it to be.

Remaining still, she looked up to the windows of the house, hoping to find Aubrey staring down at her, but there was nobody behind the glass. She faded to the street, putting her back against the brick wall and pulling out her phone. Hitting redial, she listened to the automated message on the other end.

"Aubrey, it's me. Where are you? I'm at your place now. Call me back when you get this message." She didn't want to sound too irritated with him, but some of it had leaked into her voice. And that same voice was back – the one that made her doubt Aubrey was ever interested in anything more than just sex with her.

He was just using you.

Men always want what they can't have, and you stupidly gave it all up to him.

He's forgotten about you.

This time, she listened to the voices. Shoving the phone back into her pocket, she looked around and started down the street. She was too angry to fade. Just then, a stiff wind blew across her face, carrying with it an unusual scent.

Her brain threw up the warning flare and her feet ground to a halt. Peering over her shoulder, she saw a man stepping from the shadows.

He started toward her, and Taer pulled a dagger from her thigh holster. Holding it steady down by her leg, she watched him, gauged him, studied him. With a small snarl, he launched himself at her. Taer lowered herself down, her thigh muscles easily complying. She remained still except for the pumping up and down of her chest. Time seemed to slow as she watched the distance between them get smaller and smaller. She couldn't see whether or not he was armed, though. When he was a mere foot away from her, she side-stepped him, performing the maneuver at just the right moment.

She watched his body fall and skid past her. He landed headfirst into a red-brick garden wall. The sickening *crunch* made her smile and the smell of blood was immediate. She had caused the first injury and men always tended to get a little pissy when that happened.

Adrian had always told her to let her opponent underestimate her. Males tended to think they could best her just because she was a member of the fairer sex, and she was more than happy to let them hang themselves with that mistake.

Her head whipped around when a noise drew her attention. Moving away from her first attacker, she kept her focus on the new male who had just come running down the street. His gaze found the other body crumpled against the wall first before it fixed on her with deadly precision. Like her first attacker, he launched himself at her too, only this time she was a fraction of a second too slow. His strong arm banded around her torso, driving her backwards. Her spine seized as she hit the cobblestones on the road, her whole back searing in pain. Her arms flopped out uselessly at her sides, her fingers releasing their grip on her dagger. The blade landed a few inches from her hand.

She gulped down on the O_2 trying to get her lungs to work again. She wheezed. Coughed. Sucked in another mouthful. As she worked hard to get her breathing under control, she saw the first man start to stir from the corner of her eye. He got to his feet slowly, shaking his head as if he were dazed. Her attention went back to the weight on her chest and she studied the face of the second man.

He had sharp features and shrewd eyes. His jaw was square with a healthy dose of stubble on it. His attention wasn't on her though. It was on the other guy.

"My brother, are you all right?" he asked.

The male stood up, swaying a little on his feet. Bending at the waist suddenly, he gripped the hood of a nearby car and looked over. Blood ran down the side of his face and dripped from his chin from the gash at the top of his head. The taste of metal hung on the air. "I'm fine," he replied through gritted teeth.

Taer felt her heart rate start to slow. Stretching out her fingers, she felt for the handle of her knife and dragged it into her palm, sliding the blade under her forearm to hide it from view.

"Is she secure?" the injured man tacked on as he slowly straightened again.

"Yeah, I got her," the guy said, leering down at Taer.

She bared her teeth at him.

"Just come with us quietly, female, and you won't get hurt," the injured man said. Turning her head, she looked at him as he stumbled forward a step. He grimaced and clutched at his stomach for a moment. He probably had a concussion thanks to that up-close-and-personal with the brick wall.

Good for him.

As she waited for the perfect time to strike, she wondered whether she was the intended target, or whether she just happened to cross their paths as they waited for someone else.

"Get her up and let's go."

The male holding her reached under her arm and pulled her vertical. "Put your hands behind you," he commanded, pulling out black cable ties from his pants' pocket.

Taer smiled and shook her head.

"I'm not playing with you," he ground out.

"You wouldn't like the way I play anyway," she said in reply.

The guy growled and the sound turned Taer's blood to ice. "And *you* wouldn't like the way *I* play, either. Do what I say or I will present you as spoiled goods."

"My brother," the other man said in warning.

That growl returned. "Fine," he ground out, spinning Taer around so she was pinned to his body, her back to his front. Roughly, he shoved her forward until her face was flush to the same garden wall the first guy had gotten cozy with. She stilled for a moment, wanting her attacker to think that she was giving up.

"That's better," he said into her ear, his breath tickling the skin on her neck. She closed her eyes and threw her head back. Her skull connected with his, except she hadn't broken his nose as she'd wanted. Her ears began to ring as she realized she'd struck his forehead, maybe above his eyebrow.

"You little bitch," he snarled, pressing his whole body into her upper body and shoulders, forcing her in tighter into the wall. Her first hand was wrenched around from its position by her side. As he reached for the second one – the one where she had concealed the blade – she thrust the weapon down into his thigh. The steel met with some resistance before sliding through his skin.

Leaping away, he spat, "Fuck."

Taer spun around, keeping her back to the wall. She looked at the blood flowing freely down the man's pant leg, covering his hands as he tried to apply pressure. Her eyes darted to the other man who was still bleeding profusely himself. He had his hands up in front of him.

Taking aim, she threw the dagger at him and took off running in the opposite direction. The adrenaline in her bloodstream meant she wasn't fading any time soon. In the six inch heels still on her feet, she ran until her calves burned and her lungs felt like they were going to explode. She was still in the suburbs of Boston, but the sound of downtown was a constant buzz in the background. She turned down a small side-street and slumped against the side of a building. She couldn't hear anyone coming after her. She waited until her heart stopped thumping in her ears before she shut her eyes and faded back to the safety of the Eye.

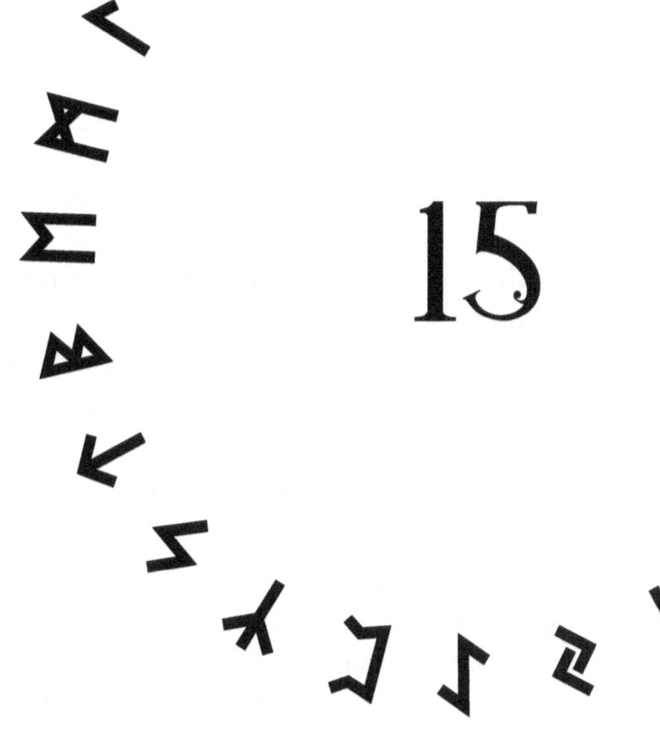

15

Boston

Loki was quietly smug with his progress. Killing Thor was just the start. It had thrown Odin off balance again, and there was nothing Loki liked more than having his blood-brother flailing.

Odin's hubris – once something Loki had enjoyed, had even encouraged – had become his downfall. He didn't need Loki's help to dismantle his world. He had done that all on his own. He'd pushed away everyone he'd ever cared about, all because he refused to change with the times, had refused to accept his position in the new world.

Once Odin's Valkyries would have protected him fiercely, even to the death, but now they would be the ones to murder him, with Loki's help. He would be successful in obtaining Bryn's feather cloak one way or another. But it was Korvain who was the roadblock he had to remove in order to strike at the Valkyrie.

And the sledgehammer to break him?

Well, that was where the light elf currently chained to a chair and unable to fade away to save himself came into play. The little Mare would come for him – was probably here right now – and when Geri and Freki got her, and when Loki sent Korvain a message conveying as much, Korvain would come for her, thus leaving Bryn unprotected. If he had made it inside the Eye once, he could do it again.

Loki laughed, seeing how each strand of his web was being woven together to create Odin's inevitable death. It had been a long time coming. Would he take his time and make the god suffer? Would he make it a slow, painful death, or a quick one? The All-Father had never shown Loki any mercy, so that really only left one option.

Drawn-out and painful.

Loki smiled.

"What's so funny?" Aubrey asked.

"I was just thinking about what I would do to Taer once I have her restrained beside you."

The only physical sign that his words had any effect was the slight flair of the light elf's nostrils. "I don't know why you're doing any of this. I've never even met Odin before."

"That is extraneous to the larger plan." Loki stepped toward him, crouching down so they were eye-to-eye. "You are part of this, a simple fly now stuck in my web, even if you are unaware of it."

There was a creaking overhead – feet moving over the floorboards. The brothers must have secured Taer.

"Excuse me," Loki said cordially, taking the stairs up into the first level of the house. He found the twins in the kitchen, one rifling through the freezer, the other through the cupboard under the sink.

"Where is she?" he demanded. His question startled both of them. When they looked up, there was blood all over their faces, still trickling down from the wounds to their heads. "What the fuck happened?"

Geri looked down at the floor. "She got away."

Loki blinked, and when he opened his eyes again, he found one of his hands was wrapped around Geri's throat, his fingers tightening. He turned his head to speak to Freki. "I think I must have misheard you; you said she got away?"

"She did," Freki replied, his eyes fixed on Loki's fingers wrapped around his brother's throat. Loki eased off, letting the other god go and stepping away.

"How could you have failed?"

Geri rubbed his throat. "She was a lot stronger than we thought."

Loki growled in frustration, squeezing his hands into fists to stop them from wrapping around Geri's throat again. He walked to the other side of the kitchen. "What good are you two if you can't do a simple task?"

"We'll try again," said Freki.

"I don't even know why I agreed to let you help me. I don't *need* you. You're only here because I took pity on you both."

Loki turned and stared at the door leading to the basement. He would make sure Taer returned to the house. He would give her something that would have her running back here.

Turning back to the brothers, he said, "This is the last chance I'm going to give you. Failing me in this seals your deaths. Do you remember the light elf we saw at the club the other night? I don't know how he found me, but I need him gone."

They both nodded in unison.

"Good. Now, I have some other business I need to attend to. Go."

Walking back to the basement, Loki looked over the array of tools he'd collected. He picked up a small hacksaw and tested the teeth against his thumb. Blood welled instantly.

He turned to Aubrey, showing the male the blade.

"What do you think would make Taer come faster, a hand or a foot?"

16

Rhys was looking for a shadow in an already darkened room. At least that's how it felt. Wandering aimlessly around Boston, searching for a god he had no way of finding, was aggravating his beast. The brief interlude with the waitress in Chicago had left him suffering more than he had before. Now he was walking on the edge of a cliff, and it was a perilous and sharp drop to the bottom.

Adding to the feeling that he was losing control was the tidal wave of grief over Galen's death he was trying to hold at bay. He couldn't do it for much longer though. Coupled with the rage he constantly carried with him, Rhys was a loaded gun with a hair trigger.

In an attempt to distract the beast clawing at him, Rhys found himself fading to the Eye again. He stepped into the darkness formed from a blown streetlight across the other side of the club. The same Valkyrie as before was guarding the door, her shrewd eyes studying everyone who passed by her.

Blood, his beast demanded on a snarl, pushing its will onto Rhys.

No, Rhys spat back, although why he was speaking to it, he didn't know. It had never listened to him before. He stayed and watched the club for as long as he could before he couldn't take it any longer. The voice in his head was becoming more and more insistent, and everybody had their limits. He knew he couldn't take another human. The last one didn't know how close she'd come to meeting the thing he shared his body with.

Rhys shuddered.

With one final look, he faded to the War Hammer. Inside he was enveloped by the sounds, smells and sights of the old world. Sidling up to the bar, Rhys ordered some ale and watched the other patrons for a while. Since the Fall, a lot of the gods – especially the Aesir – had trouble adjusting to things. Other beings like the elves had had no trouble at all. Many of them had jobs in the human world. Many humans wouldn't have known if their kid's teacher was a light elf, or whether their dentist was actually an ice giant. The fire giants, on the other hand, had to be a little more selective in where they showed their faces.

And the oldest profession for the humans also happened to be the oldest for the gods, too. Rhys's gaze latched onto a goddess who was moving through the room, stopping to touch a man's shoulder and whisper in his ear before moving on to another.

She wasn't dressed in modern clothes. Instead she was wearing a light, sheer fabric reminiscent of a Greek peplos. Deep emerald in color, it was cinched in tight to her narrow waist, accentuating her bust and hips. Rhys perused her body, lingering on all the right places, letting her know he was interested in what she was selling.

She came to stand in front of him, meeting his heated gaze with one of her own. "One hundred for a hand job. Two hundred for a blow job and," she stepped into the hard line of his body, dropping her hand to cup his dick, "five hundred to do whatever you want to me."

"I sometimes get rough," he replied, half hoping the warning would scare her off.

"Most men do," the goddess replied. "Come on. I have a place close by." She started to walk away, but Rhys pulled her to a stop. She gave him a questioning look.

"I don't have long." It wasn't a lie, but it wasn't exactly the truth either. "Bathroom?"

"Al has a room upstairs that he lets me use sometime. We can go there." Indicating with her head, she said, "There's a set of stairs in the back. Meet you in a minute. I just have to check in with someone first."

Rhys walked through the bar. Even though the place was busy, and it was standing room only, there was one table set in the corner, partitioned off from the others. Nobody was sitting there, but it seemed like it was reserved for someone in particular.

Whatever. Get what you need from the female and get out of here.

A minute passed and the goddess returned. With a smile, she took Rhys by the hand and led him up the stairs. When she came to the door at the top, she unlocked it and stepped inside. Shutting it behind them, Rhys looked around. It looked like some kind of training room.

"Do you want to get started right away?" she asked, drawing Rhys's attention away from a set of daggers displayed on a board on the wall.

He nodded.

"Great. I do almost anything, but I draw the line at rope bondage and drawing blood."

"I just need to be in control, and . . . sometimes I get lost in the moment."

The goddess nodded as if she'd heard it before. Fuck, she probably had. "No problem." With a sly smile, she started to untie her dress at the waist and then undid the clasp on her shoulder. The sheer fabric fell to the ground, pooling around her feet like a soft puddle. She had a body that would be considered too round and soft for the human's standards of beauty, but for Rhys she reminded him of what a real woman looked like.

"What's your name?" he asked, wondering where the question had come from and why he cared.

"Ava." She started touching her breasts, plucking at her nipples then snaking her fingers down toward the apex of her thighs. Rhys really didn't need the encouragement. In two short steps he was standing in front of her, gripping both of her wrists. He walked her backwards until they hit the wall. Spinning her around, he pressed himself against her spine.

"Oh!" Ava gasped, grinding her ass into his groin in appreciation.

He felt the beast stretch out in his mind. Ignoring it, he leaned forward, nipping at the goddess's neck. She groaned, panting theatrically. Forcing his hand between her and the wall, he felt for her sex and slipped two fingers inside without priming her first. Her inner walls clenched tight. Pumping his fingers in and out a couple of times, he waited until she was wet enough before fumbling for the zipper on his pants. He hated having to resort to sex every time he felt he was losing grip, but it was better than the alternative. All it meant was that Rhys never really enjoyed the act anymore – it was just something he had to do.

Ava whimpered when he removed his fingers from her so he could roll on the condom. She wiggled her ass, silently begging him to enter her. He didn't want to take her against the wall though; there wasn't enough maneuvering room. Even though his beast howled in protest, Rhys stepped away. Ava looked at him over her shoulder. Even though she'd probably been fucked by thousands of men before, her cheeks were still flushed and her eyes were blazing with lust.

"What's wrong, baby?"

"Nothing," he replied, growling softly to himself when he heard the gravelly quality to his voice. He looked around the room, spotting a large military-style footlocker. Pointing at the thing, he said, "Place your forearms on the top of that, keep your legs straight and clasp your hands together in front of you."

Ava's eyes darted to the container and she sauntered over to it; the swing of her hips was hypnotizing. When she was in position, Rhys laid a hand on the curve of her ass and spanked her once, hard. The goddess moaned in approval. Anchoring both hands on her hips, Rhys lined himself up and slammed home, shunting her forward and causing the footlocker to move with her.

Moving his hips back, he slid almost all the way out before slamming himself back in. Ava's whole body quivered with the motion.

"Harder," she panted.

Rhys obliged, retreating and surging forward once more until all he could hear was sex. All he could smell and taste was sex. The beast rushed forward, trying to take over the pleasure. With gritted teeth, he forced it back and reclaimed his control. He had always been afraid of this part of himself, and the beast knew it – took advantage of it – but now there was no one else to help Rhys if he gave into the animal's base desires.

It was all on him now.

If aggression increased its strength, it would surely stand to reason that calmness would placate the animal. Rhys had never tried to quiet it before. In his mind's eye, he pictured himself calming it with softly spoken words. He approached it slowly, running his hand lightly over its head and the back of its neck. He was surprised when the usually tense animal relaxed under his strokes. A low, coarse rumble sounded from its chest – almost as if it was purring. But Rhys knew it would only truly be content once he had found his release.

His pace increased, his body slamming into Ava's with more and more power. If she'd been human, he would have broken something.

"Pull my hair," Ava urged.

"What?"

"Pull my hair," she repeated.

Without losing his rhythm, Rhys leaned forward and fisted her hair, dragging it to the side and pulling her neck into a strange angle. Ava groaned.

He was getting lost in the sensations, knowing his release – and the promise of peace – was coming. The goddess continued to make all the right noises. Rhys came with a roar that was animalistic and primal. Ava wasn't too far behind him, but for all he knew, the sound was fake.

As always, it only took a few moments for the veil of calm to fall over Rhys. The beast retreated from the front of his mind, but it wouldn't stay there for very long and Rhys would have to go through all this again. At least he hadn't hurt this one. Perhaps he could control this side of his nature.

Sliding out of her body, Rhys disappeared the condom and pulled out his wallet. He placed five hundred dollars on top of the footlocker in front of Ava's face. She straightened, swiping the money up in one fluid movement. She counted it, smiling at Rhys when she saw the twenty percent tip.

"Thanks, baby. Come find me anytime." She picked up her dress, putting it on just as quickly as she'd taken it off, and left the room.

Rhys followed her out five minutes later. He kept his head down as he made a beeline for the door. At least one problem had been taken care of. Now all he had to do was deal with one more. He started walking, not knowing where he was going.

The night was cold and as he breathed in the chilly air, he got lost in his thoughts once more. When he finally looked up, he found himself on State Street, standing in the shadows of the Old State House. The streets were empty, which should have been his first clue that something wasn't right.

He stopped, squinting at his surroundings, wondering whether the shadows were shifting as he thought they were. His beast snarled in warning. Rhys was about to fade away when he was tackled to the ground. A large body landed on him, pushing all the air from his lungs. Before he could focus on the weight on top of him, he was kicked in the face, his head snapping around and connecting with the asphalt. His vision fuzzed out, and he could taste blood on his tongue. He swallowed it down, the dark liquid fueling his beast.

With renewed strength, he pushed the guy off and sent him into the side of a parked car. The alarm began to blare, the flashing lights illuminating the face of his attacker.

It was someone Rhys had never seen before. With his fists clenched at his side, Rhys was ready for whatever the guy was about to do next . . .

He wasn't, however, ready for what happened.

As if on replay, he was tackled back to the ground, and this time he did get a good look at the guy.

He looked exactly like the first.

Fucking twins?

He tried to recall if he'd ever encountered the pair before. Fisting his attacker's shirt in his hands, Rhys threw him over his head and then jumped to his feet. Standing side-on, he kept both men in his line of sight. Number One had recovered, but was shaking his head like he could still hear ringing in his ears. Number Two was only just getting up now. He had a cut above his eye, which made Rhys's beast lick its lips in rabid appreciation. He dug his nails into his palms, attempting to refocus his thoughts.

Rhys's eyes darted from side to side, watching, waiting for the pair to strike. He had no doubts that they would come at him at the same time. But for a few seconds, nothing happened at all . . .

Number One moved in, distracting Rhys by throwing punches at his face and around his midsection. Absorbing the hits, Rhys bided his time, finally finding an opening where he could strike at his opponent's throat. Staggering back a step, Number One gasped for air. Rhys only had a moment to enjoy the triumph as Number Two jumped on his back.

In one fluid movement, Rhys threw him forward over his shoulder. Number Two landed with a heavy crunch in front of him. Number One struck back, sweeping Rhys's feet from under him. He landed heavily and awkwardly, his body twisting at a strange angle. By this time, Rhys had lost track of who was who. He looked up to find one of the men standing over him, a blade in his hand.

"Stand him up," the guy said. Rhys was suddenly vertical, standing nose to nose with one of them. His twin was standing behind Rhys, a physical barrier that meant nothing at all to him . . . but they didn't know that. The sweet smell of blood fragranced the air, and it took Rhys a second to realize it was his own blood he was smelling.

He looked down to find the dagger sticking out of his gut, blood soaking his shirt. He saw his beast shift beneath his skin, the muscles in his stomach rolling with the motion.

"What the fuck was that?" the guy still standing in front of him asked. Rhys fisted the guy's shirt at the shoulders, holding him tightly.

"You don't want to do this," he warned, feeling his beast surge behind his eyes.

The guy blinked at him, hesitating for just a moment. That moment of weakness was all it took for the animal to completely take over.

A terrifying snarl rent the air, and Rhys heard his other attacker shift nervously behind him. "Geri?" he asked, a quiver in his voice. The fear caught his beast's attention, holding it. Rhys turned around, knowing his eyes were blazing yellow and his face was changing shape. The guy backed away a step and Rhys turned his attention to the guy's brother. Shoving him away, Rhys let go of his control. With a shudder that not only rolled over his skin, but also through his veins, his blood and bones, Rhys succumbed to the darkness inside him. His muscles tore, ripping away from the bones they were anchored to. Shredded, they could reform into a body that was stronger, more designed for fighting and perfect for rending meat from bone.

One minute he was standing on two legs.

The next, he was on four, his body substantially larger than it had been before. It was covered in dark hair that insulated him against the cold Boston night. His new mouth, filled with sharp curved teeth, was just another weapon in his arsenal. His paws flexed into the unforgiving street surface, his nails scraping loudly. He was at least two hundred and fifty pounds in his wolf's body.

"Loki didn't say anything about this," one of the men said.

Rhys's sharp gaze cut to him.

Kill, his wolf demanded.

A growl left his throat.

The sound seemed to snap the other two gods back into action. They came at him at the same time, but Rhys was more than ready. He was inhaling their fear, letting it strengthen him. One of the men threw himself at him, but Rhys merely batted him away with one paw. The other man jumped on his back, plunging a blade into his side. The steel slid through his ribs and nicked one of his lungs. Rhys immediately felt the injury, but it only enraged his wolf. Bucking wildly, he threw the god off him, rounding on him with a snarl. With his teeth on the handle, he pulled out the knife still lodged in his side and dropped it to the ground. The wound throbbed in time with his heart, but the adrenaline pumping through his bloodstream was helping to stop the worst of the pain.

Rhys waited for the god to scramble to his feet before he struck; he was always one for equality, and never hit a person when they were down. Opening his mouth over the man's thigh, Rhys clamped his jaws shut, snapping the bone in two.

Hello, agony.

The guy screamed out, the sound too delicious for Rhys's wolf to ignore. He could feel his grip starting to slip. If he gave in completely to his beast, death and destruction were sure to follow. Like closing a mental fist, Rhys contained his wolf's violent urges once more. It snarled in his head, fighting the command.

Rhys's ears began to swivel as he heard the other brother get up. He readied himself for another attack, swinging around to face the enemy, seeing the blade he carried.

His upper lip pulled away from his fangs, showing the god his teeth, challenging him to take another run at him. At least the bastard hesitated for a moment. It just went to prove that there was some sort of survival instinct in there somewhere. Rhys just hoped that the god had had enough.

But he was wrong.

Once again, Rhys was on the receiving end of a launched attack. Off balance, he was driven to the ground. He snapped and snarled at the male on top of him, taking out hunks of flesh from his enemy's side. Rolling to his feet, Rhys dumped the writhing god to the ground. The smell of blood – the sweet metallic taste on his tongue – was a siren's call to the animal in him. Backing away from the pair, he squeezed his eyes shut, trying his best to keep his wolf at bay.

He forced the animal into the steel cage at the back of his mind, but before he could slam the gate shut, the wolf made a break for it. Rhys's vision changed from color to black and white with shades of gray, and like the tide coming in, when the water went back out, so did Rhys's control.

———————

When Rhys finally came back to himself, all he could see was red. All he could smell was blood. All there was, was blood. Like a river, it flowed down the gutters and into the drains; it pooled in the depressions of the asphalt. Only one body lay in a messy heap at his feet, what was left of the god's hand still twitching with the last firings of his neurons. All that remained of the body was from the chest down. Rhys's wolf had eaten the lower half.

The other god must have escaped his wolf's rage.

What had he done? Yes, he'd wanted to kill them, but not desecrate their bodies. Not even animals did that. It was kill or be killed, not kill then eat the remains. Of course, Rhys's beast was not like any animal he'd ever known. It was something else. Its soul was dark and poisonous. Its mind was driven by nothing more than thoughts of *blood* and *kill*.

He ran his tongue over his muzzle, coating it in even more blood.

Fuck, he felt so . . . dirty.

Above his head, a raven cawed, the giant black bird taking flight. There was a sharp intake of breath behind him, and Rhys whirled around to face a young woman. How there weren't any other witnesses to his destruction was a goddamn mystery. The only explanation Rhys could think of was the two gods had used some sort of magic to veil their actions. Rhys's attention went back to the girl. Her eyes were wide and fixed. She took an unsteady step back, piquing his wolf's attention.

Gods, no, no, no.

He willed the woman to stay where she was, not to move, not to run. If she ran, his wolf would follow and hunt her down.

Her foot slid back another step. Rhys snarled.

"P-p-please," she said on a whimper.

He wanted to yell at her to freeze. He wanted to force his legs to walk away. He needed to forget about her, but his wolf – glut on blood and death – was at his strongest, and would continue to be at his strongest until exhaustion took over.

The woman stared at him for the longest time. He could practically see her brain whirring, the cogs turning. She turned and ran, and Rhys was powerless to stop what was going to happen next. His huge paws and long stride ate up the distance between them. He was so close that the bouquet of her fear was enticing, driving more blood into his muscles to run faster. No less than four feet from her, Rhys's legs were cut out from under him. He smashed into the side of a building, not only hearing, but feeling the bricks crack and splinter from the impact.

He recovered quickly, a snarl in his throat.

Stepping from the shadows, the human's savior revealed herself. It was the Valkyrie from the club, the one who guarded the door, the one who had peeked inside his head. "Don't even think about it," she warned, drawing a dagger from an ankle sheath. The blade was black, matching the tattoo on her neck. "The veil is fast disappearing. More humans will be able to see you and the destruction you've caused. Don't add another body to your list of kills."

She was speaking to Rhys as if he were a man rather than a wolf. When she'd looked into his head, had she seen what lurked beneath his skin and muscles, seen what was buried in his blood and bones?

"Shift back," she commanded, the sound of her voice raking against Rhys's sensitive eardrums.

If only it was as easy as that.

He shook his head.

"Fade then," she ground out. "I've seen what you're capable of. Get out of here. I won't leave until you do."

A sob leaked from one of the shadows, and Rhys realized they still had an audience. The humans didn't know about the creatures and gods of the Nine Worlds. That was the way it had to stay. With his hold on the wolf strengthening, Rhys turned and loped away from the scene of his disgrace. He felt sick to his stomach to think that he would have killed that woman. The only crime she was guilty of was being in the wrong place at the wrong time.

He ran until the city was far behind him. Distance ceased to exist. All Rhys knew was direction. He didn't slow until the smell of car exhaust and garbage was a memory and the scent of pine and white oak was sublimely overwhelming. The noise of the expressway was a dull drone in the background, but at least he'd found an escape. He didn't know whether anyone had seen him as he'd left the city. He'd tried to stay in the shadows and under the cover of trees and shrubs.

His claws protracted into the loamy soil, and he let out a breath that was more about relief than anything else. In this kind of environment, Rhys didn't mind being in his wolf's skin – he only got edgy when there were humans around. His start in life had not been peaceful. Rhys never knew his mother was. She had abandoned him as a baby, leaving him in the care of guardians.

He'd asked who his father was a hundred times, and a hundred times the answer was *we don't know* but not before they shared a look which was loaded with words that would never be said, never be revealed.

It wasn't until his thirteenth summer that he had his first shift. The whole incident was pain wrapped in confusion and tied with a bow of murderous rage. He had fled into the woods, living like the wolf that had taken over his body. He had hunted anything that would fill his stomach – other light elves included.

After that first time, Rhys had removed himself completely from society. It wasn't hard to do. His guardians thought he was dead, and he had no friends who would come looking for him.

He had barely seen twenty summers when Galen had found him being beaten by a group of light elves. Rhys was stronger than them all combined, but he had wanted to die. He'd grown weary from sharing his body with the wolf; he was tired of the constant battle for control.

Death would have been welcomed.

But Galen had saved his life, and so Rhys pledged himself to the Mare, promising to protect him always.

And now he was dead, and Rhys had failed. All he seemed

capable of was bringing pain to whoever was close to him. As a wolf, his harsh bark of laughter was more of a huff, but the derision was still the same. He didn't even know why he bothered to try. He thought he brought destruction when he let his beast take over, but he was wrong. Even as a man, he was equally as dangerous. That was why becoming a contract killer seemed to be the most logical career for him – he could get paid for doing what he seemed to do naturally.

He shook himself from the thoughts, and got lost like he had that first time he'd shifted. For hours Rhys's wolf roamed around the forest of tall fir and maple, tracking the scents of white tail deer and of a coyote. It wasn't hungry. It just wanted to stretch its legs for a little while. Now that it was free, it was going to take advantage of it.

It was only when the sun was starting to rise that the beast gave into its exhaustion. Retreating deeper inside Rhys's mind, it finally let him fully take back the reins. The shift happened immediately. Just as before, muscles and tendons tore and knitted back together again, and he was left panting and naked on the forest floor. His whole body ached as he stood, and even after a quick stretch, he could still feel every bruise and every cut. His punctured lung was healing. He looked down to inspect the belly wound he'd got before the shift. All that remained was a puffy red scar.

Shutting his eyes, he thought about the cheap hotel room he'd rented while he was in Boston. The pull of the fade was a welcome one, and a moment later he was standing on the threadbare green carpet, staring at the nicotine-stained walls. He walked into the bathroom to get a better look at himself. His eyes were solid blue with no hint of his wolf peering through. With any luck, the beast would be satisfied with its little romp . . . until the next time

Rhys had to fight and kill.

He sighed.

Two words: vicious cycle.

It was always the same.

Turning on the shower, he ignored the cold tap and made sure the water was as hot as he could get it. He washed the blood from his body and then fell into bed with the towel still wrapped around his waist.

Trapped.

Odin felt so damn . . . trapped.

He paced the length of his Oriental rug. All he could think was that Loki had the advantage now. Anger suddenly bubbled to the surface. His arm swept out, knocking his whiskey glass off the mantel and sending it crashing to the floor. Crystal shards were violently propelled all over the rug and hardwood floor, crunching under his shoes as he continued to walk back and forth.

He should *not* have been the one cowering inside his apartment.

He was the All-Father. People had feared him. People should *still* fear him.

Odin's eyes returned to the TV screen playing mutely, watching to see if there were any more messages from Loki. He knew it wasn't the last time he would hear from the trickster god. His only hope was that Rhys would find him before Loki could strike at Odin again. If the light elf failed, Odin had no doubt the next person he would be mourning would be Bryn.

Slumping into the wing chair, the All-Father rubbed at the tension headache forming. His entire plan hinged on Rhys. And he hated it.

He hated leaving the fate of his life in the hands of another. Standing up once more, he moved to the window overlooking Boston Common and opened it wide. Cold air swirled inside, piercing through his clothing and sending a chill through his body. Turning his face toward the sky, he closed his eyes and called his ravens back to him. Odin only had to wait a few moments until he heard the familiar sound of wind cutting through feathers. Huginn landed on the sill, his talons clicking on the stone.

Offering out his hand, Odin brought the bird to his shoulder, tilting his head to the side as he looked into Huginn's mind. The raven had been flying throughout Boston and further to the north in search of Loki, yet had found no trace of the god. Perhaps Muninn had had better luck.

Odin looked out the window once more. The bird was invisible as it flew through the dark night sky, landing silently and unexpectedly on the sill on the next window over.

"Come," he commanded, holding out his arm. The raven landed easily, walking up his arm to sit on his other shoulder. "What have you seen?"

The raven cawed, letting Odin into its mind. He watched what had unfolded on the Boston street, growing more and more incensed with every second that passed. The attack on Rhys had been bloody and violent, but that was not what upset him. What really made him angry was that it was his own wolves who had attacked the light elf. Granted they were no longer his anymore, but Geri and Freki had been his loyal servants for over one thousand years. After the Fall, he had changed them into men in order for them to thrive among the humans rather than simply exist as wolves in the woods. What he couldn't figure out though was whether the pair were acting alone, or whether they'd been sent by someone. If Loki had found out about Rhys, he would try to kill Rhys before Rhys could kill him. And if that were true, he obviously had no idea that Rhys was really his grandson.

The images were suddenly gone and Odin let out a breath. The last thing he had witnessed was Freki running while Rhys consumed Geri's body – a grisly and oddly satisfying scene for Odin to watch. There was one absolute that he'd learned, though, and that was that Rhys was not progressing in his search for Loki as quickly as Odin would like. If anything, it looked as if he was waiting for Loki to fall into his lap. It was clear that intervention was needed and Odin *would* intervene, risking himself in doing so.

Maverick watched the wolf disappear into the night, its inky fur blending in with the shadows. She'd seen the light elf lurking around at the club again and had decided to follow him. After about half an hour at the War Hammer, he'd left, only to be attacked by two gods who had thrown up a veil to keep the humans from seeing anything.

She hadn't exactly been sure it would listen to her – it was a killer through and through – but she had to take the chance. She could see from its aura that it was mindless, feral, and feeding off its base instincts. It had been ready to kill that woman. But Mav had also seen its second aura, the golden one that gave away its identity. That aura belonged to the light elf who had been asking about Loki, although now she wasn't sure he was just a light elf. He was a shape shifter for sure, but only the most powerful of gods were capable of taking another form like he had. In fact, she only knew of two: Odin and Loki.

With a thought, she faded to the alleyway beside the Eye and stepped up to the back door. She punched the code into the keypad and stepped into the hall.

"What did you find out?"

Mav looked up to find Korvain standing in the doorway to Bryn's office. She respected the Mare a lot, especially since he'd saved Bryn from Loki the first time around. "He's a shape shifter."

Korvain's expression darkened. "How is that possible?"

"There are more things in this world beside gods and goddesses," Bryn gently reminded him.

Mav waited for Korvain to wrap his head around the information. "How do you know?"

"I saw him transform into a huge wolf."

"A wolf?" This was from Bryn. Mav looked at her leader and shrugged. Of all the shape shifters, the wolf was the most common.

"What caused him to shift?" Korvain asked. He'd stopped pacing to stand beside Bryn, wrapping an arm around her waist and pulling her close to his body. His aura suddenly exploded with brilliant red, the starburst decimating his usual gray.

Mav looked away, fixing her attention on Bryn instead. "He was attacked by two gods. The elf stayed in human form for a long time, but it looked like it was taking a toll on him. When he shifted, it was fast. I think I barely blinked and then he was a wolf the size of a small car."

"Was it a random attack?" Bryn asked. "Do you know who the two gods were?"

"I didn't recognize them, but one of them was called Geri. I assumed the other was Freki. I also heard Loki's name mentioned, so I don't think it was random."

"Those two are . . . *were* Odin's wolves. How can they be human? And why are they serving Loki?"

"I don't know," Mav replied. "The elf killed one of them.

He tore him apart and partially ate the body. The other brother escaped."

"Could they have helped Loki to kill Thor, too?" Bryn said, looking from Korvain to Mav.

"It's a possibility," Korvain replied. "Where's the shifter now?" He was back to pacing.

"I told him to leave."

Bryn looked startled. "You actually spoke to him?"

"As a wolf, yes," she conceded. "I told him to fade, but he shook his head. I don't think he's able to while in his other form."

"Where did he go then?" Korvain barked the question at her.

"I couldn't tell you."

Bryn walked up to Korvain. "We need to find him," she breathed.

"I will," Maverick said. Bryn turned. "I'll find him," she repeated.

"He's dangerous."

Mav folded her arms over her chest. "It doesn't matter. If he's looking for Loki, he's doing it for a reason. He did say he wanted to kill him. As far as I can tell that's a good thing for us. He's not our enemy. We should be helping him."

"I don't think it's possible to kill Loki," Bryn said. "But you're right." She nodded at Mav. "Find him. Loki still needs to pay for what he did to us."

"And what about Odin?" Korvain's dark voice was amplified in the long hallway. "Loki is obviously still looking for him, which means he must be trying to get to you." He inclined his head in Bryn's direction. "Whichever way you look at it, you're still the key Loki needs."

"I know." Bryn sounded bitter. "Even without being involved in my life, Odin still manages to fuck it up for me."

17

Midgard – 806AD

Anxiety spiked, making Tove's stomach turn. The last three weeks had gone too quickly for her. Summer was behind them now, fall firmly set in place. The end of the good weather also signaled the end of her life, as far as she was concerned. The ceremony joining her and Floki together was tomorrow. No matter how hard she tried to petition her father, he wouldn't listen to her. He'd said that her marriage to Floki would strengthen the weakened bond between their family and his. Halvdan needed to have a strong ally by his side as more and more chieftains were rising up against him.

Soren touched the side of Tove's face, jerking her out of her own thoughts. "Are you thinking about tomorrow?" he asked gently, his fingers skimming down her arm. Goose bumps broke out in his wake, leaving her shivering. He had snuck in after her father had gone to bed and they were sitting in front of the fire in the great hall, sharing what would be their last night together before she became Floki's wife.

"Aren't you?"

He nodded sharply, his jaw tight. She knew he was holding back the words he'd been repeating for weeks now. He'd been trying to convince her to run off with him, to just leave and marry him and live somewhere far away, but Tove's sense of duty and love for her father prevented her from doing that. She loved Soren, but she loved her father more.

"If you would just—"

"What?" she interrupted sharply. "Leave? Be a coward?"

"You wouldn't be a coward," Soren tried to reason. Tove had thought seriously about his request, and for half a minute she thought it was possible to simply disappear and leave her responsibilities behind. The only problem was that she knew her sense of obligation would eventually win out. Her mother had been a shield maiden – she had been honorable, and she was well-known, beloved and respected for that honor. Tove wanted to be like her more than anything, and if that meant agreeing to an arranged marriage, then she would. After all it had worked out between her parents. Perhaps she could find a small measure of happiness with Floki.

"I would be, Soren," she replied, turning to face him. The golden glow of the fire illuminated half his face, making him look like a god of Asgard and a demon of Muspelheim at the same time. She touched his face, smoothing away the wrinkles on his forehead, trying to erase the scowl that had permanently set in the moment her father had told them about the betrothal. "I have to obey my father in this."

Soren's normally kind brown eyes took on a sharp edge. "And

what about me? What am I supposed to do, Tove? Celebrate your marriage? Wish you luck and a happy life together?" He surged to his feet, pacing along the skins they'd been lounging on. "Because I won't do it. I *can't* do it. The moment I see Floki, I will want to wrap my hands around his neck and squeeze the breath from his lungs."

Me too, she thought hopelessly. The worst part of this whole thing was that Soren would be left behind. Both of their hearts will be broken, but if she was honest, hers had broken the moment her father had told her she was to marry someone else. She had no choice; she was the chieftain's only daughter. She sighed. "I should try to get some rest before tomorrow."

Soren stopped pacing and faced her. "You're giving up on us." He stated it so forcefully that she knew he believed it.

"Never," she whispered. "I'll always love you – until my hearts stops beating, it will belong to you."

The fire crackled and hissed, embers shooting into the air as a log fell. Soren's gaze fell onto the flames. "I won't be there tomorrow. I won't watch you give yourself to another."

No, no, no. He was her strength; his love was keeping her going, and would continue to keep her going through her life. But she wouldn't tell him. She wanted him to have the freedom to choose – something she wasn't able to do. "Okay."

"Okay?" he spat, raising his voice slightly.

"What do you want me to do, Soren?" she asked, exasperated.

Grasping her arms, he pulled her into his embrace. She melted into the feel of his strong chest, placing her ear against his ribs to listen to his heart. "I want you to leave this place. Tonight. Now. We'll go west. I can take a boat and we can sail until we hit the shore of Northumbria."

Tove stayed quiet, absorbing every last second of her time with

Soren. When she pulled away, she could see that he knew this was the end. The look in his eyes was foreign, hard and unforgiving – nothing at all like the warmth and love she normally saw there. Stepping out of his arms, she retreated a few steps. "I love you."

He opened his mouth as if he was going to say something, but in the end he just shook his head and walked from the hall. Tove watched him go, feeling the tears pooling in her eyes and trembling on her lashes. She understood why he couldn't stay. It didn't make the hurt any less, though. Wiping the tears from her eyes, she promised herself they'd be the last she would cry for the life she could have had with Soren.

Floki Dalgaard was her future . . .

Her bleak, dark future.

———————

At dawn, Tove was awakened and taken to the bath-house. There, one of her mother's oldest friends informed her of her duties as a wife, gave her advice on the best way to live with a man and other religious observances she had to make as a married woman. She was stripped of all her old clothing, and the *kransen* – a gilt circlet used as decoration on her loose hair – was removed. Symbolically, this was the biggest change. Tove had walked into the bath-house as a maiden, and when she walked out, she was ready to become a woman.

By mid-morning, the sun had still refused to come out from behind the clouds. Perhaps the gods were reflecting her mood onto Midgard. Nobody else seemed to notice it though. All around her, the villagers were excited. Marriages called for great celebrations and great celebrations called for great feasts. Food was being prepared and animals that had been slaughtered the previous day were already roasting on fires. Her father had chosen to forego the week-long celebration of her marriage – a small consolation to her, she felt.

"Let's get you dressed," someone said behind her. Tove drew in one more breath of air and turned to see Aslaug standing there. The girl was perhaps only two years younger than her, and beautiful in her own way. She had also been Tove's personal servant for the past four years. She followed her into her sleeping area, stopping just inside the room. Her father was waiting for her there, sitting on the edge of her bed. His expression was solemn and in his lap was a rectangular wooden box.

"What's that, father?" she asked, approaching him slowly.

Halvdan's fingers caressed the carving in the lid lovingly, a small smile appearing on his lips. "This was the dress your mother wore on our wedding day." He looked at her. "I think she would want you to wear it." Placing the box onto the bed, he stood up and approached her. Kissing her forehead, he said, "I'll leave you with Aslaug to get ready."

Aslaug stepped close to Tove and started to undress her, stripping away the ankle-length woolen dress and the linen dress underneath it.

"Are you excited?" Aslaug asked.

"No," Tove answered, surprising herself with her honesty.

"It is a good match."

She looked at the girl. "For who?" she asked acidly.

Her curt reply left Aslaug with nothing more to say. When Tove was in her mother's dress, a brooch was attached at her throat before the girl started brushing out Tove's long hair. After today, she would never be able to wear it loose and uncovered. It was just another reminder of her fate.

After Tove left her room, she was escorted to the grove where the ceremony was to take place. A sow was sacrificed to Freyja to ask for her blessings for fertility, and then she got her first good look at the man who was to be her husband.

Floki was shorter than her by a good few inches. She would have to stoop to kiss the fool. He was losing his hair despite only having seen five more summers than her. All his features seemed too small for his long face, and his eyes were cruel. But all of those things she could ignore. The thing that held her attention more was the cloak of dark pink and dark green – two colors she associated with negativity and resentment – hovering over his head. Once more her stomach clenched into a tight knot.

The entire ceremony was a blur after that. She recalled exchanging swords and rings, but could not remember saying the vows. The next thing she knew they were feasting in the great hall at her home. She ate the food and drank the wine but she did not taste a thing. More than once, Floki leaned over, placing his hand high on her thigh and whispering in her ear, "Are you not having fun, wife?"

She said nothing. She just watched the way his aura flared with irritation.

Unable to remain beside Floki any longer, she left the table and went to speak with some of her father's supporters, catching part of their conversation about the upcoming harvest of their barley crop.

"There won't be enough to see us through," one of the men said. "The summer was too hot and we planted too late."

Another said, "But surely Dalgaard will be willing to trade with us now."

"I will ensure Floki's father trades with you," she told the men with a warm smile.

"Mistress?" Aslaug said softly.

Tove apologized to the men and turned her attention to her servant. "Yes?"

"It's almost time. I'm going to prepare your bed with the linens from your dowry. When I'm done, I will come and collect you."

Tove nodded to the servant girl and tried to focus on the conversation again, but all she could think about was what was to come. Soon she would have to lie with her husband for the first time, and the thought was terrifying.

She glanced in the direction of the long table up in front of the dais. Her father was whispering something to his advisor while Floki's father seemed to be watching everyone in the room. Her gaze settled on her husband. She expected him to be watching her, but his attention was on Aslaug as she left the hall. His aura shifted colors. After a beat, he stood up and followed her out.

"Oh, no," Tove whispered. Without excusing herself from the conversation, she hurried after them both, but an older man she had never seen before stopped her.

"Congratulations, Tove, on this special day," he said. She gave him a small smile, and started to step past him when he added, "You know, I was at your parents' wedding too. Now *that* was a feast to remember."

"Thank you, sir. But you must excuse me." She walked away without waiting for his reply and slipped into the hallway at the back of the house. Just outside her bedchamber, she was brought to a dead stop. Aslaug's screams made all the hair on the back of Tove's neck stand on end. Pushing aside the skins which had been hung for privacy, she stepped into the room.

Floki had Aslaug pinned against the mattress, her skirts up around her waist, the bodice of her dress ripped down the middle so her breasts were exposed. He slapped her hard across the face before entering her body forcefully. Aslaug screamed again, and

Tove could see blood where they were joined.

"Please," Aslaug begged softly, tears streaming down her cheeks. "Don't."

"Shut your mouth. They'll hear you."

"I already heard you," Tove said, finally finding her voice.

Aslaug's eyes widened when she saw Tove. "Mistress, I—"

"She begged me to take her," Floki spat, pulling Aslaug up from the bed and holding her in front of him like a shield. Aslaug was shaking, holding the torn dress to her body. This man was even more of a coward than Tove had first thought. "She's your servant, which means she's also mine now."

"It doesn't work that way, Floki." She took a step closer, looking the girl in the eye. "Aslaug, come to me."

Floki's grip tightened, causing Aslaug to cry out in pain. "No. She stays here with me."

Tove watched his aura flare again. His desperation was scrubbing out his lust. "Let her go, Floki, and I won't mention your indiscretion to my father."

"Nobody will be talking about this to anybody," he replied, suddenly pulling out a knife and bringing it to Aslaug's throat.

"No!" Tove cried, throwing out her hand to try and stop him, but she was too late. He ran the blade across Aslaug's throat like she was a sacrificial goat. The wound gaped, and blood welled. He pushed Aslaug aside as she dropped to the ground, gasping from breath. "No," Tove whispered, watching her servant's eyes go dull. She refocused on Floki, the ember of her anger flaring to life.

The bastard was smiling at her. "I'll tell everyone that she was trying to steal from me."

"Why?" she asked. "Why didn't you just let her go?"

"Because she was my property, just like you are my property, and I can do what I like with it." He stalked toward her, gripping her upper arm and pulling her close. She could smell the ale on his breath, she could see his malice cloaking his shoulders. "Turn around and bend over," he said.

"Excuse me?"

He held the knife to her throat. "I am your husband. Do as I command."

He meant to take her now, like this? Aslaug's body was not yet cold, yet like a pig in rut, he wanted to mount her. Even though she wanted to fight back now, she had learned that biding your time for a more advantageous position was sometimes better. Appearing to yield to his will, she turned toward the bed.

Floki placed the knife on the edge of the mattress and gripped her hips from behind. "See, that wasn't so hard, was it?" he said into her ear.

In one swift motion, she scooped up the dagger and spun around to face him. She had caught him by surprise, but his shock soon turned to conceit. He actually laughed at her.

"Knives are not meant for the hands of noble-born girls," he said, chastising her. "Give it to me."

"Never," she spat.

Floki's rage crackled, filling the air with clouded red. He lunged at her, trying to drive her onto the bed. She couldn't move in time, landing heavily with him on top. One hand cinched shut around her wrist, his other hand trying hard to remove the dagger. She always slipped out of the way though; the gods were on her side. She swiped at him, drawing first blood on his upper arm. He struck her, his fist landing on her cheek. Thrown to one side, pain exploded through the side of her face, dazing her for a moment. Floki tried wrenching the knife free, but she knew if she was disarmed, he would take her by force.

Drawing on her inner strength, Tove pierced his belly with the knife, feeling his body yield to the sharp blade. Floki started to scream, but before the sound could build, she threw her hand over his mouth, stifling it. He fell onto his side, his hands clutching at the wound. Blood streamed from between his fingers, dripping onto the floor. Getting to her feet, she looked down at him.

"You will never touch me again." Her words were drawn out by her rage. She wanted him to know that she wasn't going to let him hurt her, nor any other woman again.

He looked up at her, hatred reflected both in his eyes and in the colors forming around his head and shoulders. "You have started a war you have no hope of winning."

That may be. Her father didn't have half the number of able-bodied warriors that his father did. But he did have her. She would die for her father and to die in battle was the most honorable way. Crouching beside Floki, Tove moved his hands out of the way. He was too weak to fight her, moaning when more blood spewed from his stomach.

"I will make you pay for this," he spat weakly. Despite his fatal injury, despite the clear disadvantage, he was still defiant until the end. She ignored his idle threats though. She'd been willing to marry to him — for her father, for her sense of duty, for the survival and prosperity of her father's rule. But she was not willing to allow Floki to rape her servant and then rape her. She could see now what kind of a man he was, and she would not condemn herself to that life, no matter the consequences.

Taking her dagger, she slid it into the wound and twisted. Floki ground his teeth together, his nostrils flaring as pain swept through him. Pulling the knife out, she held it against his throat.

"You are a pig, and you will die like a pig," she told him, running the blade across his throat. Blood flowed like a river down his chest, and each pump of his heart only made the blood gush faster. Tove watched the life leak from his eyes, feeling nothing but satisfaction.

When his chest had stopped pumping up and down, she got to her feet. She stumbled out into the hall with the dagger still in her hand. Blood covered her dress, chest, arms and legs. Nobody seemed to notice her arrival though. They were still drinking and eating, enjoying the music. Tove looked around, searching for her father.

She started walking through the throng of revelers. People stopped what they were doing when they saw her, a hush falling over the room with every step she took. When she was finally in front of her father, it took him a moment to notice her.

"Tove?" He stood up from his chair, his eyes taking in the blood, the dagger, the hard glint of satisfaction and determination in her eye. "Are you hurt?" She shook her head. "Your eye . . ."

She touched her left eye, feeling the swelling. She shrugged slightly.

"What of Floki?" Vadik Dalgaard, Floki's father, asked.

Tove looked him in the eye. She would not back down from this. "He is dead."

Vadik stood up, shoving the table away as he did. Food and mead fell to the floor. The dogs ran in and started eating what had fallen before being chased away by servants.

"Who killed him?" It was a demand from a chieftain, from a man who rarely didn't get what he wanted.

Raising her chin a fraction, she said, "I did." Her voice rang around the room.

The noise in the room returned, except it wasn't joyful anymore. Anger polluted the air, shouts of outrage coming from the Dalgaard camp. Vadik stalked toward Tove, taking her by the throat and lifting her off the ground. The dagger dropped from her hand. Her fingers scrambled to loosen his grip.

"You killed my son," Vadik snarled, his aura exploding with black striations. He started walking her backwards, toward the central hearth. She could feel the heat intensify with every step. With the air slowly being squeezed from her body, her vision started to darken. She gasped, desperately trying to suck in another breath. She could feel her eyes staring to bulge, the pressure of her blood forcing them out.

Vadik grunted right before blood started to drip from the corner of his mouth. Tove looked down to see the tip of a spear sticking out from under his ribs. Over his shoulder, she saw her father. His mouth was a twisted grimace, his eyes fierce. Vadik's fingers finally loosened from around her throat. Her feet hit the ground and she sucked in a deep breath, feeling her lungs burn. Vadik dropped to his knees, his momentum carrying him forward. Tove stepped out of the way, seeing her father's enemy fall headfirst into the open flames.

The smell of burning flesh was instant and choking.

She looked back at her father and nodded. All of that happened within a split second, because the next thing she knew, swords were being drawn and spears were made ready. Vadik had brought a third of his warriors with him to the wedding; Halvdan only had a dozen. The men crowded around Tove and her father, protecting their chieftain and his only living child.

"No," Halvdan boomed, pushing through the bodies of his fighters. "I will fight with you, not cowering in the corner." He rounded on Tove. "You," he said, pointing at her, "find safety with the other women."

"Father—"

"No," he roared. The fighting had already started, their men already falling. Her father turned around and thrust his spear into the throat of one of Vadik's men. "I won't lose you too," he shouted over his shoulder. "Go!"

A servant began tugging at Tove's arm, urging her backwards. "Come, mistress." Harried and scared, the girl went to lead her away, but Tove wouldn't go. She belonged here with her father. She had caused this. She had been training to fight since she was six years old. Finding a discarded sword, Tove picked it up and entered the melee. She blocked one strike, sweeping up the dagger she had dropped and burying it into the neck of another enemy.

"Why won't you listen to your father just this one time?" a familiar voice yelled.

Tove turned her head. "Soren? What are you doing here?"

He strode toward her, his eyes roaming over her face and body, taking in all the blood covering her.

"It's not mine," she whispered as he dropped his ax and cupped her face between his hands. "It's not mine."

"You need to get out of here."

"I—" Over his shoulder, Tove saw one of Vadik's men coming toward them. "Soren!"

In one fluid movement, he picked up his ax and swung it in a dangerous arc. The head landed in the center of a man's chest, cleaving through it. Yanking the weapon free, Soren took her hand and dragged her away from the fighting. In the relative safety of the shadows, he said, "We're outnumbered."

"I know."

"Then leave with me. Now. We can just run away and—"

Tears threatened to fill her eyes, but she blinked them away. "I can't."

He growled. "Gods, Tove, why can't you forget your damn honor for once? You won't survive this." He gestured angrily to the fighting. "Come away with me and we can have the life we've dreamed about."

Could she just leave? Could she never see her father again? Tove searched him out. He was fighting two men at once, successfully cutting down one with his sword before impaling the other with his spear. That was when she noticed his movements were a lot slower than normal. He had a large wound on his thigh and another on his head. He was injured, and her whole world seemed to shift. She had never seen him as anything other than a strong, vibrant man, and now…

Now she saw the reality of her decision.

Turning back to Soren, she kissed him on the mouth and said, "I'll love you until my heart stops beating."

She ran toward her father, toward the small group of fighters still trying to protect him. Gods, there were only five men left. Even as she joined them, another two were killed. She threw herself at their attackers, deflecting their strikes and making her own blows count. She immediately moved on to another and another.

Tove felt untouchable, as if Tyr himself was guiding her hand. She took down another six men when a loud cry stopped her. Turning, she found her father on the ground holding onto his side. The man he'd been fighting was standing over him, sword in hand, ready to make the killing blow. She ran toward the pair, her eyes and mind completely focused on reaching her father.

But something made her feet stop moving, and it wasn't until she was on her knees did she realize that she'd been struck down. Impaled through the back by a spear, her attacker placed his foot on her shoulder and pulled the weapon free. Blood foamed from her mouth as she watched the man move to stand in front of her. Reaching out, he plucked the dagger from her hand and held it to her throat. Vaguely, she thought she heard Soren scream her name.

"This is for my brother and father," her attacker said.

And then, all Tove knew was darkness.

18

"Where the hell have you been?"

Taer cringed and turned around, placing her back against the door of the club. Korvain was standing farther up the hall. His intense gaze traveled down her body, scrutinizing her in her tight dress and six inch heels.

"Anytime now," he added with a growl.

She let out a breath and tilted her chin up. "Just out."

He strode forward, took her by the arm and dragged her toward Bryn's office, making her stumble in the ridiculous heels. The door slammed shut behind them, the sharp sound making her jump. She pulled free of his grip.

"What's your problem?" She wanted to rub the ache away from her arms, but didn't want to let him know just how much it had hurt.

"Did you go out to see *him*?" Korvain demanded, eying her outfit in disgust before prowling around the room.

"What if I did?" she spat, raising her voice.

He stopped with his back to her. His shoulders rose and fell, and the shadows around the room moved with them.

"I'm not going to pretend that I don't know what you two were doing together earlier." Taer shifted uncomfortably, a new feeling of regret creeping in. "But I am going to tell you this," Korvain said, pinning her in place with his menacing stare. "He sells drugs and whores in the human world. He kills indiscriminately and he *will* hurt you."

His words should have shocked her, and in a small way they did. That version of Aubrey was a foreign concept. She knew the Aubrey who helped her train to kill her tormentor, who made her whole body light up just by being in the same room as her. He was the male who had made her want more, who had made her crave.

But now he was just the man who'd taken what he'd wanted and left her.

Stupid, stupid, stupid, Taer.

"Are you hearing me?" Korvain demanded.

It didn't matter; she was done with Aubrey. "I hear you," she replied.

He nodded. "Good." He turned to leave the office, pausing at the door. "It's late. You should get some rest."

Taer agreed that it was late, but she wasn't in the mood to sleep. She was in the mood to have a drink. "I have something I have to do first."

"Just don't leave the bar."

"Why not?"

Korvain's jaw bulged for a moment. "Just trust me on this one, Tay. Stay in the Eye."

"But—"

"I'll explain later," he said dismissively. "I have to get back to work."

When he left the room, he left the door ajar. Alone with her thoughts, Taer's mind went back to Aubrey, even though that was the last place she wanted it to go. She needed a way to forget about how she'd made an effort to look good for him. She needed to forget how he'd stood her up, and as the music of the club trickled through the open door, she realized just how to do it.

Heading into the Eye, she walked straight past Mason standing guard at the bottom of the stairs, and made her way up to Raven. Brushing aside the curtains, she scanned the room, her eyes settling on Dex as he poured a drink with a flourish. He winked at the girl he was serving and took her cash.

She walked over to the bar and sat down. Dex sidled up on the other side.

"Taer, you are looking good, sweetheart," he said with a suggestive grin.

"Thanks," she said curtly. "Can I get a drink?"

His lifted his eyebrows. "Sure. What do you want?"

"Anything, as long as it's strong."

Dex set about making her a drink, mixing in triple shots of vodka and a coffee-flavored liqueur. He topped the whole thing off with soda and handed her the tall glass. She eyed it dubiously. "What is it?"

"A dirty black Russian. A friend of mine got me hooked on these a while back."

Taer took an experimental sip, then threw the rest of it back and put the empty glass onto the bar.

"Another?" Dex asked, surprised. Taer nodded and he started mixing.

By the fourth drink, she was starting to feel a buzz. Dex had bounced between her and the customers for well over an hour. It was starting to slow down now though, so he was spending more time talking to her.

"What's up, Taer?"

"What makes you think something's wrong?"

He gestured to the empty glass in front of her and gave her a questioning look.

"It's nothing," she replied, looking down at the shiny black bar top.

"Does it have something to do with that guy who came in before, your boyfriend?"

"No."

Dex gave her a sad smile. "Look, if you want to talk about it, I'm here."

"I don't want to talk about it. I want to get blind fucking drunk."

He grabbed a bottle of tequila and two shot glasses and placed them down in front of her. He filled them and held one up. "To getting blind fucking drunk then."

Taer couldn't help but smile at him. She picked up the other glass and knocked it against his. The liquor burned on the way down, and she scrunched up her face, slamming the shot glass back down on the bar.

Dex sucked some liquor off his thumb. "You want to go out after I finish up here?"

Did she? Not really, no, but the alternative was going to bed, and she knew she'd go and see Aubrey in a moment of weakness. "Yes."

He grinned, showing all his teeth. "Great. Let me finish cleaning up and we can leave. I'm meeting some friends at another club."

Taer blinked at him and looked around. Raven was completely empty. Her brain was so foggy thanks to the alcohol that she hadn't noticed the place had closed for the night. That was good though. She didn't want to think. She didn't want to feel.

Numbness was what she was chasing.

"You ready to go?" Dex asked a few minutes later. She nodded and slid from the stool. "Do you need a coat or anything?"

"I'm fine," she said, stumbling a little.

"Whoa, take it easy there, sweetheart," Dex said, taking her by the elbow. He tucked her hand in the crook of his arm and guided her down the stairs. She'd drunk too much. She knew that, but she didn't care. She was blissfully unaware of everything and that was just what she wanted right now.

By some miracle, both Korvain and Mason were nowhere in sight so leaving the club was easy. They just walked straight out the front door. Outside, the wind whipped around them and Taer wished she'd bothered to go and get a coat. She peered up at the sky, thinking that it could snow at any time.

"Where are we going anyway?"

Dex pulled her closer and threw his arms over her shoulders. "That will be a surprise."

When they arrived at Whiskey Saigon, Taer groaned. She had pretty much sobered up on the walk over. Dex knocked on the door of the club, blowing into his hands to warm them up while they waited.

He knocked on the door again, putting his hands up on either side of his face to peer through the glass.

"Maybe you got the wrong night?" Taer asked.

"No, they're in there. The lights are on." Banging on the door, he yelled, "Yo, Cash, let us in, man."

She watched a man approach from the other side of the door, his eyes fixing on her. He was a lot taller than Dex with long face, high cheekbones and a mop of blond hair. If she didn't know any better, she would have guessed he was a light elf.

"I didn't know you were bringing someone," Cash said as he opened the door. His dark eyes studied her carefully, and Taer returned the favor. Up close, she could see her assumption had been right. He gave her a nod, then looked at Dex.

"She's cool. Who else is here?" Dex took Taer's hand and pushed past Cash. The color palate inside was moody, the walls covered in rich black and red wallpaper. All the seats at the banquet tables and at the bar were black leather with a red trim. The bar itself was smooth and dark with large red pendant lights hanging overhead. Up ahead, sitting at the far end of the room, was a group of three people – two guys and one girl.

"Tay, this is Steve, Paul and Laura. Guys, this is Taer," he said, making a sweeping gesture toward the group. Laura was the only one who didn't smile at her.

"Hey," she said. Dex gestured to one of the free chairs. It was facing the wall, and all of her instinct told her not to take it, but then she remembered that Darrion was dead, and she no longer had to worry about a threat coming at her when she least expected it. She sat down, still turning the chair so it was side on to the door.

Old habits.

Conversation started up again when Cash joined them at the table. He sat beside Taer, so close that she could feel the warmth of his body.

"What was your name again? Taer?" he asked in a low voice, keeping the conversation between them.

"Yeah."

He gave her a sideways glance. "My real name is Tarathiel, but I haven't used that name in over a thousand years."

"Still Taer," she replied, earning herself a small smile.

"What are you two talking about?" Dex interrupted, sliding his arm around her waist. She stiffened at his touch, but forced herself to relax.

"How much of a dick you are," Cash shot back. He got up and went to the bar, reaching over the top and retrieving a bottle of champagne and two glasses. The light elf held out the bottle to Taer. She shook her head.

"Can I get you something else then?"

"A soda will be fine."

With a nod, Cash stood up again and jumped over the top of the bar.

He returned with her drink. Taer sipped at her soda, watching them all. Cash rarely joined in on the conversations, but he watched Taer though. She felt his eyes burning into her. It seemed as if he wanted to say something to her, but he was biding his time.

After two hours of absorbing the noise of the conversation, she stood up, drawing Dex's attention.

"Where are you going?"

"Home," she replied.

He downed the last of his drink. "I'll walk you."

"No. It's fine."

"It's late. You can't walk home alone."

She smiled at him, the way she would to a small naive child. "I think I can look after myself."

He frowned, obviously thinking he was being chivalrous.

Cash burst out laughing. "What she's saying is that she's not interested in anything you want to give her."

Dex scowled, his alcohol-fogged brain working hard to keep up with the conversation. "What? No, I was just offering to—"

"Dex? I'm good." Taer turned to Cash. "I'll see you later."

"I'll walk you out," he replied.

This again? "I'm a lot tougher than I look."

Cash stood up. "Yeah, well, I have to lock up after you."

He followed her to the door, opening it up for her. Cold air hit them both in the face. Over his shoulder, Taer could see Dex watching them, his expression hard. "Don't worry about him. He's just been talking about you for a while now. To be honest, I didn't even think you were real," Cash said. "Are you two . . .?"

"No."

"Dex wants there to be something more."

"Well, that's not going to happen," she snapped back.

Cash put his hands up in front of him, grinning. "Put the claws away, kitten."

Taer shook her head and stepped out into the cold night. As she turned away, Cash grabbed her arm. Without conscious thought, she palmed the dagger from her thigh holster and pressed it to the elf's throat.

He laughed, completely at ease with having a weapon extremely close to a major artery. "I knew there was more to you."

"What do you mean?" she asked, pressing the tip in closer, dimpling his skin.

"I heard there was a female in Darrion's latest quinary. I thought it was bullshit."

"Darrion is dead."

Shocked registered on Cash's face. "When? How? Who?" He fired the questions off quickly like he knew the guy personally.

"Less than twenty-four hours ago."

"Who killed him?"

She pulled her arm from his hand, but kept the knife in place. "You're looking at her."

If she thought he'd been surprised before, it had nothing on the look on his face now. "You?"

"Are we going to have a problem here? Because I have no issue with ending your life just like I ended his." Taer was prepared for a fight. She was ready. She was more than ready. She had a fuck load of anger still and no outlet, but if Cash wanted to volunteer for the job, she would oblige him.

"We don't have a problem." Unbuttoning his shirt, he shrugged it from his shoulders. Taer eased off when he turned to expose a tattoo spanning the width of his back. *Death before dishonor* – Darrion's words, Darrion's contract with his Mares.

Slowly, Taer lowered her arm. She should have known she'd run into one of Darrion's assassins sooner or later. Living with her brother and Korvain, she had been shielded from a lot of the politics of the guild, including the other assassins that Darrion had bound by blood contract.

He turned back around, his expression thoughtful. "I figured something had happened. I couldn't feel his pull anymore."

She shrugged.

"How did you manage to kill him?"

Taer re-sheathed her dagger. "I found his weakness."

"A weakness indicates that the bastard had a heart to start with."

"He did have a heart. It was black and I made sure it stopped beating."

Cash's lips flexed into a smile. "I guess I owe you one then."

19

Loki placed the filleting knife back onto the tray. Blood covered the entirety of the slim blade and it was even creeping up the handle. Resting both hands on the edge of the workbench, he bowed his head and let out a breath. Blood hung in the air, hugging every particle in the wooden stairs and the beams above his heads. It would linger too, that smell. It would soak into the very bones of the house, making the place abhorrent for anyone who set foot into it.

After the brothers had failed to secure Taer, a layer of rage had begun to manifest. Unfortunately for Aubrey, he had been on the receiving end of that rage. The elf didn't make a single sound, even when Loki began peeling the skin from his toes. He thought skinning someone alive would be enjoyable, but without the satisfaction of hearing his victim's screams of pain, their pitiful moans for mercy, he had found the entire exercise distasteful.

Loki's shoulders tightened when he heard the last step on the stairs creak. "Is he dead?" he snarled.

"No," Freki replied, his voice low.

Loki whirled around to find the god covered in blood. "What happened? Where's Geri?"

"Dead. The light elf is—"

"So you failed." Loki spoke over him, cutting off the excuses he didn't want to hear. "You and your brother both said you wanted to help me. First, I asked you to capture the female Mare and you failed in that. Second, I asked you to kill one light elf, and you couldn't even manage that. Tell me, Freki, why do I even keep you around?"

The god looked down, his brows drawing close together. "I'll try again."

Loki snorted derisively. "Don't bother. I'll take care of him myself – something I should have done before."

For a minute, they simply stared at each other. "What do you want me to do now?"

"You failed me. I want you to go."

"But—"

Loki pulled a gun from the holster at the small of his back and took aim, training it between Freki's eyes. "I have no problem sending you to Hel to join your brother."

Freki's eyes narrowed, his jaw jumping violently. "As you wish." The god disappeared from view, leaving Loki with an unconscious Aubrey and some time on his hands. He had no intention of torturing the elf if he was wasn't awake to enjoy it. His gaze drifted around the room. Blood was congealing in puddles around the chair, more was spattered on the walls.

He approached the workbench, looking at his dangling carrot sitting there. Things were taking too long. Aubrey's little Mare needed a hint, and he knew just the thing that would clue her in to her lover's demise.

Finding a small box, Loki emptied its contents, dumping the small bottles of oil onto the ground. Lining it with some rags, he set his gift inside, then placed the box into a cardboard box, completing the illusion.

Loki faded to the Eye. Shifting his appearance, he became a generic UPS driver, changing his clothes to the drab brown uniform the company employees wore. All that was missing was the van the humans associated with the delivery service. He had already boxed up Aubrey's hand, the parcel tucked under his arm as he stepped off the curb and approached the bouncer at the door.

The human took in his uniform and the box. "Deliveries out the back," he said, jerking a thumb at the alleyway beside the club. Wordlessly, Loki followed the directive and walked down to the side door. Not much had changed since he'd last been here, except it seemed as if security had been improved. Instead of a simple camera above the door to identify whoever was there, there was now also a keypad to gain entry.

Loki knocked twice and stepped back.

The steel door opened, revealing the Valkyrie he'd spoken to in the club when he'd been in disguise before. The dancer was dressed in a sheer pink gown with a feather trim that hit her upper thigh. Underneath the garment, she was wearing lingerie the same shade of pink.

"Can I help you?" she asked.

"I have a delivery."

The goddess's eyes fixed on the box, an excited look forming in her eyes. "Who for?"

"Taer," he replied, watching irritation replace her excitement.

She held out her hand. "I'll give it to her." Snatching it away from him, the Valkyrie closed the door in his face.

Loki shook off his disguise and moved from the alleyway. Turning the corner, he walked down the street, his footsteps echoing off the pavement. It was busy, the evening just starting to pick up. The sound of the passing traffic nearly drowned out every other noise, but there was one that brought him to a stop.

Air skimming over feathers.

A sharp beak snapping.

He looked behind him, then tilted his head back. A black bird dropped from the sky, swooping down toward him. With its beak clicking together in warning, Loki batted it away. He would have considered it a freak incident, except when a second bird dove down and grabbed a chunk of his ear, he knew it wasn't simply a coincidence. Loki hissed in pain, placing his hand over the wound. And as he watched the bird fly away into the cold night, he felt the first trickle of blood seep between his fingers.

"Odin," Loki growled under his breath. His blood-brother was stooping to new lows by sending his ravens after him. He ducked again when he heard the other bird coming in to attack for a second time.

"Don't move," Freki warned. Loki stilled, hearing the distinct sound of metal cutting through air. There was a sharp snick and the wet squelch of impaled flesh. The raven dropped at his feet, a knife sticking through its neck. Loki glanced over his shoulder to see Freki walking toward him.

"I'm impressed," he said, as the other god stopped beside him. "I thought I told you to go."

Freki grunted and bent down to take back the dagger. "This is Odin's bird."

"Was," Loki corrected. "It's dead now, thanks to you. Perhaps you are still useful to me."

20

Rhys had never felt this in control before. After his wolf had been allowed out and given free rein to kill at will, it had retreated back into his mind. It was silent now and Rhys almost felt . . . normal. He had returned to the Eye in the hopes that he could see the Valkyrie again. And luckily for him, she was working the door. He waited to cross Tremont Street, watching for a break in the traffic. He finally saw one, but had to start running when a cab unexpectedly pulled out. He flipped off the driver as he stepped onto the curb.

The blaring horn drew his unlikely savior's attention as she let a group of women into the club. Rhys approached with his hand held out to her. After a beat, she took it and they shook.

"I just wanted to thank you," he said, meeting her eyes. "And to introduce myself. I'm Rhys."

She dropped his hand and turned her attention back to the next person in line. She motioned for the guy's ID. "Mav and what for?"

"For what you did last night." The human standing in front of Mav smirked and Rhys glared at him. "Is there somewhere else we can talk?"

Mav didn't hesitate. "Yeah." She handed the ID back to the human, then touched a button on her collar, speaking under her breath. A moment later, another security guard turned up. "Follow me," Mav told Rhys as she stepped into the club.

Rhys's eyes darted around the busy room as the Valkyrie led him to the other side of the bar. He bumped into a number of people on the way, but didn't bother to apologize. When they finally waded through the crowd, Mav opened up a door and ushered him through. They stepped into a long, empty hallway, the door slamming shut behind them.

"I'm glad you came around tonight." Her statement caught him off guard. She looked at him over her shoulder. "We need to talk."

He followed her until she stopped at a closed door. She knocked and then opened it. Inside, a woman Rhys could only assume was Bryn was sitting behind a desk, her attention bouncing from a pile of paperwork in front of her to one of the computer screens.

"He's here," Mav said.

Were they expecting him?

Bryn looked up, her eyes assessing him carefully. Mav went to close the door, but the other Valkyrie stopped her.

"Korvain is coming." A moment later, a large shadow stretched across the open doorway. Rhys turned his head. He'd heard of Korvain before – he was rumored to be the last full-blooded Mare – but Rhys hadn't ever seen him. His very presence in the room seemed to fill it completely. Rhys shifted back a step as the guy stalked inside.

Bryn said, "Sit down. Please."

He looked at the chair the Valkyrie was gesturing to. He slowly lowered himself into the seat.

"Can I get you a drink?" Bryn offered, leaning back into her chair.

Rhys shook his head, watching as Korvain perched himself on the edge of the desk and eyeballed him.

Bryn said, "Look, let's not waste each other's time here. We know what you are." Rhys said nothing, only kept his steady gaze on her. "Mav's told us you're looking for Loki. Why?"

He balled his hands into fists. Just the casual mention of Galen's killer made his rage surge. If he let his anger get the better of him, his wolf would awaken and the cycle would start again. He bowed his head and took a deep breath. "To kill him."

"Why?" Korvain's question drew Rhys's attention, and the two of them just studied each other for a moment. There was absolutely no reason not to share information. Rhys had nothing to go on – not Odin's location, and not Loki's.

"He killed my best friend."

The shadows around the room trembled and the lights dimmed, flickering a little. "Why did he kill him?" the Mare asked in a dangerously low voice.

Rhys shrugged. "I'm not sure."

Bryn leaned back in her chair, the leather creaking. "How do you know Loki was the one to kill him then?"

"I was told as much."

"By who?"

"Odin."

Bryn sat forward. "When did he tell you this?"

"A couple of days ago, in Chicago."

"What did he say exactly?"

"He told me Loki killed Galen, but—"

"Wait," Korvain interrupted. "Did you say Galen?"

"Yes."

"The same Galen that worked for Henry Craine?" Bryn demanded.

How could they have known that? He let his silence do the talking, and apparently it was saying a whole lot.

Maverick entered the conversation. "He came around here with an offer to buy a portion of the Eye, apparently at Craine's request."

Rhys turned around in his chair. "I wasn't aware of that. All I knew was that he'd been sent here alone by Craine. When he returned, both Galen and I were supposed to come back here to . . ." His words drifted off.

"Come back here to?" Bryn prompted.

"That must have been when Loki killed him. That was the last time I saw him." Rhys said the words to himself, remembering the meeting where he'd been dismissed so Craine could speak to Galen in private.

Korvain and Bryn shared a look before the Valkyrie said, "I'm not following."

Rhys spoke quickly, afraid that if he didn't get the words out now, he never would. "Craine said he wanted to speak with Galen alone. Galen told me to go home. I did, but Galen never returned. We were supposed to leave Chicago that night to come here."

"Why were you coming back? To offer me another deal?" Bryn said.

Rhys's eyes found Korvain. "Our orders were to kill him."

The Mare reached for a curved blade strapped to his chest and pulled it free of the sheath. His lips were twisted into a snarl, the scowl on his face fierce. "I'd like to see you try," he growled.

Rhys shook his head. "I don't know why Craine wanted you dead though."

"In what capacity were you working for Craine?" Mav asked, drawing everyone's attention. Bryn was standing up behind her desk now, and Korvain had pulled another blade free.

"Wet man," Rhys replied cautiously.

"So, you and Galen were hired killers. Craine wanted Korvain gone so he asks you two to do the job, only Loki kills your best friend before you can." Mav talked the whole thing out, her brain obviously coming up with the next logical part of the puzzle — something Rhys hadn't been able to do. She ran a finger over her tattoo, and her black sword was summoned. She held its tip so close to Rhys's skin that he could feel the coolness of the blade. "Tell us why you're really here, Rhys."

He could feel a cold sweat break out on his brow. "I told you, to kill Loki," he said, his voice steady and even.

Bryn looked above his head. "Is he telling the truth?"

He held his breath for a moment. How would Mav know whether he was being truthful or not? His pulse raced until finally the Valkyrie lowered her weapon.

"Yes," she said, her voice low and coarse.

Bryn sat back down again, resting her elbows on the blotter. "All right, Craine wanted Korvain gone, but I can't understand why. He had nothing to do with negotiations, only I did. Did he want to get rid of my security to scare me?"

"I . . ." Rhys paused. "I had no idea what Craine was thinking."

"What if we're looking at this the wrong way?" Mav said. "What if Craine was really Loki? What if Loki was pulling Rhys and Galen's strings all this time? That would make the plan to get rid of Korvain make more sense. With him gone, Bryn, you would be more vulnerable. Loki kills Craine and takes over his life. He then uses Galen to try and get inside Bryn's inner sanctum without drawing attention, because as far as everyone else is concerned, he's just a human businessman sending his associate to negotiate a deal."

"Why would Loki want to kill Bryn though?" Rhys asked.

"To get at Odin," Bryn said. "It's no secret that those two are enemies. He was just looking to strike at the All-Father by getting to me."

"Which is why the bastard has to die," Korvain tacked on through gritted teeth.

Rhys said, "That's why I'm here, but there's just one problem … I have no idea what Loki looks like. All Odin told me was that he was in Boston."

"Could he be pretending to be Galen?" Mav asked.

"Sending Galen failed once. He wouldn't use his identity again. Loki would have tried another line of attack," said Bryn. She sighed and glanced at Korvain. "Odin is the only person who can decisively tell us where Loki is, and he and I are not on good terms right now."

"I'll talk to him then. I just need to know how to contact him." Rhys's voice held an edge of desperation he hated to hear. This was the closest he'd come to getting answers since arriving in Boston.

A heavy silence fell over the room. "Bryn," Mav started. "Odin would come here for you. He'd do anything for you."

The Valkyrie laughed derisively. "Yeah, especially if that anything directly benefited him." Bryn's jaw bulged for a moment, before she ground out, "I'll think about it."

A knock on the door drew their attention. Mav opened it and a young woman stepped inside. In her hands was a cardboard box. Her green eyes seemed to be fixed only on Korvain, and when Rhys looked at the Mare, he noticed how rigid he'd become.

"Taer, what is it? What's wrong?"

The woman, Taer, shook her head, and tears welled in her eyes. She opened her mouth to speak but only a sob came out.

Bryn stood up. "We'll be in touch," she said, dismissing Rhys.

"Come on. I'll walk you out," Mav said.

Rhys stood and followed her from the room. She stopped at a metal door that he assumed led outside. "Thank you again," he said.

She studied him. "You changed forms quickly. I've seen my fair share of shape shifters, but never any who could shift so quickly."

He shrugged. The truth was even he didn't know why he could change skins so quickly. His whole existence was a mystery he had never been able to figure out.

"If we find out Loki's location before you, I'll call you. What's your number?"

He recited the digits, feeling his phone vibrate in his pocket when she dialed it.

"That's mine." She held out her hand to him. They shook and Rhys left the club. Grit crunched under his boots as he walked to the entranceway of the alleyway beside the club. He stepped out onto the street, joining the heavy flow of foot traffic. Not wanting to be penned in by all the warm bodies, he maneuvered himself to the outer edge, moving swiftly along the gutter beside the parked cars. Just as he passed a Mercedes S550, the rear window retracted and his name was called out. Odin opened the rear door. "Get in. We have something to discuss."

Rhys checked his surroundings before getting into the back.

Odin looked different from the last time he'd seen him. It wasn't his clothing, it was more his physical appearance. His face looked more haggard – wearier somehow; there was also a great sadness about him.

"You are yet to find Loki."

That was not the opening statement Rhys was expecting. "I . . . I cannot find him without help. I don't even know where to find him; I don't know where to look."

Odin put his hand up, stopping him. "I know. I've been watching your progress."

"You have?" And Rhys had not sensed him?

"I also saw the fight between you and my former guards, Geri and Freki."

"I killed one of them," Rhys said. In his mind's eye, he saw the blood, saw the half-eaten body.

"Geri was always the weaker fighter," Odin said off-handedly. "Freki, on the other hand, was much better at judging his opponent. He must have seen that you and your wolf had the upper hand when it came to strength. And no doubt he went sniveling back to his new master to inform him of Geri's death."

"Loki," Rhys breathed. His beast shifted beneath his skin.

Odin nodded. "Loki."

"Where is he?" Rhys was desperate to know. He needed to avenge Galen so he could finally leave. With his best friend dead and Craine no longer giving him orders, Rhys feared what he would do if he were to stay in a large city like Chicago or Boston. Perhaps he would escape to one of the national parks out west and live in a small wooden house he would build with his own hands. Maybe he could go to Canada or Alaska and live out his days away from the temptation of hot blood and warm skin.

Odin handed him a piece of paper. "Loki is here, at this

address. He has a prisoner he's using to expose Bryn by luring her bodyguard away from her. Loki must be stopped before his prisoner's usefulness is used up."

Rhys looked at the paper, memorizing the address. Although his beast was telling him to strike now and strike hard, Rhys also knew the benefit of getting help when he needed it. He was under no illusions that Loki would be a formidable opponent. If he had Mav by his side, he was sure he would at least have a slim chance of killing him.

"When will you attack?" the All-Father asked.

"Soon."

Odin nodded, and twisted his body around to face the front again. Rhys took the hint and popped open the door and stepped out onto the street. The car was accelerating before the door shut, seamlessly pulling into the flow of traffic.

Rhys retraced his steps back to the Eye. Mav was at the front door, working. Pulling out his phone, he punched out a quick text message and she glanced at her phone briefly. Her eyes found his. She jerked her head toward the club and he crossed the road.

"How did you find this out so soon?"

"Odin found me."

She arched an eyebrow. "He just walked up to you and provided the information?"

He shrugged. "More like he pulled up alongside me in a car and told me."

He didn't blame her if she found it hard to believe. He couldn't quite believe it himself.

Changing the frequency on her radio pack, Mav said, "Rhys has found Loki." There was a beat of silence. "Okay."

A man dressed in black appeared a moment later. Mav handed her radio equipment over to her replacement and stepped out onto the sidewalk.

"Do you need any other weapons?" Rhys asked as they turned down the alleyway beside the club.

"No. I'll meet you there." She faded to the address he had texted her. Rhys did the same, rematerializing beside her.

He looked up when he heard a raven caw. The bird was sitting on top of the red brick wall Mav was staring at. It surrounded the house and was covered in creeping ivy that concealed a door. Stepping forward, she peered through the small crack between the door and the frame.

"What can you see?" he asked.

Mav stepped back. "Take a look for yourself. I'm going to see if there's another way in."

Rhys stepped up to the gate and looked. On the other side was an empty cobblestone courtyard. The air shivered then and Mav reappeared.

"Anything?"

She shook her head. "I didn't see any wards either."

"You want to just fade inside?"

"At least into the courtyard."

Standing in Bryn's office, Taer's hands were still trembling. Only minutes earlier, she'd opened the box and discovered something unspeakable. Behind her, the door shutting made her jump. Korvain took a step toward her.

"Tay, what's in the box?" he asked, his dark gaze dropping to her hands. She felt the tears run down her cheeks. She bit her lip and looked back at him.

"It's . . . It's . . ." She couldn't say the words.

He took the package from her – his eyes still fixed on hers – and placed it on the desk. He pulled her into his chest, holding her close while she gave into her emotions. His strong hand rubbed circles over her back just like Adrian used to do.

"What's in the box, Taer?" Bryn asked this time.

Swiping her hands under her eyes, she said, "Open it."

Bryn moved to do just that, but Korvain said, "I'll do it." Her mouth pressed into a tight line like she didn't like being told what to do, but she nodded and sat back in her chair. Korvain pulled away from Taer and cautiously flipped open the flaps with one end of his karambit. He peered inside before turning back to Taer.

"Whose is this?"

She sucked in a deep breath. "Aubrey's."

"You're sure?"

Taer met his eyes. "Yes. That's his ring."

Bryn stood up to look in the box. Her eyes darted to Taer. "How did you get it?"

"Kara said UPS delivered it."

"There aren't any tracking stickers on it," Korvain said, getting a better look at the top of the box.

"I know," Taer said. "I thought that maybe Aubrey had dropped it off thinking I was pissed off with him."

"Why would he think that?" Korvain asked suspiciously.

Fuck. She shrugged. It was better to stay quiet than incriminate herself any further. Korvain growled, but turned his attention back to the box.

"I have to help him," Taer announced.

"No." Korvain's emphatic response wasn't unexpected, but it still angered her.

"I have to."

"No," he snarled, whirling on her and gripping her by the upper arms. "You still don't understand who he is, do you?"

She squared up to him. "You obviously think you do," she spat back.

Impossibly, his eyes darkened. "He's involved with Venezuelan drug lords. We have no idea who has him – human or god – or what they want."

"A human wouldn't have him," she replied evenly. "If it was a human, he would have faded away. It has to be a god."

His brow furrowed suddenly. "Fuck," he said, releasing her to start pacing in a tight line.

Taer watched him, growing more and more anxious. Korvain never lost his cool. "What is it? What have you just thought of?"

He looked at her then at Bryn. The Valkyrie's expression was pinched as she had obviously come to the same conclusion as Korvain had.

"What?" Taer demanded. If they knew something, she had to know what it was. She had to save Aubrey.

"Thor was murdered tonight," Korvain said, finally coming to a stop in front of her.

"So? What has that got to do with Aubrey?" Her voice rose, the edges of her tone threaded with building panic.

In a calm voice, Bryn said, "Loki killed him, and then left a message for Odin."

"I thought Loki was still imprisoned under the earth."

"He was," Korvain murmured. He scrubbed the back of his head. "Do you remember how I told you about some other Valkyries being attacked and killed about a month ago?"

She nodded. Taer had been heavily focused on her training at the time, but she did recall hearing something about it.

Korvain perched his large body on the corner of Bryn's desk

and took out one of his karambits from the holster criss-crossing his chest. He pressed its curved edge against his thumb, and if Taer didn't know any better, she would have said he was beating himself up over something.

"Well, Loki was behind those attacks too. We killed him." He frowned and looked at her. "At least we thought we killed him. It turned out we were wrong. Somehow he survived, although how that was possible we have no idea. In any case, he's back now and it looks like he's going after Odin again."

Taer could see Korvain was trying to paint the whole picture for her, but there were still some spots missing. "Why does any of this involve Aubrey?"

Bryn pulled open her desk drawer and took out a small bottle of liquor. As she unscrewed the cap she said, "Loki is trying to kill Odin, which means he'll be coming after me first since I'm the All-Father's only weakness." She took a quick drink.

"So, you think Loki has Aubrey?" she asked, looking to Korvain for the answer. None of this was making any sense to her.

He nodded. "It's a possibility."

Taer thought back to the ambush she'd found herself in earlier. Could that have just been a coincidence as she'd passed it off to be, or was there something more to it?

"But why would he take Aubrey?" Bryn asked. "He has no direct connection to me."

Taer thought it through and her head began to swim. The answer forced her to put her hand on the back of the chair to steady herself. Aubrey *didn't* have any connection to Bryn . . . but Taer did. It wasn't a random attack. It was planned. "Gods."

"Tay, what is it? What's wrong?"

"Me," she whispered.

"What?" asked Korvain.

"Loki wants me."

His expression hardened. "That's a pretty fucking thin theory, Tay."

"No, it's not." The more she thought about it, the more it made sense. "Think about it: Loki is back. He needs to get to Bryn, but you're standing in the way. So, how could Loki get rid of you?"

Korvain didn't have to think for very long before snarling, "By distracting you with Aubrey. That bastard must have been watching us – all of us – this whole time, just looking for a weakness he could exploit."

Taer shook her head. She'd been very careful about going to see Aubrey for training. Not once had she sensed she'd been followed or was being watched. It didn't matter though. The outcome didn't change. Aubrey was being tortured and mutilated, all because of her. She thought her serving of guilt in getting her brother killed was enough to last her a lifetime, but she was wrong. Knowing she was also responsible for Aubrey's suffering confirmed her need to save him. He'd been the one to save her, and now the situation had been reversed. Without him, she never would have defeated Darrion and – even though she'd sustained some permanent damage along the way – she had still avenged her brother.

"I need to get him back."

"How are you going to do that?" Korvain shot back. "You don't have the first clue where he is."

She squeezed her hands into tight fists at her sides. There was a way to find out, but it meant doing the one thing she feared. But for Aubrey she would do it. "I'll find him."

In her room, Taer took out her phone and brought up Aubrey's contact info. Dialing, she put the speaker to her ear. She didn't expect him to pick up, but was hoping Loki would so she could find out if her suspicions were correct.

It rang once, twice, three times . . .

She couldn't stop her hands from shaking.

It continued to ring until it went to voicemail, and she left a message. She didn't know where he was being held, but she knew she had to at least try to get him back. It was clear to her now that as soon as he'd arrived back in Boston, something had happened to him. Sitting on the edge of her bed, she put her phone on the nightstand and then lay down.

Although it had only been a matter of days since her dream-walk into Darrion's mind, her stomach twisted with the thought of doing it again. A familiar fear started to creep up on her, poisoning her mind. She tried to beat it back by telling herself this wasn't the same as with Darrion. But no matter how many times she repeated the words, it did nothing to stop her stomach churning and bile twisting up her throat.

She blew out a breath and closed her eyes, focusing her mind on Aubrey. He was hurt. He was in danger, and she was the only one who could locate him. She tried to relax. She had done this before. It was familiar. It was prescriptive. She knew that once she tapped into Aubrey's mind, she would find a hall where she would walk through a door. If the person was trained in protecting their mind, there would be a shield here, but for him, she would walk straight into his psyche.

Feeling the shift between realities, Taer opened her eyes and blinked at the empty hallway she'd found herself in. Her heart thumped impatiently under her ribs. She started to sweat. Her eyes darted around the hallway, feeling as if the walls were closing in on her. She sucked in a breath, and it felt like sucking air through a straw; she simply couldn't get enough oxygen into her lungs.

Fear.

Fear was debilitating.

It was unjustified though. Taer held all the power in this realm, or at least she thought she had until she'd stepped into Darrion's mind. He had hurt her, had caught her unaware and shattered her fragile confidence.

"But Darrion is dead," she said to herself, letting the words join the many others she'd said before. "He's dead and you're not."

The walls seemed to retreat even though they hadn't really moved at all, and she found she could breathe again. She looked to her right. There was a door there now. She turned the handle then stepped over the threshold and into Aubrey's mind. Her foot hit the black-and-white checkered tile he had in his kitchen. From where she was standing, she could see the light was on in the basement. She opened the door, her nose filling with the scent of leather and lemon cleaner. It was just like the first time she'd gone down there. She knew there would be racks filled with weapons and sparring mats on the floor. Walking down the stairs, her heart was racing, her mind screaming at her to go back, to get out. It was Aubrey she was going to see, but she still couldn't shake the fear Darrion had instilled in her. Even in death, he was a cancer in her life.

But she would cut him out.

She focused her thoughts once more, recalling the way Aubrey's scent of cinnamon was so strong while they were in the storage closet together. She looked deeply into his pale gray eyes, she kissed him, sucking his bottom lip into her mouth and biting down. She heard him groan her name, lighting a fire within her body. She burned for him, and when he touched her, she combusted.

On the very last step of the stairs, she stopped. Aubrey was standing a few feet away, a sword in his hand and a savage expression on his face. His eyes were wild. Taer stopped breathing, hesitant for a moment.

"Aubrey, it's me," she said.

He said nothing.

"Aubrey?" Taer took another step closer, causing his eyes to narrow. Her eyes flickered to the sword in his hand; his fingers had tightened slightly. That was when she realized he was whole and seemingly unhurt. Of course that would be the case. She didn't know what he looked like now. Although this was Aubrey's dream, she was controlling it, so she would naturally conjure up the image of Aubrey as she had last seen him. He lowered the weapon, his body no longer held taut, although she could tell he was not relaxed. He looked away, toward the back of the room. His name escaped her lips on a bare whisper.

Aubrey's gray eyes penetrated her as his gaze swung back, but . . .

He wasn't really seeing her, was he?

Taer licked her lips. Aubrey couldn't see her. He couldn't even hear her. Her mind raced. What did this mean? Had Darrion somehow broken her, negating her ability to dream-walk? Her gaze swept the floor before meeting Aubrey's eyes once more.

Then, with a cry, she was violently ripped from his mind.

21

Sacrifice.

Odin had had animals and people sacrificed to him many, many times over the centuries. The humans begged him for victories in battle, for a longer life, for good crops, and greedily he'd accepted the blood that was spilled in his name. He gloried in it. He reveled in the light fading from the eyes of his offering, whether it was the pure blue of a slave girl, or the rectangular pupil of a goat.

But he never understood it – not truly . . .

Not until this night.

As he stroked the inky feathers on Muninn's back, he mourned the loss of Huginn. Muninn cawed softly, the sound somber. Odin had known either one of the birds could have been killed, but had hoped that one would survive the attack on Loki. He understood what he'd had to do – in order to finally be rid of Loki, he would have to stop running and hiding. He would have to risk himself, and whether or not that risk would be worth it would not be revealed until the end.

"For Bryn," he said under his breath. He'd been saying those two words ever since feeling the death of his raven, but he was struggling to believe them. Yes, he knew what he was doing, but it didn't mean doubt hadn't crept into his mind. After all, he'd been alone for nearly a century. Isolation had hardened him even further than before, and all of that could be blamed squarely on his blood-brother. Odin had started traveling the road of solitude after Baldr's death – killed by Loki's trickery and treachery. His world had spiraled after that – the Fall had come, and although he had his Valkyries for a time, they too inevitably left him. Perhaps he hadn't been the easiest person to serve, but he only had good intentions wherever Bryn was concerned.

Muninn's haunting, low caw sounded again. At least Huginn's sacrifice had not been for naught. Muninn had tasted of Loki's flesh, finally giving Odin the ability to track the Trickster despite shielding his location from him. As soon as he'd found out where his blood-brother was hiding, he'd spoken to Rhys, giving him the information he needed. The elf was the only one who could end Loki's life – to end his grandfather's life. Did Odin feel bad for keeping that information from Rhys? No. It was a means to an end. And he would do anything to keep himself and Bryn safe.

He wondered whether the elf had already arrived at the house where Loki was. Was Loki already dead, or was the fight still raging? He looked at the raven.

"Go, now. Return at the conclusion."

Muninn took flight, leaving through the open living room window. The All-Father watched his remaining raven disappear into the night, fearing it would be the last time he would see the bird.

22

Valhalla – 807 AD

Tove woke to the smell of roasting pig, the sweet scent filling her nose. Was she still at her wedding feast? Her eyes opened slowly, the sight of huge fires burning in stone hearths coming into focus. She sat up, alarmed. Where was she? The hall was huge, larger than any building she had ever seen before. Vast columns held the roof in place, the white stone carved with depictions of great battles. Tove thought she also saw all of the greatest gods in the images too – Odin and Thor, Tyr and Freyja. They had their spears and swords drawn, engaging in fierce battles with Fenrir, Surt and Nidhogg. The ceiling was thatched with golden swords and spears, all of them reflecting back the warmth of the fires. In front of her were long benches with tables – all of them empty.

Standing up slowly, she shuffled forward a few steps, expecting to feel a lancing pain through her back. She had been impaled by a spear, hadn't she? Her memory was foggy, like the battle that had broken out in her home had happened years ago rather than minutes. She came to a doorway, the width of it large enough to fit at least eight hundred soldiers through, shoulder to shoulder. Through the opening, she saw two wolves standing on either side. One turned and snarled at her, making her take a step back.

"They won't harm you."

Tove spun around. A beautiful woman with long blonde hair was standing there. Her eyes were a curious mix of two shades of blue.

The woman smiled at her warmly. "And I won't harm you either. You are safe here, Tove."

"How do you—" Tove stopped, startled by the guttural sound of her voice. Bringing her hands to her neck, her fingers brushed past a thick scar running across the front of her throat.

The woman's serene expression darkened for a moment. "I'm sorry about that. I tried to get him to heal all of you, but he wouldn't."

Tove swallowed. "Who wouldn't?" She recoiled at the harsh timber. "Where am I? What is this place?"

The woman shook her head, giving her that same friendly smile again. "I'm being so rude. Let me introduce myself. I'm Brynhildr."

Tove could feel her eyes widen. "The Valkyrie?" she whispered.

Brynhildr shrugged almost sheepishly. "The one and only. And Odin was the one who wouldn't heal your throat."

She almost swallowed her own tongue. "The All-Father?"

Brynhildr nodded and held out her hand to Tove. She took it, feeling a power flow through the goddess's fingers and into her. It gave Tove an inner strength she didn't know was flagging. "I'll take you to him. He wanted to see you when you woke."

The Valkyrie led her through another large doorway and into a hallway inlaid with more golden shields and spears. Along the walls were stone statues, although Tove didn't recognize any of the faces. Tove's bare feet moved soundlessly across the stone floor, following Brynhildr deeper into what she could only assume was a vast building. "What is this place?" Tove hated the sound of her voice, but she needed answers too badly.

"Valhalla."

Of course she had heard of Valhalla before; it was the great hall of the dead located in Asgard. If she was there, it would mean she was . . .

"Am I dead?" The Valkyrie didn't slow, didn't turn, didn't answer. Tove wasn't sure Brynhildr had heard her. "Brynhildr?"

"Yes."

Dead? "How long have I been gone from Midgard?"

The goddess stopped walking, drawing Tove to a stop. "No more than three hours of your human time. Time passes differently here though. Here, in Asgard, you have been sleeping – recovering – for a week."

Tove's head started to spin. "What of my father? And Soren? Did they survive the battle?"

Brynhildr started walking again. "I'll let Odin tell you. He has his reasons for doing things, and I'm sure he'll explain everything to you."

Tove started to follow Brynhildr again. They arrived at a door that looked no different to any of the other hundred they had already passed. The Valkyrie knocked before entering, not waiting for permission. Inside, a large fire burned in a hearth against the wall. Animal skins layered the floor, keeping the room warm. On the opposite wall to the fire was a large bed, and against the window directly opposite to where they were standing were a table and bench.

There was a man with his back to them, his head bent over something she couldn't see. He had dark hair and the shoulders of a warrior. This could not be the All-Father. He was supposed to be a wizened old man with long gray hair and a beard. Brynhildr cleared her throat, drawing attention to them. The man turned, and Tove immediately felt as if she was standing in front of the sun. There was so much power, so much radiance coming from him. He had one green eye, the other was just a simple black orb. He approached them, stepping up to Tove and inspecting her closely. She could see her fearful reflection in his glass eye, and it was unnerving.

"You're awake."

"I am," she replied softly.

His gaze fell to her throat, and he softly thumbed the scar. "I'm sure Bryn told you I did not see fit to heal this wound." She nodded, feeling his thumb sweeping back and forth along her skin. "Has she told you why?"

"No."

Odin's eyes traveled to Brynhildr for a mere second before his lips flexed into a smile. "Why did you kill him, your husband?"

Tove licked her lips, unsure what to say. Did he already know the answer before she spoke it? "He was not a good man."

His head cocked to the side. "Go on."

"He raped and killed my faithful servant and then tried to rape me also."

"But he is your husband. Who are you to stop a man from getting something he desires?"

Tove bristled. "He *was* my husband and just because a child wants to touch a fire, it does not mean you should let them."

Odin's features hardened, causing Tove's heart to race. Had she spoken out of turn? She only relaxed when the god threw back his head and laughed. The sound boomed around the room.

"I can see why you were watching this one, Brynhildr."

She had drawn the attention of the gods? Tove didn't know whether that was a good or bad thing.

Odin continued, "If you are to join us here, you must abandon everything from your former human life – your family, your friends, everything that you know, including your name. Forget it all. That is the only way to truly become one of my Valkyries."

Tove blinked dumbly. "Your . . . Valkyries?"

"Did you think I simply brought you back to life for no reason? You are here to serve me." Odin touched his chin thoughtfully. "Your new name will be Gunner. It means 'battle'." He looked her over speculatively. "After what your actions caused, it seems like a fitting name."

Tove licked her lips, nervous for a moment. "Odin, what of my father?"

"Dead." Odin went to the fire, staring into the flames. "He was struck down moments after you were killed."

"Where is he? If he died during battle, he should have been brought here to Valhalla."

The All-Father didn't even acknowledge her. "He died cowering from his enemy, begging for mercy."

His words lit a fire inside Tove. Halvdan was not a coward. Her father was feared for his ferocity on the battlefield and he was respected for his even-handed rule. Her hands curled into fists at her sides, the urge to defend her father still as strong as it had always been. It was only Brynhildr's hand on her shoulder that stopped her.

"You will not win against him." It wasn't a warning she was

giving. It was just advice. Tove turned to look at her.

"What about Soren? Did he survive the battle?"

"No."

"Take her to see what the consequences of her actions were," Odin said. "Let her see what she brought down on her own people." Tove glowered at the All-Father. He glared right back. "You can hate me. I did not want to save your life."

"Why did you do it then?" she spat.

The god looked to Brynhildr. "You have her to thank. She was the one who wanted you."

"Come," Brynhildr urged, taking Tove by the arm and leading her away. Brynhildr led them out a large doorway and outside into a courtyard; the sun was shining down on them. Tove shielded her eyes, her gaze falling on a gilt tree. Its bark, its branches, even its leaves were gold. There seemed to be a glow coming from within the trunk too, lighting it up from within.

"Close your eyes, Gunner." The new name jarred Tove, but she had to think of herself as Gunner now. "Good. Now I want you to think about your old village. Imagine yourself standing in the market. Smell the smells, hear the sounds."

Although she didn't understand why, she shut her eyes and let the memories come. The sound of hawkers calling out above the din of the crowd filled her ears, the smells of fresh fish and cooking meats surrounded her, dragging her back to when she'd walk through the market, looking at everything, sampling mead from traveling merchants and tasting the sweetest plums and strawberries.

"Open your eyes," the Valkyrie instructed. Tove did, gasping when she saw where they were standing. The buildings surrounding them were nothing more than glowing embers and charred wood. The ground was black as well – scarred – and the scent of burned timbers sat heavily in the air.

"Where are we?" Tove asked, staring wide-eyed at her surroundings.

"Your village."

She turned to the goddess. "What happened?"

Brynhildr's dual-ringed eyes tracked over what remained of Tove's home. "Vadik Dalgaard's warriors, the ones who survived the fight in the great hall, swept through the rest of the village, raping and pillaging as they went. When everyone was dead, and the ones who had fled were cut down, they set fire to every building." She met Tove's eyes. "Your home, as you knew it, is gone."

Tove started shaking her head, trying to deny what she already knew was truth. "No," she whispered, her voice dropping down to a low, hard rasp.

"This is the reason Odin would not repair your throat. He said you could live the rest of your immortal life with the reminder of what you did. He never wanted you to forget."

Tears formed in Tove's eyes. "Why?"

Brynhildr sighed. "The All-Father gave his eye at Mimir's Well in order to know everything there was to know. That knowledge is a burden he lives with . . . Let's just say he likes to make others feel his pain sometimes."

Tove was speechless, but she could see the god's reasoning if she squinted at it for a long time: she had made a decision — a decision which had repercussions much larger than she could have foreseen or ever imagined. It didn't make it better though. She had killed her father. She had killed Soren. She may not have been wielding the sword, but she was responsible. She looked around, seeing the ghosts of everyone in the village. Their lives had ended because she couldn't accept — no — *wouldn't* accept her father's ruling.

It was all her fault. She felt ashamed of herself for being so selfish. She wasn't worthy of calling herself Tove Norling.

"Why did you save me, Brynhildr?" Her words were nothing but a hoarse whisper.

"Bryn," she said. "Just call me Bryn. Only Odin calls me by my full name, and only because he knows it annoys me. And the reason is simple. You are a fierce warrior, and I can see some of myself in you." Bryn touched Tove's cheek softly, briefly, before letting her hand drop to her side. "Come. There is nothing but waste and desolation here."

Letting out a breath, Tove closed her eyes. The smell of smoke, ash and death disappeared completely, the scent of ale and slow roasting meat taking its place. She opened her eyes to find herself standing in front of the gold tree once more.

Tove stepped away, wrapping her arms around her stomach. "I wish to be alone for a while."

Bryn's eyes studied Tove's face, searching for something. She nodded. "I'll take you to your chambers."

As they walked through the halls of Valhalla, the sounds of a great feast drifted through the corridors with them. Passing the largest doorway, she could see hundreds of men drinking, eating and fighting, the scuffles lasting no more than a few moments before each man would sit back down again and drink some more.

They continued on to a quiet hallway where Bryn stopped at a huge ash door. "This will be your room." Bryn pushed on it, revealing a room filled with furs, a large bed and an immense hearth. "There's some new clothes for you in the trunk at the foot of the bed."

I don't deserve any of this, Tove thought grimly.

"If you need anything, just knock on my door – my room is

right next to yours."

Tove nodded, counting down the seconds until she could be alone. When the door finally shut behind her, she stripped off her mother's torn and bloody wedding clothes and held them in her hands for a few moments. Even though it pained her, she threw them into the hungry flames. As she watched the fabric burn, she thought of her old self burning with them. She decided that she would embrace her new name, her new life.

Looking around, she saw a platter of fruits and a knife on a nearby table. She picked up the knife, testing its edge. The blade bit into the skin on her thumb effortlessly. Tipping the fruit from the platter, she looked at the polished surface, seeing her face reflected back. The image was distorted and crude, but it would be sufficient to her needs.

In front of the fire, she propped the dish up against the stone hearth and sat before it. Taking a hank of her hair in her hands, she brought the blade up, pressing it close to her scalp. Her blonde hair came away from her head easily. It was almost like skinning an animal. Tove stared at the blonde locks, letting the fine hairs sift through her fingers. They fell to the ground, dusting the furs on the floor.

She looked at herself in the platter once more, seeing the huge patch where her hair had once been. She took another bunch in her hands and sheared it off, letting it fall. Again and again she did this, her actions more and more frenzied. With every movement of the blade, Tove felt more distanced from her former human life. Like her clothes in the fire, Tove was being burned away, revealing something new, some*one* different.

When all her hair was gone, she studied her reflection. The scar across her throat was stark and that was just the way she needed it to be. She would wear the injury for the rest of her life. She would be reminded of her folly for the rest of her life too. She was no longer Tove, daughter of Halvdan and the shield maiden Bodil.

She was Gunner.

She was one of Odin's Valkyries.

23

Aubrey's eyes opened slowly, and oddly he wasn't in any pain. He tried hard to focus on the wall in front of him. His weapon racks weren't empty like the last time he'd seen them, but full of daggers and swords. If only he could reach one of them, he would be able to fight his way out of this whole fucked up situation. He flexed his hands then bent his elbows, and was surprised to the see the chains were gone.

What's going on?

He stood up, anticipating his knees would buckle straight away. When his feet hit the sparring mats, his toes flexed into the pliable material and anchored him in place. He looked around expecting to find Loki there with the next instrument of torture in his hand.

But he was alone.

Only his unsteady breathing was keeping him company. His eyes fixed on the ceiling when the boards on the first floor creaked as someone walked across them. His heart rate broke into a gallop, all the moisture draining from his mouth. It only took him a second to arm himself, finding the katana he had used when he'd last sparred with Taer.

There was another loud creak and the door to the basement opened. He prepared himself for the battle with Loki. There was very little chance he could win, but he'd be damned if he didn't go down without a fight. Lightly trodden steps preceded down the stairs, the wood moaning in protest.

Aubrey rolled his neck, working out the kinks. Modulating his breathing, he willed his heart to slow. Although he wanted to inflict maximum pain on the god, he had to remember what he'd told Taer: remain detached from emotion because emotion can get you killed. And right now, Aubrey was nothing but a ball of hate and anger, all directed at the Trickster.

The sound of footsteps got closer, but he still couldn't see Loki's legs or torso as he descended. What the fuck was going on? He stepped forward. The distinctive *thunk* stopped, right on the final tread. He studied the stairs, still seeing nothing.

"I'm losing my goddamn mind," he muttered under his breath, shaking his head. He lowered the sword, but his muscles refused to relax. A few tense seconds passed before he tore his gaze from the bottom of the stairs, looking to the back of the room, expecting to see all the tools Loki had been using on him for the past few hours . . . or was it days? He hardly knew anymore.

His heart suddenly bounced into his throat as his gaze returned to the stairs. He could have sworn he'd heard Taer calling his name.

"Wake up, wake up, sleepy head."

The voice that called to him was disjointed and cruel. Aubrey's mouth began to ache. He wiped at his nose when he felt something running down his face. It was blood – his blood. Soon after, the whole left side of his face throbbed in agony. There was a dripping sound, and when he looked down, there was a pool of blood on the ground to the right on his body.

"Ah, there you are," said that same voice, only this time, it didn't sound incoherent. He recognized it straight away.

Loki.

Aubrey's eyes cracked open slowly, a rolling wave of pain crashing against him. He tried to wipe the blood from his face, but the chain still binding him to the chair stopped the motion. His elbows screamed in protest, forcing him to press his lips together tightly. He must have lost consciousness, but at least he wasn't in any pain there. Unlike here.

The god laughed. "I hope you were dreaming of somewhere far, far away from this place because that is all it will ever be: a dream." Loki crouched down in front of him, making sure he saw the electrodes in his hand. "It's all right to scream, you know. In fact, I think I'd rather enjoy it."

"Why?" Aubrey croaked, his voice hoarse from thirst and suppressed cries.

"You're still asking the same question." Loki stood up and stepped away, moving behind Aubrey's chair. "If I were you, I'd be asking things like, 'what can I do to make you stop?' Of course, the answer is nothing." He stepped back into Aubrey's line of sight. His gaze was cold and detached. "There is nothing you can do to make me stop what I'm doing. In all this time you have not once screamed, or wept or begged me to stop. I take that as a personal challenge." Loki smiled and the sight of it made Aubrey's skin crawl.

Aubrey swallowed, the motion like sandpaper covered in glass shards down his throat. There was a very good chance he would die here in his basement, but at least he would know Taer was all right, that she hadn't been dragged into the situation. Loki had said he'd wanted Odin, and however Taer played into the plan, Aubrey would make sure Loki would never get her.

The god took a dagger and cut open Aubrey's bloody shirt, pushing the sides away to reveal his chest. He attached a clamp to each of his nipples, then connected one of them up to a car battery near his feet. When Loki was satisfied with the connection, he looked up at Aubrey.

"Scream if this hurts, won't you?"

He was on the verge of connecting the negative battery cable when someone burst through the door at the top of the stairs and started to descend. For half a second, Aubrey hoped it was Taer – that she had figured out where he was – but that hope was crushed when a male voice said, "They're here."

Loki pulled back, turning his attention to the man standing at the bottom of the stairs.

"Where?"

"In the courtyard."

Loki's smile was maliciously triumphant. "It sounds as if your little Mare is here with all the cavalry."

Aubrey would have fought against the chains – as hopeless as it was – if he'd had the energy, but he was physically drained. He'd lost too much blood. His body had endured too much. Regeneration was possible, but without the proper rest and recovery, which he was severely deficient in, there was very little chance he would make a full and complete recovery.

"What do you want me to do?" the other god asked Loki.

"I want you to finally prove your worth," Loki said. "I want you to redeem yourself."

The guy nodded and climbed the stairs once more. Loki turned back to Aubrey and smiled, disconnecting the battery cables. "I think I've thought of something else that will make you scream even louder."

24

Mav had barely been standing in the courtyard for more than a few seconds when the hairs on the back of her neck stood on end. Someone was waiting for them. Rhys appeared beside her a moment later and she glanced in his direction, seeing his body stiffen and his nostrils flare.

"Near the south side of the house," Rhys said in a low voice, his eyes flashing gold. "Sonofabitch. It's the same guy who attacked me with his brother."

He pulled out a dagger from his thigh holster and stalked toward the front of the house. A moment later there was a grunt and Rhys was thrown backwards. His dagger skittered across the cobblestones, coming to rest against the brick wall. He was back on his feet in an instant, a growl bubbling from his throat.

Freki stepped from the shadows then, his brows drawn low and his mouth pressed into a hard line. In his hand, he held a knife, his deadly focus on Rhys. "You'll bleed for killing my brother."

"And you'll bleed for me," Rhys replied, his eyes darting down to Freki's weapon. He pumped his hands into fists at his sides. "Just like Loki will bleed for Galen."

Mav watched on, wondering how Rhys would fair without a weapon of his own, looking for a signal from Rhys that he needed help. The pair started to circle one another, each waiting for the other to make the first move. It was Freki who finally attacked, driving the blade in the direction of Rhys's stomach. Rhys wrapped his hand around Freki's wrist to stop him, but Freki simply switched hands and plunged the steel into Rhys's back twice. Rhys roared in pain and retreated. Blood soaked through his shirt immediately, spreading too quickly.

Mav drew her sword, preparing to end it. She took a step forward, but stopped when Rhys turned his head to look at her. His eyes were yellow and she lowered her arm. His wolf was probably in control right now, and she had no idea what it would do if she approached with another weapon. She touched her tattoo, recalling the sword.

Rhys's attention went back to Freki. He bared his teeth at the god and advanced once more. Freki thrust his knife toward Rhys, only this time Rhys managed to intercept the strike, pushing it away. Then he planted his other hand on Freki's face, shoving him back. Freki stumbled, but recovered quickly.

Rhys glanced at Mav once more, their eyes meeting before his gaze darted to the dagger he had lost. Mav nodded in understanding and faded to the other side of the courtyard to scoop up the weapon.

Clearly growing frustrated, the god charged at Rhys yet again, stabbing wildly. Throwing his arm across Freki's chest, Rhys fisted his shirt and held him off, maneuvering his body to the opposite side of Freki — away from his weapon hand. There was a scuffle as Freki tried to make the blade sink home and as Rhys avoided the slashes. Rhys motioned to Mav for his dagger then. She threw it to him.

Reaching around Freki's body, Rhys thrust the blade into the god's midsection. Mav could smell the blood immediately. Freki howled in pain as Rhys fell to his knees and ran the blade across Freki's Achilles tendon. Freki dropped like a stone. Rhys grabbed the back of the god's shirt and dragged him into the middle of the courtyard, throwing his body down hard. Immobile, Rhys loomed over Freki's supine form. The god remained defiant, but Mav could see his aura had changed from confident to doubtful.

"What are you going to do to him?" she asked.

Rhys's head wrenched around. Mav stared into his wolf's eyes for a long minute before he started to stalk toward her; Mav's pulse raced. Fearful for the first time, she watched and waited to see what Rhys would do next. Was his wolf in complete control, or did Rhys still have a finger on the steering wheel?

When he was only a foot away from her, he raised his hand. Mav was ready to reach for her sword if she needed to, but when his nostrils flared slightly, his expression changed and he lowered his arm down to his side again. With his intense gaze still locked on her, she watched the golden hue in his eyes start to bleed away.

"Are you good?" she asked.

He nodded. "Never felt better, actually. Do you have a dagger?"

She pulled the sister blade to her sword from inside her jacket and handed it to him. He looked it over appreciatively before walking back to Freki. The god had been trying to drag himself away, but Mav knew for a fact that there was too much adrenaline in his system – that he was too hurt – to fade.

Planting his foot on Freki's chest, Rhys stopped him. Freki's eyes widened and he looked to Mav.

He begged, "Don't let him do this."

"I can't control his actions."

Moving with speed, Rhys drove Mav's dagger through Freki's left shoulder, pinning him in place. Freki's scream had not even finished echoing around the yard when Rhys did the same with his dagger, plunging it through the god's other shoulder.

Standing over Freki, who was staked out like a frog in a high school science class, Rhys pulled open the pinned god's shirt. Checking him for more weapons, Rhys pulled a butterfly knife from his ankle. He flipped it open, studying it.

Freki licked his lips. "Please. I was just following orders."

"And now you're just collateral damage," Mav said.

Rhys raised his hand over his head and drove the four and a half inch blade through Freki's sternum and started hacking his way down to his belly button. Freki screamed for the first few seconds then fell silent. Rhys worked quickly, breaking the ribcage and pulling out all the internal organs, removing them with skilled hands. He laid them beside the body where pools of blood quickly filled the grooves between the stones.

When Rhys stood up, Mav thought she would see his wolf peering out through his eyes, but she didn't; he was in complete control of himself.

"We need to find Loki," he said.

She summoned her sword and moved to the front door. She would have faded inside if she thought the element of surprise was on their side, but Loki clearly knew they were there if he'd sent Freki out first. She wrapped her fingers around the round, brass doorknob and twisted it sharply to the right. The locking mechanism broke with a sharp snap and the door swung open. Her fingers flexed around the handle of her sword briefly before she stepped inside. Rhys followed at her back, moving silently.

Mav's eyes skirted around the large reception rooms to the left and right of the entranceway.

She turned her attention to the set of stairs leading up to the second level of the house, listening hard. Touching Rhys on the shoulder, she pointed first to him then at the roof.

"I'll look around down here," she informed him in a low voice.

Rhys started up the stairs, his bloody back disappearing around a corner at the top of the landing. Mav walked silently through both reception rooms before exploring the rooms at the back of the house. Her booted feet hit the black and white tiles of the kitchen, where she found flecks of fresh blood on the floor. Turning her attention to the basement door, she reached out and touched the handle. With a sharp exhale, she twisted the brass knob.

The door swung inwards and she stepped away as the overwhelming smell of blood drifted out. Mav waited for her senses to come back online before starting down the stairs. A few steps in and she heard the sound of chains clinking, but she pushed on. The first thing she saw as she stepped onto the concrete floor was someone sitting on a chair in the center of the room; they were surrounded by blood, but she forced herself to take in everything — to *see* everything. At the back of the room was a workbench with tools scattered all over its surface. The opposite wall was bare, but there were some nails and boards in the walls where something had once been stored.

Taking a step forward, she got a better look at the male in the chair. Her lips pressed together into a hard line as she recognized who it was — the light elf who had visited Taer at the club. Walking behind him, she found his arms were bound with chains that were covered in the runes to prevent fading. When her gaze fell on the void where his hand used to be, everything slowly started to make sense.

This was why Taer had been so upset – Loki must have sent her the elf's hand. But why would Loki use him? What purpose did he serve? She touched her tattoo and her sword disappeared. Taking out her phone, she punched out a text and pocketed the device. She watched the elf's chest carefully, waiting for the rise and fall. He was still alive – for now – and she had to get him out of here.

Searching the workbench, she found a pair of bolt cutters buried under some other tools. Pulling them free, she lined up the blades on the chain. As she brought the handles together to cut through one of the links, her shoulders tightened. Moving just her eyes, she looked around the basement once more.

And realized she wasn't alone.

Pulling back, she stood up to her full height. Her head jerked around as movement in her periphery caught her attention. She watched as someone emerged from the shadows under the stairs.

Loki.

Mav's senses sharpened with the instantaneous adrenaline dump. She hadn't seen the Trickster since before his imprisonment under the earth. His appearance hadn't really changed other than being a little thinner than before. But there was one thing that was very different – the crazed look in his eyes.

"If you're in the house, Freki obviously failed – not that I'm surprised."

She flexed her hand around the bolt cutters down by her side. He took a step toward the workbench, and Mav moved her body subtly to keep him in her line of sight.

"I was hoping that Taer would be the one to come, but you will do just fine. You'll serve your purpose just like all the other Valkyries who have come before you."

It seemed like a lifetime, but it was only five weeks ago that Loki had murdered nearly half of Odin's Valkyries – Mav's sisters in arms. The scars were still fresh. The pain was still real. Her fingers cinched tightly around the handle of the bolt cutters. The muscles in her arms contracted without thought as she lifted the weight of the tool and hurled it in Loki's direction. Loki moved at the same time, his action quickly followed by a sharp and immediate pain through Mav's left forearm.

She ground her teeth together and looked down to find her wrist impaled by a dagger. Her worst fears were confirmed when she attempted to flex the fingers; she had absolutely no movement in her hand. The tendons had been severed. Loki started to laugh, drawing her attention. He had another dagger in his hand, and he let her see it briefly before launching it in her direction.

Pain shot through her shoulder, traveling into her chest and down to her fingertips. The second blade had penetrated through the muscle and had hit bone. With gritted teeth, she mentally fought back the pain, fought back the fear, and concentrated on fading away. It was a long shot, but she managed to rematerialize in the kitchen; she was simply suffering too heavily from the effects of shock to go any farther. Exhaustion hit her immediately and she slumped against the counter at her back. There was an island bench between her and the door now, and above it was a suspended pot rack filled with copper pots and skillets in varying sizes.

A few tense seconds passed. The wounds to her wrist and shoulder were throbbing in time with her heart. Blood gushed from them both and her vision started to fuzz out at the edges. Then her eyes latched onto the outline that formed in the air on the other side of the island as Loki materialized.

Awkwardly grasping the dagger in her shoulder with her only

functioning hand, she removed it. Mav remained silent, breathing heavily through the pain. She felt more blood run down her arm, back and chest, her tank top doing little to soak it up. Steeling herself again, she did the same with the knife in her wrist. She couldn't help but scream this time as she pulled out the blade. With sweat breaking out on her brow, she summoned her sword. Fighting with it now would take its toll on her though; she was running at fifty percent capacity with the injuries she was carrying.

Even though it used her flagging strength, Mav faded closer to Loki, simultaneously swinging her sword in the hopes that the blade would hit its target as she rematerialized. The Trickster was obviously anticipating this though and moved closer to the island bench. Maverick lunged forward, her black sword swinging in a deadly arc through the air. Loki snatched a large skillet from the pot rack in an attempt to deflect her attack. She knocked the cookware aside and thrust again.

Loki took down another pot and another and another as Mav knocked them all free from his hands. With all the noise they were making, she expected Rhys to come running in any minute. Gods, she hoped that he would. She didn't know how much longer she could keep this up.

Loki backed away, increasing the gap between them. In an effort to conserve her energy, she let him. She watched him carefully. Loki started smiling at her, raising his hand and wiggling his fingers at her. Mav frowned; she couldn't understand what he was trying to show her except for his bloody hands. He brought the digits to his mouth and slid them inside. As she watched, Loki's face and body began to change.

The entire transformation happened slowly – subtly – but there was no doubt who she was now looking at. It was as if she was staring into a mirror, except this new version of herself didn't have a sword tattoo on her neck.

"Gods," she whispered. Her brain was having a difficult time putting together the information. With gritted teeth, she held her sword in front of her again. The pain was like a high-voltage shock through her veins, leaving her weak and shaking. With a hoarse cry, she ran at Loki once more. With quick, sure movements, he swept up two pots from the ground and stopped her advance. With the blade of her sword sandwiched between the copper-bottomed cookware, the god yanked back.

Mav's grip tightened around the handle, but she was exhausted. The sword slipped through her fingers, leaving her to watch her weapon fly through the air and land on the other side of the room with a loud *clang*.

Loki moved swiftly, tackling Mav to the ground. His advantage didn't last. Mav used the last of her strength to flip the god over. But Loki wasn't giving up easily. With his hands curled into fists, he started striking her in the face. She tried to return the favor, but the pain from her shoulder soon eclipsed her desire to inflict as much damage she could.

Without warning, she was jolted off Loki. Mav's ears started ringing and her lungs emptied of breath as she tried to pinpoint the cause of the searing pain in her stomach. She touched just to the left of her navel, her fingers coming back bloody. She looked up to find Loki smoothly climbing to his feet. Seeing the smirk on Loki's – *her* – face as he took a step closer made her blood run cold. Her gaze dropped down his body, noticing the gun in his hand.

"You know, I didn't think it would be this easy," Loki said. Holstering the weapon behind his back, he walked to where her sword was lying a few feet away. Despite the pain, Mav smiled. Nobody could touch it but her – not even Odin had that ability.

But without hesitation, the Trickster easily picked up the sword.

Mav's eyes widened, and her heart started hammering beneath her ribs. "That's not possible," she whispered.

He studied the weapon then looked at her. "I can assure you it is possible. I have taken your blood into my body. I am you in every way, which means that my hand can touch your sword – can wield your sword. I don't even need your cloak to kill you now. All I need is this."

Her eyes darted down to the black steel of her sword. She had longed for death for a long time after Soren and her father died. There was a time when she'd wanted to turn her own blade on herself and just end it all . . .

But she never could. Bryn had given her a second chance at life, and she'd sworn she'd spend it protecting the Valkyrie who'd saved her in more ways than one.

Mav wasn't ready for Loki when he swung the blade at her, but despite this, she dodged the blow, slowly rolling across the floor and dragging her body away with her less injured arm. With each movement, pain rocketed through her. She was getting light-headed from the blood loss, but she knew that even a tiny scratch from her sword could kill her instantly. She got to her feet with the help of a cabinet handle and lurched for the kitchen doorway. She staggered through it, only partially aware that Loki had started to laugh. In the dining room, her foot got caught on the Oriental rug beneath the table and she stumbled. Loki was on her in an instant. He rolled her over onto her back and brought the tip of her black sword to her throat.

She was going to die and she had only two thoughts. The first was how relieved she was that she was being killed in battle.

And the last was of Soren.

———————

Rhys's head jerked up at the sound of a gunshot. The scent of fresh blood blanketed over the other scent that he'd been able to smell as soon as they'd set foot into the house.

Kill, his beast whispered. Rhys shook his head and tugged a little tighter on the reins of his self-control. For the first time he could remember, he'd managed to stop himself from shifting – from wanting to shift – once blood had been spilled. Out in the courtyard, he had felt like losing control, but knew he would endanger Mav's life if he did. So, like before with the goddess at the War Hammer, instead of fearing his wolf and putting distance between them, he'd embraced it. He'd run his hands over its shoulders and back, soothing it. The animal hadn't relaxed completely, but it had stopped scratching to get out.

Rhys crept to the bottom of the stairs, letting his senses roam. The smell of blood was getting stronger. Outside, a raven's haunting call rang through the night. Checking the rooms immediately to his left and right, he found his way to the dining room. He paused at its threshold, seeing a shimmer hanging in the air. It was just like when he'd been attacked in the street by Geri and Freki. Someone had put up a veil of magic then, and they had again now. Stretching out his hand, his fingers breached the magic. The veil dissolved instantly – like popping a bubble – revealing Mav's body on the ground. He approached her slowly, looking for any signs of life. But her chest was still.

"She's dead," a cruel voice said behind him.

Rhys spun around and stared at the man who was casually leaning against the wall. He had his arms crossed loosely over his chest, one foot placed over the other. He was the picture of calmness. "You don't recognize me, do you?" Rhys shook his head and the other man's face changed to Henry Craine's. "How about now?"

"Loki," Rhys hissed. Mentally, he loosened his grip on his wolf, letting the animal come forward, letting it take control.

Loki spread his arms wide. "The one and only."

"You killed Galen."

"I've killed a lot of people," Loki replied offhandedly, staring at his nails. "But the person who I really want to suffer, who I really want to die, is a lot harder to get to. I have to kill or maim a lot more people in order to get to him, and I'm afraid that you are one of those people."

"Was Mav one of them too?" Rhys spat. His wolf shifted beneath his ribs, the movement drawing Loki's eyes.

"Yes," the god replied, his eyes still firmly on Rhys's chest. "She was." He disappeared from sight. Rhys's wolf snarled and snapped inside his head. He spun around to find the god holding a gun. He had it trained on Rhys's heart. "Did Odin send you after me?"

Kill.

Rhys was on board with that idea, but he had to calm his racing pulse before he could fade. When he didn't reply, Loki began to laugh.

"Of course he sent you after me. My blood-brother has always been very good at delegating." He took a step closer, bringing the muzzle of the gun flush to Rhys's chest. The cold metal penetrated through his shirt. "What did he say to finally make you come after me?"

"You killed Galen," Rhys repeated, only this time, his wolf added its voice to his. The sound was a layered growl.

Loki narrowed his eyes as he studied Rhys. "For once, it wasn't a lie he told to get his way."

The wolf bared his teeth at the Trickster and jostled for position in Rhys's head. Rhys tightened his metaphoric grip. "So you admit that you did kill him? When? After Craine – *you* – said you had to speak with him in private?"

Loki answered with a sharp nod, and Rhys could feel all the rage he'd been holding back surge against the wall in his mind. That would fuel his wolf, but he wouldn't shift yet. He couldn't fade in his other form, but he was confident he could control himself.

Rhys smirked, enjoying the look of confusion of Loki's face for that brief moment, and then faded just to the right of him. With his hand over the top of the gun, he pulled down hard, throwing Loki off balance. Rhys snatched the weapon away and faded to the farthest reception room. He opened up the closest window and tossed it out.

Move, his wolf warned. He ducked to the side, hearing the air whistle as a blade aimed at his neck flew past. It missed his carotid by less than a quarter of an inch. Behind him, a mirror hanging on the wall shattered.

He recovered in time to deflect another blade and maneuvered himself into a better position. He scooped up Loki's knife, and held it out in front of him.

Rhys and Loki circled one another, each looking for a weakness in the other's defenses. Rhys struck quickly, trying to catch Loki unaware, to see if he panicked or not. The god remained calm, his free hand brushing away each move effortlessly.

Rhys took a few steps toward the grand piano, and Loki followed. The god lunged and slashed at Rhys's dominant arm. Blood sprayed, running down his arm in thick rivers. Beneath his ribs, his wolf shifted impatiently. Behind his eyes, he could feel it looking out.

Loki frowned and Rhys took the moment of distraction. He attempted to stab the guy, but only succeeded in running the tip of his blade over the other god's chest. His skin split open and blood soaked into his shirt.

Rhys's wolf became stock-still. In his mind's eye, he could see it was sniffing the air – taking in the scent of Loki's blood. The moment of silence was shattered when the animal inside went berserk, thrashing wildly, attempting to rake its claws through Rhys's skin. A growl bubbled from his throat, the sound cutting off when Loki tackled him. They landed on the glass-top coffee table. It shattered under their weight, glass skidding on the hardwood floor. Bringing his arm up, Loki started to stab wildly – his intended targets Rhys's throat and chest. Only a few strikes landed, but they were deep. Blood flowed freely, running down the side of his chest. Rhys backhanded Loki, making his head snap sharply to the right. Loki turned back to him slowly, tweaking his jaw.

"You'll have to do better than that," the god taunted.

Ignoring the bite of glass in his back, Rhys made a club with his fists and slammed them into the center of Loki's chest. There was a loud crack. The god sucked in a sharp breath and keeled over, rolling onto his side as he struggled to suck in enough oxygen.

Rhys got to his feet and disappeared the dagger that Loki had been using. With such force that Loki's body was shifting a foot each time, Rhys repeatedly kicked the god while he was down, then fell to his knees, straddling Loki's waist and landing blow after blow to his face. Blood sprayed when his nose broke and blood started to foam from the corner of Loki's mouth. When Rhys finally stopped, Loki's face was unrecognizable. Rhys looked down to find his knuckles busted open and bleeding. Climbing off the body, he sat back on his haunches and wiped his mouth with the back of his hand.

His head whipped around when he heard a tapping at the window. He looked up to find a raven on the sill. It cawed once and took flight. Rhys fell back onto his ass, resting his arms on his raised knees. He bowed his head, letting out a deep breath. Silence blanketed the house, and there was something so peaceful about it.

"You can't kill me."

Loki's barely whispered statement made Rhys lift his head. The god's eyes were open, and he was grinning at Rhys, baring teeth that were covered in blood. Rhys's wolf growled. Scrambling back onto his feet, Rhys cocked back his arm and swung again, but his fist went straight into the hardwood floor; Loki had faded. The wood splintered and jagged shards became lodged in his hand. More of his blood joined the growing puddle on the floor. He stood up, looking around the room. Where had the bastard gone? In his mind, he saw his wolf's head lift to the air. Its nostrils flared and its fangs flashed as it picked up Loki's scent.

Courtyard.

From outside came the sound of gunfire. Rhys quickly went to the piano and yanked up one of the wires then faded into the courtyard. Loki had recovered his gun and was now taking aim at the raven sitting on the courtyard wall.

What is he doing?

Quietly, Rhys wrapped each end of the piano wire around his fists a couple of times and tested the tension. There was hardly any stretch in the wire itself, the sharp snap of steel punctuating the night. Fading, Rhys looped the cord around Loki's neck from behind and applied pressure. Loki jerked in surprise, his finger flexing on the trigger; another round went off. Rhys pulled back hard, and the god stumbled. Loki dropped the gun, bringing his hands to his throat in an attempt to pry off the garrotte. Rhys increased the tension, his muscles straining to keep up the pressure.

Loki gasped and his legs began to give out. He landed heavily on the cobblestones, and Rhys followed his movement, falling to his knees too. Loki struggled to ease the tension, but Rhys wasn't about to give the god responsible for Galen's death the opportunity to survive. Loki's breathing became shallower and shallower.

Like hell you can't be killed, Rhys thought darkly.

He waited until the god had become completely still before he released his grip. Loki fell forward, landing violently face-first onto the ground. Rhys let the wire unravel from his fists. It tumbled to the ground beside him, covered in Loki's blood.

He looked up when he felt eyes on him. There, on top of the wall, the raven was watching everything. "Get out of here," Rhys said. The raven cawed once, but didn't move.

Behind, his wolf snarled urgently.

He turned around to find Loki clambering to his feet. There was a thick slash running along the front of his throat from the piano wire and blood was pouring from the wound.

"Fuck."

Loki smiled, his lips twisting into a grotesque sneer. "I told you," he whispered, his voice distorted.

The god disappeared from view.

Behind, his wolf warned.

Was his wolf *tracking* Loki? Rhys's thoughts refocused when the god jabbed the muzzle of the gun into his lower back. "I could put a bullet in your spine right now and there wouldn't be a damn thing you could do about it."

The raven cawed again, and the pressure eased just as Loki

growled, "I'll teach you to spy on me, *brother.*"

Rhys turned around in time to see the bird flap its wings, taking to the air with a long throaty cry. His ears rang when a bullet exploded out of the gun. The raven fell from the sky, landing on the cobblestones, blood pouring from its chest.

Loki swung the weapon back to Rhys. Staring down the barrel of the weapon, Rhys faded to the other side of the wall. Tense, he waited for Loki to follow. When he didn't appear beside him, Rhys realized that the god couldn't track him. He faded back, rematerializing behind the god. He raised his arm to stab Loki between the shoulderblades, but Loki spun around, knocking the knife away. It clanged to the ground.

Loki snarled and disappeared from view. Rhys followed his wolf's lead, hunting down the scent of Loki's blood. He rematerialized and looked at his new surroundings. It was dark, but it looked like they were underground. He had no idea if they were even still in Boston. An ominous sound rumbled through the thick concrete walls, and he watched the dust fall in waves ahead of him. That was when he caught sight of Loki.

The god looked over his shoulder when Rhys started after him. Raising the gun, Loki took aim. The flash from the muzzle was almost blinding in the darkened space. Rhys staggered back a step as the slug hit him in the shoulder. It took a moment for him to regain his equilibrium, but nothing would calm his wolf now; it was pulling violently against the symbolic chain Rhys was holding it back with.

With an almost deafening roar still resonating in his head, Rhys let some of the chain's links glide through his fingers. Although he had the power to contain the vicious beast, in this moment, he didn't want to. He wanted to inflict as much damage as possible. Moving faster than he ever had before, Rhys batted the gun from

Loki's hand and aimed a clenched fist at Loki's shoulder. Rhys had intended to simply shatter the clavicle – and he did – but he hadn't expected to find his hand completely embedded in Loki's body.

Loki's green eyes seemed to widen as he, too, realized what had happened. Suddenly, they were fading, only he wasn't in control of it – Loki was. With his wolf so very close to the surface of his subconscious, he could smell Loki's panic as he tried to fade away from him.

Rhys looked down at his other hand and found that his fingernails had somehow partly transformed into his wolf's razor-sharp claws. He looked back into Loki's eyes and finally released all control. With a loud snarl bursting from his throat, Rhys brought his transformed hand up and shoved it into Loki's other shoulder. The god screamed and tried to scramble away. Rhys felt his body bending to the will of his wolf, could feel the first twinges of his muscles and tendons tearing.

The shift happened quickly, and it felt like Rhys was being hit by a freight train. His body quadrupled in size in the space of a heartbeat. His arms and legs, his torso and head all became his wolf's. He could feel his fingers buried in Loki's flesh change shape – become bigger, become more deadly. Purposefully he flexed his wolf's toes, feeling the muscles in the other god's body yielding to the dagger-like claws replacing his fingernails. His skin began to prickle then as tens of thousands of follicles pushed through. The black fur grew within seconds, covering him in a thick coat.

Loki collapsed under the heavier weight, falling backwards so that his skull slammed against the ground and exposed his throat. Rhys stared into his eyes, seeing the black wolf that shared his soul staring back at him.

"It's impossible," Loki said, his eyes so wide Rhys could see the whites.

Rhys tore his front paws from Loki's body. The sound that left the god's throat was an unnaturally high keening. Blood sprayed into Rhys's face, and he leaned down to drink from the river of blood gurgling from the wounds.

"It's not possible," Loki said again, repeating the words over and over. Placing his large paws on the god's chest, Rhys flexed his claws and punctured the skin. More blood flowed, and with it, so did Rhys's sense of justice. He started to dig into Loki's chest cavity, breaking through the protective sternum and ribcage and finding the internal organs.

Loki's heart was the first thing to be eaten. The flesh slid down the back of his throat easily. Rhys buried his muzzle in the pooling blood, lapping at it. The lungs were next. Rhys ate every organ and piece of viscera until there was nothing left but blood.

But he didn't stop there.

Clamping his mouth over the god's leg and arm joints, he dismembered him, flinging the limbs in different directions. With a low growl in his throat, Rhys looked at Loki's face. He wasn't serene in death. The look of terror was etched into every line on his face – even his eyes told of the horror. Rhys broke Loki's neck and removed his head from his body.

"Oh, my god! Someone call animal control," someone said behind him.

Rhys looked over his shoulder at a human woman who was standing about twenty feet away. In her arms was a small dog that appeared to be too scared to even yap at him.

"Don't get too close, Pearl. He could come at you too," a man warned.

"That poor man," another voice said. There were dozens of

them coming out of the shadows, and Rhys realized he was standing in a suburban street. With his wolf sated, he forced himself to shift back. Everyone gasped, and a wave *of did you just see that, that's impossible* and even one *what the fuck?* came pouring from the crowd. Naked and covered in gore, Rhys took one souvenir from the grisly scene and faded from sight.

25

O din blinked rapidly, his vision from Muninn's eyes disappearing abruptly. He had been checking in with the bird whenever he could, but with the limited vision he had, he felt this would be the last time. The sharp bang of a gun firing was still ringing in his ears, the sight of Loki holding the weapon at Muninn making his stomach twist with equal parts rage and anxiety.

He would have no way of knowing who had won the fight. From what Odin had seen, Rhys wasn't faring too well. He cursed and started to pace. He should have known his plan would fail. Loki would be too strong for the light elf. He stopped to take a long drink of cognac from the full glass sitting on the coffee table.

Gods, he had to know what the outcome was.

Striding to the desk, he picked up the letter opener and brought the point to his palm. He slashed his skin then held his hand

– palm down – over the licking flames in the hearth. Making a fist, he let three drops of blood fall. As they hit the flames, he called the name of each Norn. When the final, trembling drop had fallen, he stepped back from the fierce heat and took another sip from his glass. A few minutes passed before there was a subtle shift in the air. Odin looked over his shoulder to find all three Norns. Verdandi and Skuld were standing meekly before the fire, but Urd was lounging on the chaise with his glass of cognac in her hands.

He turned around to face them properly, seeing Verdandi and Skuld's gazes skittering to their sister before returning to him. The pair curtseyed. Urd just took a loud slurp from the glass and raised a dark brow at him – baiting him. Biting his tongue, Odin sat down in the wingback chair.

"I need to know something."

"Yes, All-Father?" Skuld said.

"Loki is currently fighting Rhys. He is the light elf who was born to the female who survived Fenrir's attack."

"Sonofabitch," Urd said. "You found him."

Odin spared her a *I'm the All-Father, you foolish woman* look and pressed on. "My ravens are dead. I don't have any eyes out there anymore. I need to know who wins. I need to know if Loki is killed." He focused his attention on Skuld since she was the future fate. "I need to know the outcome. Now."

Skuld looked to Verdandi, who then said, "The future is not set yet."

"What do you mean 'it's not set yet'?"

"The future can still change because the present is not fixed. What if Rhys avoids one blow only to receive another later on that could prove fatal?"

Odin squeezed the arms of the chair in an attempt to keep

control of his temper. His fingers digging into the plush fabric drew Urd's attention and she gave him a disdainful look. She put the crystal glass down between her feet and leaned her elbows on her knees.

"It's driving you crazy, isn't it?" He didn't take the bait. She smirked. "You held so much power once upon a time. How does it feel to hold absolutely none now?"

"Urd," Verdandi hissed, chastising her sister.

Urd shrugged and reclined once more. "It's not my fault he can't handle it."

"Urd, please," Skuld said. "If you're not going to be helpful, you might as well just leave."

She stood up, fluffing her dark hair. "Good. I've got better things to do than hang out with a washed-up god anyway." With a smile that bared her teeth, she disappeared from the room.

"You can all get out," Odin said quietly, staring at his highly polished Gucci loafers. He looked up at the remaining Norns. "I said get out. You are no help to me now."

The sisters curtsied in unison and vanished from sight. Odin sat staring into the fire after they left. Not knowing was driving him crazy. If Loki was still alive, Odin had just lost his one and only chance at killing his blood-brother. Turning his other children against him simply wasn't a possibility. Odin had absolutely no sway with any of them. In fact, he was quite sure they hated him as much as their father did.

No, the only chance he had now was to escape the city – the country even – but he wouldn't do that without Bryn. Standing up, he faded down to the Eye, sure he could convince her that this time she had no other option but to go with him.

26

Rhys faded back to the house where it had all started. The front reception room was in disarray, and he got a proper look at how much damage he and Loki had caused. All the furniture was askew, and the coffee table they both went through was nothing more than shards of wood and glass scattered all over the floor. There was a single bloody handprint on the glossy body of the piano. He headed toward the stairs, walking up them slowly. At the top of the landing, he stepped into one of the bedrooms and opened up the closet. His body had fully healed with his shift, but he was still naked. Pulling a shirt off the hanger and finding a pair of pants in the nearby tallboy, he got dressed then went into the adjoining bathroom.

Turning on the faucet, he cupped his hands under the flow. He splashed the water onto his face, rubbing at the patches of blood on his cheeks and chin. The water seeping through his fingers was pink, and he watched it swirl down the drain. Normally his wolf would be trying to get out after such a bloody battle, but not tonight. It had joined in. For the first time ever, Rhys had relished in having his beast take over.

It was . . . satisfying – far more satisfying than he thought it would be. He enjoyed the feeling of calm that had come over him once he'd relinquished control. He enjoyed the feeling of calm that still remained.

He washed his hands and turned off the water. Taking a towel from the stack beside the bath, he dried off his face and looked at himself in the mirror. He expected to see his wolf peering out of his eyes like it did at any opportunity, but it was absent. He patted the towel to his neck, then draped it over the side of the sink. He rifled through the closet one more time, finding a backpack.

Down in the dining room, he approached Maverick slowly. Her eyes were shut, and her face was peaceful. She had a wound on her left wrist, a larger one through her right shoulder, what looked to be a gunshot wound to her stomach and a small scratch on the front of her throat. From her injuries, he couldn't figure out what had killed her. Odin's Valkyries were fabled and feared, and supposedly immortal.

Dropping to his knees beside her, he bowed his head and said a prayer in the old language. He also said a prayer for Galen – something he had not done since finding out he was dead. With one arm under her head and shoulders and another under her knees, Rhys lifted her up and cradled her against his chest. He had to return Mav's body to her family. He wouldn't be able to fade with her – only the strongest gods like Loki and Odin had that ability – so he had no choice but to walk back to the Eye.

Outside, he breathed in deeply once and started toward the club, ducking into the shadows when groups of people approached. He counted the blocks as he went, thinking about what he would do now. He couldn't and wouldn't return to Chicago to do any more than collect his cash. He'd saved every cent he'd earned as Craine's wet man. At last count, he had close to seven hundred grand to his name. He wouldn't need to work for a while, and when he did, he would choose a job that required him to work alone.

He had always wanted to travel to Alaska, or far north Canada. The isolation appealed to him. He could let his wolf out more often, let it roam around. Half the time he wouldn't have to get food – he could just let his wolf do the hunting. It huffed contently at the idea.

When Rhys saw the Eye up ahead, he picked up the pace. He slid down the alleyway beside the club quickly to avoid being seen and came to the metal security door. He pounded on the steel. It swung out and a dark shadow filled the jamb. Korvain stared down at him, his expression unreadable until his gaze landed on Maverick. His lips tightened. Rhys was prepared to explain himself to the Mare, but Korvain simply stood back and let Rhys inside. He walked in, gently repositioning Mav as he did. The short distance between the rear door and Bryn's office seemed to take forever to walk. Korvain followed at his back.

Rhys stopped in front of the office and waited. Bryn pulled the door open from the inside, her eyes finding Maverick in his arms. He stepped into the room and Bryn retreated a few steps, stumbling over her feet and hitting the edge of the desk. Tears filled her eyes and Korvain was there in an instant, wrapping her up in his arms.

Rhys stood there stoically, feeling like an interloper. He knew the grief Bryn was feeling. He had felt it too, but instead of mourning his best friend like Bryn was doing, he had let his rage take control. Now that Loki was dead and Galen had been avenged, perhaps he would let himself grieve properly.

Korvain looked to him. "How? Her cloak was here."

Rhys frowned. "I don't understand," he replied looking between them.

Bryn wiped under the eyes. "It doesn't matter. Tell us what happened tonight." She stepped away from Korvain and started moving stacks of paper to one side. "Put her down."

He shook his head and hugged Mav a little closer to his chest. There wasn't any romantic connection between them, but he didn't want to let her go just yet. He felt somewhat responsible for her death even though he knew Mav was fully aware of the risks. He sucked in a breath and started at the beginning.

"What of Loki?" Bryn eventually asked.

Rhys shifted the backpack from over his shoulder, letting it fall open on the desk. Loki's head landed with a thud then rolled forward a few inches. The Valkyrie studied it, saying nothing for a long time. She glanced at Korvain and then back at Mav.

"At least he's paid for his sins."

Rhys couldn't have agreed more.

"What are you going to do now?" Korvain asked.

"I'm leaving."

"Where will you go?"

"North."

The Mare slowly approached him. He held out his arms, ready to receive Mav's body. Rhys took one last look at the warrior's face and allowed Korvain to take her from him.

"Thank you," the Mare said softly, his eyes conveying so much more than his words could have.

Rhys nodded tightly and turned. He was already out the door when Bryn called his name, but he had no intention of stopping.

His job was done.

Now, he was free.

Taer was in her room, sitting on the bed, waiting. For the past few hours, she'd kept within the safety of the club, trying to get into contact with Aubrey. She had only been able to get through to him once, but something had gone wrong; for whatever reason, he wasn't able to see or hear her.

She didn't have any idea where he was being kept, but she wouldn't give up.

In her pocket, her phone vibrated. She took the device out and read the text message that had just come through from Mav; it had been sent nearly an hour ago. It contained two words: *He's here.* Following them was an address.

Taer dropped the phone, feeling her world slow down. She was stunned. Shaking herself, she picked up the phone and re-read the message a few more times.

"He's in his house," she said under her breath. "He's in his own *goddamn* house."

Jumping up, she dropped to her knees and pulled out the box containing her katana from under her bed. The sight of the sword with its pale green veils through the blade flooded her with memories. Aubrey had given her the sword when he realized that it was her Affinity – the weapon that spoke to her, that she was born to carry. When she held it, it was an extension of her body and she wielded it with deadly precision. Sliding the leather of the back holster strap over her head, she positioned it across her chest before securing her katana behind her and stood up.

The elevator ride down gave new meaning to the word torture, and when the doors finally opened, she strode to the far end of the hall. She wouldn't allow anyone to stop her. She exited into the alleyway, closed her eyes and faded to Aubrey's house.

Out on the street, everything looked the same as it did before, but Taer could feel it was different somehow. Reaching her hand over one shoulder, she felt for the handle of her sword, taking comfort in it. Looking down, she saw a few spatters of blood on the pavement. She crouched, touched her fingers to one of the drops, and brought them to her nose. It wasn't Aubrey's blood, so whose was it?

Getting upright again, she faded to the other side of the wall. In the courtyard, there was more blood. Some had been smeared, and some had collected between the cobblestones. The largest pool, however, belonged to someone who had been left spread-eagled and disembowelled on the stones.

She blew out a breath that hovered in front of her mouth, and let her gaze travel over the scene. Something small and dark caught her attention. As she approached, she realized she was looking at the iridescent feathers of a raven. She picked up the bird. Its neck was broken and there was a small caliber bullet lodged in its chest.

Gently, she placed the bird back down. She turned to face the house once more, her stomach dropping like a stone. If this was the destruction on the outside, what would the inside be like? What would Aubrey be like? A shiver slid down her spine, but she steeled herself and faded inside.

The parlor to her right was in disarray. Furniture was broken, a mirror had been shattered and there was even more blood covering the floor. Forcing her eyes away, she drew her sword and started up the stairs, expecting to see Aubrey's captor around every corner.

She cleared the top level of the house quickly, which only left downstairs. Deep in her gut, she knew exactly where Aubrey was located; he was in the basement. Moving swiftly down the stairs, she navigated through the dining room and into the kitchen. There was more blood in both of those rooms, but her brain didn't seem to really take it in. In the kitchen, pots and pans were strewn on the floor, many of them with large dents in their sides. When she came to the basement door, she pushed away her fears that were threatening to surface. She held her sword steady while reaching out with her free hand to turn the knob on the door.

Taer took a step back, holding a hand over her nose and mouth. The stench that rolled out the door was unbearable: a combination of blood, urine and vomit. Taer had to squeeze her eyes shut to stop them from watering before she descended the stairs. If it had been anyone else down there other than her brother or Korvain, she wouldn't have gone.

But it wasn't just anyone.

Keeping up her guard, she breathed through her mouth and took the treads quickly. When she reached the bottom, she couldn't believe the scene. Her katana dropped from her fingers. It landed on the bare concrete floor with a loud clang.

Aubrey didn't even flinch. He was sitting in a chair in the center of the room, his arms behind his back. His head was bowed, his matted hair shielding his face from view. He was naked from the waist up. His chest and stomach were covered in so much blood that she couldn't tell if he had one or multiple wounds. She looked down at the pool of blood surrounding the chair, its reach about three feet in diameter. That was when she noticed his feet. Taer put her hand to her mouth to stifle the gasp. The skin on his toes and feet had been removed.

She edged further into the room, never taking her eyes off Aubrey. Her focus was particularly on the shallow rise and fall of his chest. He was still alive, still breathing, but for how much longer? How much trauma could a body go through before it would simply give in? Taer moved behind him, seeing the stump where his hand used to be. An even larger pool of blood was on the floor.

"Oh, Aubrey, what did he do to you?" she whispered. Her voice had barely been audible – even to her – but somehow he had heard her. His head jerked up, looking toward the stairs where she had been standing only moments before.

"Get . . . get out of here, Taer," he rasped. "He's coming back. Couldn't . . ." His words died, his head falling forward once more. Taer felt her lungs begin to burn, and she let go of the breath she been holding. Aubrey muttered her name a few times before saying, "Couldn't live with myself if you got hurt."

She felt tears fill her eyes and knew she had to get him out of here. After getting a better look at his bindings, she saw that they were made of steel. She turned around, searching the workbench for anything that would break, crush or cut the links. All she found were the instruments of torture Loki had turned on Aubrey. She found a hacksaw in the second drawer, its teeth still caked in blood. She felt sick to her stomach, knowing it had been the tool to remove Aubrey's hand. But she had no other choice. She lifted it from the drawer, holding it down at her side, and stood behind the chair.

When she got down on her knees, her pants instantly absorbed Aubrey's blood. Taer closed her eyes for a moment, trying not to think about it too much. She took one deep breath and opened her eyes, looking at the chain. It was wrapped tightly around Aubrey's elbows, bending them at a strange angle. Lifting the saw, she set the teeth against the metal.

"I dreamed you'd come to see me," Aubrey said under his breath.

Taer stilled. Was he conscious?

"I dreamed it, and if it was true, it would have become a nightmare. I can't . . . I won't allow that bastard to harm you."

"He didn't," she replied just as softly. She waited for him to respond but he was silent. "I'm going to get you out of here."

Taer drew the saw back, feeling the teeth bite into the chain. Pushing it forward, steel flakes began to rain onto the bloody puddles. Tears streamed down her cheeks, dripping onto her shirt and her hand as she pushed and pulled the saw's teeth across the chain. She was almost through when Aubrey's head jerked up again. He turned so she could see his profile. He had a frown on his face along with a black eye and a busted up lip.

Recognition dawned and his eyes widened. "Taer? What are you doing here?" he asked, panic threading through his hoarse voice. "You have to get out of here. This is exactly what he wants. Just leave me here. Go."

She hushed him gently. "It's all right. He's not here. You're safe. I'm going to get you out of here. I just have to—"

"No!" He jerked his arms, making the saw skip out of the channel it had made. "He'll come back. He always does."

He grunted as he shifted his arms again. The tendons in his neck bulged with the effort, but he was only causing himself more pain. Growing more and more agitated, he tried to stand up, a strangled cry bursting from his throat. Taer watched on helplessly. "Aubrey, please, listen to me. Loki's not here. I can help you, but you have to calm down."

More tears fell, her own helplessness adding to her personal pain at watching the man she loved work himself into a frenzy. He was hallucinating. He thought Loki was still there in the house. She did her best to soothe him, but nothing she said was getting through. She tried to place her hands on his shoulders, but that only agitated him more. He bucked in his seat, throwing her back. She stumbled over her feet, landing backwards into the workbench. The tools rattled, their combined sound terrifying her. Aubrey became stock-still, his shoulders tensing up.

"No. Please, no. Don't hurt her. Do whatever you want to me, but don't hurt her. I beg of you!" His strained voice rang with both conviction and anguish. "Loki, *please*."

Taer sobbed as her heart broke for him. Had he been damaged too much? Would she ever see the Aubrey she once knew again? Turning her back on him, she stared at the wall, drawing in a few deep breaths. She had to get him out of here. She didn't know whether Loki was coming back, or when. Perhaps he was already back in the house, and all the noise they were making was alerting him that she was down here. She had to move quickly, but with Aubrey acting the way he was, she couldn't see how.

That was when she noticed it on the bench: a syringe already loaded with a clear substance. It must have been dislodged when she bumped into the table. She picked it up. With no idea what was actually inside the barrel, she was taking a huge risk.

But what other choice did she have?

Aubrey was still thrashing in the chair when she turned back around. She jabbed the needle into his neck and depressed the plunger. In an instant, his whole body went slack and his head slumped forward once more. Dropping the used syringe to the floor, Taer picked up the hack saw and started cutting the chain once more. It only took her a matter of minutes to free him, but that was the easy part. Now she had to figure out how to get him out of there.

Carefully taking one of his arms, she drew it over her shoulder and lifted him. He weighed a lot more than she thought and her legs buckled under the pressure. Repositioning him a little better, she turned toward the stairs and started the ascent. Every muscle in her legs was protesting, but she ignored it all.

"Just get to the front of the house," she told herself. Once she got there, she would get to the courtyard and she would continue to give herself small goals. By the time she reached the courtyard, though, she just couldn't handle the weight anymore. For a fleeting moment, she thought about reaching out to Korvain, but he wouldn't come – not for Aubrey.

Jostling his body to one side, she reached for her phone and unlocked it. She tapped into her contacts, scrolling through them, trying to find a likely ally, when she saw a name she hadn't personally entered. Biting her lip, she hit the call button.

"Taer," Cash answered smoothly on the other end. In the background was the sound of people laughing.

"I'm calling in the favor you owe me."

Her demand was met with silence. Finally, he said, "What can I do for you?"

27

Odin yanked at the bottom of his suit jacket and stepped off the curb. He looked around at the revelers walking the streets of Boston. Every single one of them was unaware of what was happening, unaware of the stakes. The line outside the Eye was probably snaking around the corner, but he barely spared it a glance on his way down the darkened alleyway. Stopping at the steel door, he raised his fist to knock. A mechanical whir sounded above his head, and he looked up to find the security camera moving. He gave a tight nod in the direction of the CCTV and stepped back from the door.

A moment later, light spilled out as the door swung open, landing on the ground at Odin's feet.

"I was wondering how long it would take for you to come here," said Bryn.

He gave her a warm smile. "We need to talk." She stepped back from the door. "Thank you," he said with a nod.

Inside Bryn's office, he took a seat, unbuttoning his jacket and crossing his legs at the ankles. After shutting the door, Bryn walked around her desk and sat down, pulling open one of the drawers.

"Drink?" she asked, showing him the bottle of 42 Below.

Even though the last time he asked the question, he was given an icy reception, he still said, "Got any cognac?"

She gave him a tight smile and picked up the phone. She punched in a few numbers. "Mist, we got any" – she covered the speaker with her hand – "What do you drink?"

"Courvoisier."

"Courvoisier? Yeah. Can you bring it back here please?" Bryn hung up and took two glasses from the drawer, placing them next to the vodka. Odin was surprised she was being so civil. The last time he'd been there, she'd been combative and hostile. Perhaps she had seen the error of her ways.

There was a knock on the door.

"Come in," Bryn said. The door opened. It was Mist. Her eyes darted between him and Bryn quickly.

"All-Father," she said softly. "What are you doing here?"

"I—" he started.

"I invited him here in the spirit of cooperation," Bryn said, speaking over him. He glanced in her direction and raised an eyebrow. She didn't acknowledge him at all. Instead, she stood up to accept the bottle from the other Valkyrie. "Thanks. That's all for now."

Mist nodded slowly after staring at Bryn for a long moment. When they were alone once more, Bryn poured them each a drink and picked up Odin's glass, handing it to him. She perched on the edge of her desk, crossing one ankle over the other.

"I must say, I'm pleasantly surprised by your behavior, Brynhildr."

She gave him a tight-lipped smile. "Like I said to Mist, I invited you in in the spirit of cooperation."

"And reconciliation, also?" he asked, taking a shallow sip from his glass. The cognac trickled smoothly down his throat.

"Something like that." Bryn watched him over the rim of her own glass. "Why did you come here tonight, Odin?"

He had decided before he'd even arrived that he would tell Bryn the truth about his visit. He could lie to many others, but he still struggled to do so with Bryn. Leaning forward, he placed his glass down on the desk, purposefully taking his time to turn it around so the logo of Odin's Eye was facing out. Bryn's blue eyes darted to the glass and then back to him.

"I have some bad news."

"You always seem to be the bearer of bad news."

He started to loosen his tie, but stopped himself. "Loki is coming for you again." He paused, waiting for her shocked response. When she did nothing more than look at him, he continued, "For the past month, I've been watching him. I followed him to Chicago. I watched him play with the lives of the humans, but I couldn't understand why. Whatever his motive, I knew it would lead back here."

"And to you," she added.

He nodded. "He came back to Boston, but I have a plan. I found out how to kill him – to make sure he could never attack us again."

"How?"

"He can be killed by a true blood relation."

She placed her glass of vodka beside his drink. "Well, that makes him invincible, as I see it. His children would never turn on him."

"Yes, that's what I thought also. But I discovered that his son, Fenrir, fathered a child while in his human form. The boy survived to adulthood."

One of her pale brows rose. "Loki is a grandfather?"

"He is."

"How did you find this out?"

Odin gave her a reproving smile. "Brynhildr, truly, you ask this of me?"

She grunted. "So, you found the chink in Loki's armor. What good would that information be if you don't know who his grandson is?"

He brushed some lint from the bottom of his trousers. "It's more than a chink. I've exposed his throat."

"And how do you suppose you'll get Loki's own flesh and blood to become the weapon to kill him?"

Odin sank back in his seat, resting his elbows on the armrests and steepling his fingers together. "It was surprisingly easy, actually."

"You know who he is? You've spoken to him?"

"Yes."

Bryn's brow furrowed and she stood up, walking out of his line of sight. "You lied to him."

There was disapproval in her voice. He didn't like to hear it. He sighed. "It was a means to an end, Bryn."

"Yes, everything seems to be explained away as 'a means to an end' with you," she replied softly.

He shut his eyes briefly, wounded by her distaste for his actions. She couldn't see that everything he did was for her. "It was necessary."

"Again, a phrase that you seem to use excessively to excuse your actions."

He bit the inside of his cheek and let the comment slide. "The reason I came to speak with you is to tell you that the grandson failed. Loki killed him. Tonight. Which means that time is of the essence. We need to leave."

"*We?*" she shot back incredulously. She walked back to her desk, and Odin could see that her eyes were red. Had she started crying? "I don't know how I'm a part of your plans."

"Bryn, please, you don't know this, but we're indisputably connected – irrevocably bound together."

"Oh, I know about that, Odin. I know that your life and mine are intertwined."

He tried to keep the shock from his face. How had his greatest secret become known to her?

"Loki told me when he imprisoned me," she said. "He told me that if I die, you die. It's as simple as that. Everything you have done in the name of 'protection' has been a falsehood. You're a self-absorbed sonofabitch, and I'm ashamed that I served you so loyally for all those years."

"Bryn—"

"No!" She was trembling now, her face twisting into a fierce scowl. "Enough of the lies." She marched around to the other side of her desk, producing a backpack. Upending it, something bloody landed on the desk's surface.

Odin sat forward to get a better look as the object rolled, finally coming to a stop directly in front of him. Loki's unseeing gaze seemed to penetrate him, but he couldn't take his eyes off the dismembered head. For so long he had wanted this, and now that it had finally happened, he wasn't sure what to say, what to do.

"How?" he croaked.

"Rhys killed him."

His head jerked up. "*Rhys* was here?"

She nodded. "Yeah, Rhys – *Loki's* grandson. He came here hoping to locate you. He needed more information on where to find Loki. You obviously intervened at some point, and . . ." She sucked in a breath. "Mav went with him."

"When did this happen?"

"No more than half an hour ago."

"He's dead," Odin whispered to himself. He could feel the triumph starting to bubble up in him. He was finally free of Loki. He wouldn't have to look over his shoulder anymore; he wouldn't have to wonder whether an attack was coming. He felt so light – all the weight, all the fear, had been taken away. He looked up at Bryn, smiling broadly, but the Valkyrie's expression was dark.

"Mav went with him to find Loki," she repeated.

"And they did find him," he replied. "Clearly."

"Yes, but at what cost?"

He was puzzled. Where did cost come into the equation? Both he and Bryn were still alive. Nothing else was important.

"She's dead. Loki killed Mav."

Odin wasn't moved by the news. Maverick had joined his service only at Bryn's request. If he had had his way, he never would have let the girl be resurrected. He would have done anything for Bryn – would still do anything for her. "Sometimes people get killed in wars."

Bryn's jaw jumped. "This wasn't *her* war. It wasn't any of *our* wars. It was *yours*, Odin."

He brushed her comment off with a shrug, reaching for his drink again. His eyes lingered on Loki's dead eyes. "Sacrifices have to be made."

Bryn hadn't been the only one to lose people. He had lost his wife. He had lost his son. But he would sacrifice them all again if Bryn could live.

"Yes, they do."

The air seemed to shiver then. He turned to look at her. She had summoned her golden sword. "What are you doing?" he asked blithely. She had made threats against him before, but she could never go through with it. She loved him too much.

"Something I should have done a long time ago."

He stood up, laughing. "What do you plan to do, Brynhildr? Strike me down here, in your office? What possible reasons could you have to harm me? I have saved you from the threat of Loki. I alone have made it safe for you, for us."

Her free hand clenched into a fist. "You don't get it, do you?" she spat. "None of this would have happened if you had just taken responsibility for your actions. Months ago, when Loki first came for you, you could have stopped him. But you were a coward, too conceited to see that you were the problem – not the solution."

He waved his hand through the air, pushing away the very notion. "None of that matters anymore. It doesn't change the fact that Loki is now gone from our lives."

Silence settled on the room, and Odin could see Bryn was coming to see his point of view. Her expression lost its hard edge and she actually smiled a little.

"You know what? You're right." She lowered her sword hand and he nodded.

Leaning forward, he picked up his glass and took another sip, enjoying the lingering flavors of vanilla and caramel after he swallowed. "I knew you'd come to your senses."

He turned his head when something caught his attention – light reflecting off something shiny and metallic. "Bryn?"

She raised her sword.

"Bryn!"

The last thing Odin saw was the look of satisfaction on his beloved first Valkyrie's face.

———————

The momentum of Bryn's swing twisted her body around. Straightening, she looked over her shoulder. Odin's body was crumpled on her office floor, his head lying about a foot away from his neck. She hadn't needed to be so brutal with her strike – a mere graze would have killed him – but all her anger and hurt from seeing Maverick's limp body cradled in Rhys's arms had demanded that she make Odin's ultimate death more dramatic than just a scratch.

The room was silent with the exception of her harsh breathing and the occasional buzz as the CCTV screens changed views. She didn't know what she would feel when she finally struck down Odin, but the giddiness bubbling up inside her seemed out of place. Should she even be happy he was dead? Shouldn't she be mourning his loss, or feeling guilt for murdering him in what was cold blood? He was her father, after all. She shook her head.

"No, he wasn't your father," she said aloud. "He killed your paternal father. He was just a poor stand-in."

Calling back her sword, she picked up the phone from the desk and punched in the necessary numbers to get Korvain.

"Bryn, what's wrong?" he asked.

She cleared her throat. "Odin's just been to see me."

"What did he want?"

"He came to ask me to leave with him. He didn't know Loki had been killed. He was fucking blind to what was going on. He was simply trying to protect his own ass . . . again."

A growl vibrated down the line. "If I could, I'd kill that bastard myself."

"I'm afraid I beat you to it," she said hollowly.

There was a beat of silence before Korvain asked, "What did

you say?"

She looked at Odin's body on the floor. "He's dead. I killed him."

The connection cut. Bryn placed the receiver back into place and sat down in her office chair. She watched the door, knowing that Korvain was about to burst through it. As she waited, she thought back to the conversation she'd had with Odin. When he'd said he'd found Loki's grandson, everything seemed to click into place: Rhys could turn into a wolf because his father was Fenrir, Rhys could follow Loki because they were related by blood.

Her gaze jumped back to the door when the handle of her office door was lowered. Korvain stepped into the room, his dark eyes taking in the bloody scene. They quickly turned to her.

"Are you okay? Are you hurt?"

Her smile was shaky, but she already felt better for having him in the same room. "I'm fine. He didn't even see it coming."

He studied her face for a long time before getting down onto his haunches to get a better look. "Nice work," he murmured. Standing up, he asked, "What are we going to do with the body?"

She stared at Odin for a long minute. "We'll burn it."

Standing on a beach on Plum Island, just north of Boston, Bryn cleared her throat. She, along with Korvain, Mist and Kara were standing there with the calm North Atlantic at their backs and the shadowed moon lighting the water. A few feet away was the funeral pyre they had all helped to build in order to give Mav the goodbye she deserved. They'd placed Maverick's body on top of the wooden structure, each of them whispering their final messages to the Valkyrie who'd been such an integral part of their group for so long.

Bryn nodded at Kara, signaling her to start singing a prayer in the old language. It was haunting to listen to, making goose bumps break out on Bryn's skin. The lapping waves behind them complemented the halcyon quality of Kara's voice. Along with the salt spray, the smell of smoke surrounded their little gathering and Bryn looked around at the remaining Valkyries standing in a half circle around Maverick's funeral pyre. With Eir back at the club, tending to the wounds of Taer's friend Aubrey, it left Mist, Kara and herself to remember Maverick.

Their fallen sister had been dressed in an outfit similar to what she wore while in Odin's service. It wasn't meant to be a homage to Odin – rather it was meant to represent the sorority they'd shared for over a millennia. Kara finished singing, her voice cracking over the last word. Mist wrapped an arm around her waist and pulled her close.

"Does anyone have anything they want to say?" Bryn asked quietly, leaning back against Korvain's chest. She had already said everything to Maverick after Rhys had left her office. There simply wasn't anything else she could say now to make the pain lessen.

"I do," Mist said. She began to speak about Mav's professionalism and how much she respected her. Bryn felt the first tear slide down her cheek, and there was nothing she could do to stop the rest that came. Her whole body began to shake, and she would have collapsed if it weren't for Korvain's strong arms around her waist.

When Mist had finished, Korvain chose to speak. His words vibrated through his chest and into Bryn as he did, and she closed her eyes as he talked about Mav and how she was the perfect soldier and the most loyal friend. When he was done, he squeezed Bryn briefly before stepping away. He came back with a torch for each of the Valkyries. As one, they held the flames directly underneath the pyre, waiting until the kindling caught. Despite the wind, the fire took quickly and gray smoke started to billow out from between the brushwood. The flames were small, but they grew quickly, licking at Mav's body. Nobody said a word as the fire consumed her.

Bryn looked up at the night sky, watching the smoke rise to join the stars. They remained there until all that was left were Mav's ashes. Bryn collected them in Mav's ash wood box – the same box containing her feather cloak – and closed the lid.

Mist asked, "Where will you take her?"

Bryn wiped under her eyes and took a deep breath. "I'm taking her home – back to the village where she grew up – but not before we attend to some other business." Turning to Korvain, she said, "Can you please go and get him?"

"Who?" Mist asked as Korvain faded away from sight.

Bryn looked both Mist and Kara in the eyes. She sighed. "Odin."

"Odin's coming here?" Kara asked.

"Odin's dead," Bryn said. "I killed him." She held her breath, waiting to see what the other two would do. Would they hate her for her actions? Would they blame her? She couldn't lose them over this – especially not since she had lost so much in the last couple of months.

"What?" Mist said.

"When?" asked Kara. She wrapped her arms around her torso. "How?"

"Last night, after Mav was killed. He came to me, begging me to leave with him. He thought Rhys had failed to kill Loki. He was just saving his own ass again. And . . . I just . . . had enough." Bryn's gaze dropped to the box in her hands. "He's responsible for getting Mav killed." She looked up again. "And he's responsible for killing the other girls over a month ago. If he'd just had the guts to step up and take responsibility for his actions, then none of this would have happened."

For a few minutes, nobody said a word. Bryn's stomach twisted, anxiety working it into tight knots. When Mist finally approached her, Bryn didn't know what to expect. The other Valkyrie slid her arms around Bryn's waist and started to cry into her shoulder. Relief washed over Bryn as she realized it was okay; they didn't blame her.

Over Mist's shoulder, Bryn could see Kara approaching them. She opened up her arms for Kara to step into the embrace, and then, together, they cried. Bryn didn't know whether it was for the loss of Mav and the others that had come before her, or whether it was for Odin's death, but the one thing she did know was that it was cathartic.

They all pulled away when Korvain returned. Over his shoulder was Odin's body, draped in a sheet. He started toward them, placing the All-Father's body down onto the stones littering the sandy shore. Odin would have no pyre. He wouldn't have the honor of a proper funeral. Korvain handed Bryn the pillow case containing his head.

"What's in there?" Mist asked, pushing some hair behind her ear.

"His head," Bryn replied, stepping away from the others.

"Gods, what did you do to him?" Kara asked, taking a step closer.

"I made sure he couldn't possibly survive." Bryn's response was clipped as she upended the case. Odin's head fell out, hitting the stones with an audible squelch. It came to rest beside his waist.

Bryn returned to Mist and Kara's sides. She looked out at the horizon, seeing the spot where the sun would rise. It was barely a dull glow, just something far away and intangible, but soon it would explode and rain light over them all. They had no time to waste; they couldn't risk being seen by the human authorities. "Do it."

With a nod, Korvain pulled a bottle of lighter fluid from his pocket and emptied it all over Odin's body and head. From the other pocket he produced a lighter. The small flame looked impotent next to the pyre that had burned before, but it didn't really matter. It would have the same effect, eventually. Bryn watched Korvain crouch down, touching the lighter to the trail of fluid he had made leading toward the body. The flame hungrily ate the accelerant, bringing it closer and closer to Odin. Bryn found herself holding her breath, bracing herself to feel the heat of the blaze . . .

Unexpectedly, there was a crash of thunder across the ocean just as a brilliant flash of lightning struck Odin's body. As the peel of thunder faded, a new sound replaced it: the cries of hundreds of ravens. The sound filled the air and Bryn reached out to clutch Korvain's hand as he came to stand beside her, her fingers cinching shut around his. What was she seeing? Was it even real? Quickly, she glanced around at the faces of the Mist and Kara, seeing they were just as dumbstruck as she was.

In the pre-dawn light, hundreds of ravens were taking to the sky. Their feathers scraped together as they all fought each other to escape the shroud that had been covering Odin's body. The gray sky was soon overwhelmed by the birds, each of them crying out, each of them disappearing into the mist over the North Atlantic. Just as the last bird disappeared from view, the sun broke free on the horizon. Its light grew stronger with every second that passed, revealing the untouched sheet still holding the form of Odin's body. The fire had not touched it. The lightning strike had not caused damage. Walking over to the All-Father, Bryn knelt down and touched his foot. The sheet crumpled onto the stones.

Odin was gone.

28

Taer couldn't sleep.

Knowing that Aubrey was injured on the spare bed on the other side of the living room wall was killing her. Eir had done her best to start healing what injuries she could, but she could not help him grow back his hand. He would forever be an amputee, and Taer didn't give a damn. She realized that as she'd stood there on the bottom step of his basement stairs. She didn't care what Aubrey looked like. Relief that he was still alive had flooded her. That reaction alone had told her all she needed to know. She loved him, because if it had been anyone else, she wouldn't have felt a damn thing.

And now all she wanted to do was be with him while he slept and recovered and healed. Approaching her bedroom door, she paused when she heard a quiet conversation between Aubrey and Eir.

"—love her?" the goddess asked.

"Does that even matter?" Aubrey replied. His voice was hard. "She saved me physically, but I'm still broken." He heaved a heavy sigh. "She should have left me there."

"She took a great risk to get you," Eir replied gently.

He was quiet for a long time. "That was her choice." His words were almost indistinguishable, but Taer heard them clearly enough. As if she had a choice in the matter. She would have moved every single last one of the Nine Worlds to get to him. Anger slammed against her common sense, and she stormed into the bedroom.

Both Eir and Aubrey's heads whipped around. Eir stood up quickly, wringing her hands together as she glanced between them.

"I just came in to give his body a little healing boost," the goddess explained. "I'll leave you two alone."

As Eir passed, she gave Taer's arm a supportive squeeze. Taer waited until the door shut before sucking in a deep breath and letting it go.

Aubrey grunted as he struggled to sit up against the pillows, wincing when he placed his bandaged arm down to give himself some leverage. Seeing him in pain now cut Taer deeper than it had when she'd seen him in the basement.

"Let me help you," she offered, forgetting her anger completely.

"I've got this," he snapped. He was clearly in pain, but his damn pride was stopping him from accepting her help. She stepped back. He was panting by the time he was upright, sagging into the pillows while sweat beaded on his brow. He looked down at the bandage wrapped around his arm. There was blood seeping through the gauze. "We need to talk, Taer."

His words left her cold. "Okay," she said with a nod. "Let's talk."

"I've been thinking about us."

"I have too."

"And I think we should put a stop to it before anything else happens."

Taer blinked, and a ringing started in her ears. Her foot slipped back a step. "What do you mean?"

He looked up at her, his gray eyes cold. "Once Eir has healed me as much as she can, I'm leaving here."

"No."

"You don't get a say in this. I told you to leave me there. I'm a cripple now because of you."

Taer frowned, anger bubbling up. She fisted her hands, but hid them under her arms. She didn't want him to see her getting angry. "Loki crippled you. I saved you."

"Saved me?" he spat. "You condemned me to a life where I'll have to look over my shoulder every second for fear of attack. You painted a target on my back."

"What are you talking about?"

"If my business associates find out that I was abducted and tortured and that I couldn't save myself, I'll be an easy target for them. They could take apart my business and there wouldn't be a damn thing I could do to stop it."

"Let me get this straight: you don't want to have a relationship with me because you're concerned your business will be taken over?" The words sounded just as ridiculous when she said them as they did coming out of his mouth the first time.

Brandishing his bloody stump in her direction, he said, "Look at me! How am I supposed to be feared now?"

Her green eyes lingered on his arm. "You want my pity?"

Angrily, he studied her face for a moment before dropping his arm. "I didn't expect you to understand."

"Understand what, exactly?" she shot back, holding her anger in check, but only just. "How it feels to be tortured?" Yanking down the neck of her shirt, she exposed both of her scars to him. "Tell me how I don't understand." When he said nothing, she thought she was getting through to him. "Stop playing the fucking victim. That's not the man I know."

"No. The man you knew died in that basement." His voice was soft – angry. "You don't know me anymore." He looked over at the black screen of the small TV on the dresser.

She wiped away the tears threatening to spill over. "Maybe I don't. And if that's true, it makes me wonder why I even bothered to save you in the first place." She turned to leave, but stopped and said, "Losing your hand doesn't change anything for me, Aubrey."

She wasn't into the whole guilt trip thing. If he said he was done, she wasn't going to try and change his mind.

That was up to him.

EPILOGUE
18 MONTHS LATER

Taer slid the sunglasses onto her face and sat on the checked picnic blanket Eir had just laid down. It was spring, and Boston Common was full of families enjoying the sunshine. It had been eighteen months since the deaths of Darrion, Loki and Odin, and an unfamiliar but much needed peace had settled over all of their lives. Everyone had found some kind of happiness. Bryn and Korvain had become parents to a little girl they had called Tove. Taer wasn't sure what the significance of the name was, but she thought it had something to do with Maverick.

Eir and Mason also became parents. Firstly to a new German Shepherd puppy called Sophie and then again twelve months later to a baby boy who they named after Mason's brother. Mist still ran the bar, but she had also started dating a human guy who had no idea who or what she really was. But it was Kara who had made the most dramatic change to her life. She quit stripping the same day Odin was killed, threw out her entire wardrobe and started fresh. She began working down in Raven the following night and she and Dex had started dating.

Taer had had a tough year and a half, though. Although Aubrey had been rescued, and Eir had done her best to heal him, he still wasn't himself. She hadn't returned to her apartment for nearly two weeks after their last conversation – that's how long it took Eir to finish healing him, and when she did go back, she was haunted by the memory of him being there. The following six months were the most difficult – adjusting to life again. After that though, she found a rhythm that worked for her. She still bartended down at the Eye and in Raven Thursday through Sunday, and in her down time she took up painting. She found it helped her purge the nightmares of her brother's death that still plagued her night after night.

When Bryn and Korvain had announced they were expecting a baby, Taer was beyond happy for them. Korvain had finally found the happiness he deserved and Bryn was finally adding to the family she loved. Baby Tove seemed to heal the hole in both of their hearts. When Taer held her for the first time, she felt a pang of regret. Perhaps she should have fought a little harder for Aubrey. But what was done was done.

In an attempt to get over him, she had started dating Cash, but it had only lasted a month. When he asked her what the problem was, her answer was simple: she was still in love with someone else. When she returned home from that final date with Cash, she texted Aubrey to let him know she was still thinking of him.

He didn't reply.

That didn't faze her though. Every time she did something she thought he might enjoy, she would text him and let him know the details.

Every time she was disappointed.

And it seemed today was no different. She sighed and crossed her legs beneath her, accepting a squirming baby Tove. Korvain sat down beside her, letting Tove wrap her little fingers around his thumb.

"How are you doing, Tay?" he asked softly.

She glanced at him briefly before looking out at the spread Mist had prepared for their picnic. Once again, she longed for more even though she didn't deserve it. "I'm doing all right."

"That portrait you did of Bryn, Tove and me is amazing, Tay. Thank you so much for painting it."

She shrugged. "Anything for you guys."

He wrapped his arm around her shoulder. "You're not happy. You haven't been happy for a long time."

Again, she shrugged. There was no point denying it.

"He's a fool," Korvain said softly before pressing a kiss to her forehead and standing up to join Bryn who was talking to Kara and Dex.

She let out a breath and looked down at the dark-haired, blue-eyed baby sitting in her lap. She squeezed her eyes shut for a moment, trying to ease the sting of unshed tears. She had cried more in the past couple of years than she ever had. It was embarrassing that a man was responsible for her new and unfortunate emotional state. But where did it stop? She couldn't keep doing this. She couldn't keep hoping he would miraculously change his mind and come back to her. She had to put an end to it. She decided that after today, she wouldn't think about Aubrey. She wouldn't text him again. She was done.

Someone sat down beside her then. "I have to tell you, Winter Fox, having a baby in your lap suits you."

Taer's head jerked up, her eyes widening when she saw who was sitting there. "You came."

Aubrey's mouth flexed into a small smile. "I came to every single one of your art exhibitions, too. Just like I came to every single thing you invited me to – even if it was just to see a movie."

"But where were you? I never saw you."

"I was there, lingering in the back, or sitting behind you in the cinema while you ate your popcorn mixed with milk duds." He closed her mouth with his finger under her chin, his touch lingering on her jaw. "I made a mistake."

She frowned. "Coming here?"

He shook his head. "Letting you walk out of my life. The reality was I was petrified to lose you. So I gave you up on my own terms."

"I don't understand."

He let his hand drop and exhaled, looking out across the grass. "If you left me, I would have known it was because I couldn't give you everything you needed. If I pulled the pin before that, I could have said anything – given you any excuse – and wouldn't have had to explain myself any further."

Taer let his words sink in. "You hurt me," she whispered.

"I know. And it was the last thing I wanted. But if you'd stayed, you were at risk of being hurt by my business associates."

"So what's changed?"

"I got out," he replied softly. "I'm going straight, as the humans say."

That made her smile. "What will you do?"

He shrugged. "There aren't many jobs out there for a one-handed man, but I'll get by."

"We could use some more security," Korvain said, startling them both out of their conversation. He leaned down and picked up Tove, holding her close to his chest. To Aubrey, he said, "If you need a job, we have one for you."

Both men stared at each other for a long while before Aubrey finally nodded. "Thanks. That would be . . . great."

Korvain grunted. "Come and see me tonight. You can start right away."

When he was gone, Taer turned to face Aubrey. She still couldn't believe he was sitting there. He looked a little thinner than before, and he was dressed simply in jeans and a tee, but to Taer, he had never looked better.

"What are you smiling at?" he asked, gently touching her bottom lip with his thumb. He grimaced and dropped his hand.

She brought it back to her face, leaning into his touch. Closing her eyes, she quietly absorbed him – his scent, his feel, his warmth. They were the things she thought she'd lost forever. "You're really here."

"I'll be here forever if you still want me."

Leaning forward, she kissed him and whispered, "Always" against his mouth.

DOWNFALL

3

GODS & MONSTERS